What is a Highlander to do when he falls for the daughter of his enemy?

Highland warrior, Blane Sutherland, has one mission: disguise himself as an Englishman, cross the border and retrieve Lady Aliah de Mowbray. Always up for a challenge, he agrees, pursuing his conquest with vigor — and trying to deny the powerful desire that eclipses him each time he touches his charge. A rogue of the highest order and a younger son, he has nothing to offer a lady but a broken heart.

And what is a lady to do when she cannot trust her heart?

Aliah is skeptical of the English noble who has come to take her to her father and sister in Scotland, but she pushes her doubts aside. Without word in months, she must make certain her family is safe, then she can return to England to join the convent to which she has sworn to pledge her life. But then her escort reveals his true self — he's a Highlander and his kisses are more seductive than the sweetest of wines.

Surrender never tasted so sweet…

Also Available by Eliza Knight

The Highlander's Reward – Book One, The Stolen Bride Series
A Lady's Charade
A Gentleman's Kiss
Men of the Sea Series: Her Captain Returns, Her Captain Surrenders, Her Captain Dares All
The Highland Jewel Series: Warrior in a Box, Lady in a Box, Love in a Box
Lady Seductress's Ball
Take it Off, Warrior
Highland Steam
A Pirate's Bounty
Highland Tryst (Something Wicked This Way Comes Volume 1)

Coming soon…
The Highlander's Lady (Book 3: The Stolen Bride Series)
Highlander Brawn (Sequel to Highland Steam)

Writing under the name Annabelle Weston

Wicked Woman (Desert Heat)
Scandalous Woman (Desert Heat)
Mr. Temptation
Hunting Tucker

Coming soon…
Notorious Woman (Desert Heat)

****

Visit Eliza Knight at www.elizaknight.com or
www.historyundressed.com

3

Eliza Knight

Dedication

To my mom, for always encouraging me to be myself!

Acknowledgements

Without the gracious assistance of many special people, this book would not be what it is today. My thanks to Kim, Victoria, Vonda, Andrea, Lizzie and Kathy! You ladies are wonderful!

Eliza Knight

The Highlander's Conquest

Book Two: The Stolen Bride Series

By
Eliza Knight

Chapter One

Late Fall
Northern England, 1297

A violent banging at the manor door startled Aliah from her studies and set Frosty, the family's monstrous Irish wolfhound, to barking ferociously. Aliah jerked backward against the oak chair she sat in, hitting her head against the ancient wood and stifling a harsh word beneath her breath.

Her father, Baron de Mowbray, had left a small contingent of men to protect her while he escorted her older sister Arbella to her bridegroom in Scotland. These men would fight to keep her safe until their very last breaths.

But who was to say they hadn't already taken that last shuddering inhale?

Aliah glanced around the room, filled with memories, but not with people. Today, her maid Glenda was her only companion. Well, Frosty as well — who in fact was a far superior protector than her maid. Swallowing her fear, she rubbed the ache from the back of her head and squared her shoulders. Strength. That was what she needed, even if the sound of someone knocking made her want to run to the opposite end of the manor and hide.

Her father should have returned a month ago. The only news she'd managed to garner was that a battle took place at Stirling Bridge in Scotland—the very place her sister was to marry.

Had the battle now come to her own door?

Aliah jumped as a strong fist once again slammed the door.

"Glenda, would you answer the door?" Aliah asked.

'Twas Saturday morning and most of the servants had gone to tend family or to enjoy themselves in whatever way they did, leaving Aliah quite alone—and at the mercy of whoever stood outside her door. Could they have dispensed of her father's guards so quickly?

Glenda, afraid of her own shadow, started to shake her head, but Aliah gave her a stern look. The woman had been driving her mad since she was a babe and ever since Arbella left, Aliah had little patience for the older woman's nonsense.

Aliah set down the book of Gaelic she'd been studying—she was determined to learn the language because she secretly believed the Scots would soon invade. Understanding their barbaric conversations was crucial. Aliah smoothed her gown and stood tall.

Glenda scurried toward the door, Frosty a foot ahead of her.

Aliah tried to find comfort in the fact that perhaps the guards had allowed whoever came knocking through the manor gates. She'd heard no clanging of metal or yells of pain. Aye, the only conclusion that made sense was, they were not enemies, but friends.

She could use a good friend. The comfort of someone she knew. Aliah frowned. She had few friends, and seldom was it that they dropped by.

So who had the audacity to practically beat down her door?

"Wait!" Aliah shouted just as Glenda touched the wooden plank barring the door.

She hurried to retrieve her bow and an arrow from beneath her chair. As swiftly as possible, she cocked an arrow and aimed it at the door. Taking a deep breath, she nodded for her maid to open it. If her father's enemies dared to come after her, they were in for a big surprise, she wouldn't surrender so easily.

An interminable amount of time seemed to pass before the door was fully open. Aliah stepped back, speechless. Standing before her was the most staggeringly handsome man she'd ever seen—and he was quite alone. Frosty growled for only a moment, quickly silenced by a motion the stranger made with his hand. What? How had he done that? Aliah struggled to keep her mouth from falling open at the man's effortless command of the dog. The animal had favored her sister, but since Arbella had left, Frosty refused to leave Aliah's side.

She felt a certain amount of betrayal at Frosty's easy acceptance of this stranger. Who in the name of God was he? And why didn't one of her father's men escort him? She'd have to speak with them about that later.

The visitor wore an intriguing cap of deep burgundy, a dark feather jutting from the side, held on by some sort of medallion. A thick black wool cloak lay open to reveal a matching tunic, and leather studded armor. White hose outlined the shape of his legs in a way that drew her eyes from his intense dark green gaze. His boots were made of soft, expensive-looking leather, and the gilded belt at his waist held a gleaming, sharp sword that was hard to miss.

Aliah allowed her gaze to travel over the length and breadth of his solid form, before getting ahold of herself.

11

"Will you shoot me, my lady?" His voice was deep, raspy, and stroked along the ends of her nerves in a way that made her want to run away and kiss him at the same time.

Where had that thought come from? She'd never kissed a man. And she never would. She'd pledged her life and future to God. Shame crawled through her making her cheeks heat with embarrassment. Even her toes felt the blush of such a carnal thought.

Aliah had to gain some control of her wayward mind. Her life belonged to the church—penance for having caused her mother's death. There was no room for kissing or men in her life. Not even for a thought.

"Apologies, sir, but one can never be too careful. I am Lady Aliah." She kept her arrow pointed at his heart, taking note of how his tunic and leather studded armor strained over what appeared to be a very broad, taut chest.

"Sir Blane of Yorkshire." He doffed his cap and bowed low, then returned upright, settling his cap back in place.

She tilted her head, studying the angles and lines of his face, taking in the pleasant smile of his wide, full lips. He didn't appear to be someone she should be wary of, but as she'd learned over the years, looks could oft be deceiving. Aliah flicked her gaze toward her maid who wrung her hands and looked ready to bolt from the room.

Deciding that for the moment he did not have any designs to harm her, Aliah disarmed her arrow and lowered the bow. "Welcome to Mowbray Manor, Sir Blane. Have you any men with you?"

"Aye, I've left them by the stables. I assure you, we come on friendly terms."

Aliah nodded, making her lips thin so as to keep them from trembling. Did he come with news of her father, of Arbella? She shivered. The news must not be good. If her father were able, he would announce his return himself. Her spirits lowered, replaced by a dull, cold pulse.

He smiled, disarming her, his lips curving in a rascally way that set her to shivering and then to quickly reciting a Hail Mary in her mind for penance.

"I come with a message, my lady. If I may?" He swept out his hand, asking permission to fully enter their great hall.

She nodded again, not sure she could trust her voice.

Glenda backed away, but Aliah quickly caught her gaze. "Fetch our guest some refreshment." She motioned for Sir Blane to sit at the long trestle table. "There is no need to wait, please tell me what news you bring."

Sir Blane pulled out her chair before taking his own seat, and she disliked how that chivalrous move made her feel warm and tingly inside.

"I come from Scotland, my lady."

She felt the blood rush from her face, but quickly recovered. There could only be one thing he needed to relay and she was positive she was not ready to hear it. Just then, Glenda returned setting down a pitcher of watered wine and two glasses. She left again, coming back several moments later with a trencher of hard cheese, a few apples and day old brown bread. After setting down the food, Glenda made a hasty retreat from the room.

Aliah poured his wine and pushed the goblet towards him, then snatched an apple from the trencher. Slicing a piece, she bit into it, hoping the man would eat and forget that she'd asked to hear the news.

But alas, that was not to be. After a hearty bite of cheese and bread, Sir Blane's green eyes met hers. "My lady, I come with a message from your father. He and your sister are well and wish you to accompany them in Scotland for a spell."

"They are well?" Her voice sounded weak to her own ears and her heart pounded against her ribs.

13

"Aye, heartily so."

Aliah released a shuddering breath. "And Arbella, is she married then?"

A strange expression briefly crossed his face before disappearing. "Aye."

What did that expression mean? "Is she happy?"

"I believe so."

But would the man say otherwise? 'Twas really none of his business whether or not her sister was happy, and if he were truly just the messenger then he wouldn't know anyway.

"How can I know you speak the truth?"

As if the sting of Frosty's earlier betrayal was not enough, the great wolfhound sidled up to Sir Blane and nuzzled him in the ribs. Absently, the man rubbed Frosty behind his ears.

"My lady, I come with direct orders from your sister. Arbella told me herself to tell you that it pained her not to have you at the wedding with her, and that she hoped you'd help her to settle into her new home."

Aliah frowned. Was he telling her the truth? It made no sense. Hadn't Arbella told her not to come before she left? So what changed her mind? Why would Arbella say such a thing? Aliah had agreed for her own personal reasons. Reasons no one knew about. If Blane were telling the truth, this would surely hinder her plans. There were only a few short months before spring and Aliah was due to present herself to Mother Superior, never to leave the convent again. Although her sister wasn't aware of that, going to Scotland to be with her sure did put a glitch in her arrangements if it meant Aliah couldn't return in time.

"Your father sent this." Sir Blane reached into his pocket and pulled out a rolled scroll.

The seal was plain wax. "My father's seal is not on this missive." Aliah handed it back, intent now on figuring out a way to escape. Who was this man and why was he trying to lure her away from her home? A sense of unease made her suspicious.

Sir Blane didn't even bat an eye. "Ah, yes. Your father knows you well. As I told you, there was a battle. He lost his seal during the encounter and bid you forgive him for such."

"Was he injured?"

The knight shook his head. "Not overly so. A few scrapes and bruises."

"And Arbella—"She sucked in a breath and held it, regaining her composure. "Was she near the skirmish?"

Again that odd look crossed Sir Blane's face. "No, she was perfectly protected."

Aliah broke the seal and read the short, two-lined note stating her presence was requested in Scotland. It was signed by her father. His script appeared shaky, but that was not alarming as he'd just been in a battle. After rolling up the parchment, she set it aside and returned her attention to her guest.

Should she trust him? Could she trust him? Her father may have been forced to sign the missive. But why? What could Sir Blane possibly want with her? If the knight had her father and her sister, taking her wouldn't further his cause. Aliah's instincts were failing her. *Saints preserve me!*

He tore off a hunk of bread, bit into it and chewed as his eyes roved over the room. She took the opportunity to study his features. His skin was darkened from the sun, and a brush of stubble covered his cheeks and chin. Aliah fought the urge to reach out and brush her fingers over it to see how rough it was. She would be doing penance for a month if Mother Superior knew the thoughts going through her mind. Pledging herself to God meant she should not care about the texture of his face. It meant that the way he smiled should not make her melt.

Aliah watched in utter fascination as his throat bobbed after taking a swallow of wine. "'Tis a homey place you have here," he murmured.

Aliah glanced away from him and stared at the walls covered in tapestries her mother, grandmother and several other generations of Mowbray women had woven. Some depicted battle scenes, victories, while others showed glorious moments in their family's history, like a man being knighted, or the birth of an heir. A few even depicted warm moments that she missed the most—especially the one that embodied her mother, with Aliah, Arbella and their brother Samuel as small children, playing at her feet—a moment that had never come to pass. The latter was sewn by her aunt some years after Aliah's mother's death as a comfort to the family. But to Aliah it was a constant reminder of what she didn't have. She still felt an empty void where the love of a mother should be.

"Aye, I suppose it is." She glanced back at him. "Is your home not so?"

He shook his head, his eyes saddening. She wanted to ask why, what made his mood change, but didn't. That would have been awkward coming from someone he barely knew. And she didn't want to offer him the chance to get more personal, even if it were only on a basic level.

His face cleared and Sir Blane pushed back from the table. "I hate to rush you, my lady, but we must be going now. 'Tis a long journey to our destination and the weather will soon be turning surly."

Glenda gasped. Aliah had not realized her maid had returned, and she threw a disgusted look in Glenda's direction. She knew what Glenda was thinking—that if Aliah were to leave she would surely die of the cold—and Aliah was also aware that it was utter rubbish. Glenda had been filling the girls' ears with rumors and terrors of the Scots since they were babes, and while Arbella had taken them to heart, Aliah knew better—but only by accident. She hadn't meant to eavesdrop, but one evening after Glenda had consumed too much wine, Aliah heard her confess to another maid that her own mother

16

had told her those things. And everyone knew that Glenda's mother was mad.

Aliah had only ever met a Scot once —a woman in fact, who'd been married to a neighboring lord, and she'd been the epitome of grace and calm. If it weren't for her Scottish burr, Aliah would have thought she was an English noblewoman. She'd begged to go with her father when he made the trek to congratulate them on their wedding and he'd acquiesced since Arbella and Samuel were both busy with their studies.

Ever since meeting the Scottish Woman, Aliah never paid much attention to Glenda's rantings. And so, she didn't mind the journey to Scotland for the cold, she minded it for another reason entirely.

"I shall need an escort."

"Aye, indeed, my lady, I shall provide you escort."

She shook her head. "No, that won't do."

He gazed at her quizzically. "Why not?"

"I'll need a female companion."

He pointed to her maid. "This one shall do."

Aliah rolled eyes at the choking noise that Glenda made. "Glenda does not travel."

A hint of knowledge glowed in his green eyes. "That is Glenda?" He nodded. "Makes sense now."

"You've heard of her?"

"Oh, aye. Your sister speaks of her often." His smile was catching and she found herself returning it.

"What did she say?"

"What manner of horrid things we—I mean the Scots— would do to her."

What did he mean by *we*?

He picked up his glass of wine and chugged it. Perhaps the slip of his tongue was the wine, or lack of sleep. If he knew of Glenda from her sister—and she could only imagine what Arbella had said—she could trust him, couldn't she?

17

"Where is it exactly that we shall travel to?" she asked.

"The Highlands, my lady."

A chill caught her and she tried to downplay the gooseflesh rising on her arms. "And what is my family doing there? I thought their destination was Stirling?"

"'Tis where they are seeking shelter. Stirling is in a bit of unrest." He waved his hand, dismissing the topic. "We must depart, my lady. Pack a satchel or two. That is all. We can send for more things if they are needed. But we must ride quickly and too much baggage will hold us back."

Aliah sensed urgency in his tone, which made her wary. But all the same, this man knew her father and sister and said he would take her to them. She needed to see that they were safe, before she was cut off from the world by entering into the church where she would take a vow of silence for a year. She hesitated for a moment. He had to be telling the truth, didn't he? She had her doubts but she didn't have any other choice but to trust him. Her father and Arbella might need her help. How could she give herself over to the church if she gave into her fears and didn't help her father and Arbella in their time of need? Reluctantly she stepped forward, tilted her chin and met his gaze.

"I will be ready within a half-hour. Would you care for a bath or some other comfort while you wait?"

He shook his head. "I thank you, my lady, for the generous offer, and while I would relish a bath, there is simply not enough time. I will see to my men and procure a mount for you."

Aliah nodded for Glenda to follow as she made her way upstairs to her chamber. Once inside, her maid broke into a terrified litany, chewing her fingernails to the quick. "My lady, you cannot go with him. You don't know who he is, and he could be a barbarian himself for all you know. He will cook you up for dinner. He could have done the same to your sister and your father — absorbed their souls — and that is the only way he knew you were here."

Rolling her eyes heavenward, Aliah threw open her wardrobe and pulled out a leather satchel that her father had given her. "Glenda, stop your blubbering. You saw yourself he was English and he had a letter from my father."

"Oh, I… Oh…" Glenda rushed around the room, doing nothing productive whatsoever. The woman opened the wardrobe wider, banging the door into Aliah's shoulder before shutting it again. She rushed to poke at the non-existent fire, then turned to mess with the coverlet on Aliah's bed. "You will at least pack your bow?"

"And my arrows," Aliah said sarcastically. She pulled a couple gowns, shifts and hose from the wardrobe and tucked them into the satchel. "Help me change into a more suitable riding gown."

Glenda clucked and tugged at Aliah's gown until she shoved the maid's hands away and finished the job herself. The woman was completely useless.

"Be cautious, my lady."

"I assure you, Glenda, I will not let any man put my bones in his beard, nor shall I succumb to death from the cold." She'd almost forgotten to get her cloak. She pulled out the black wool, fur-lined cloak, and then switched from slippers to her sturdy leather boots.

"Oh, I do hope that is the case, my lady. Arbella seems to have made it alive. Which leads me to believe you might also."

"Your encouragement overwhelms me." Aliah bit the inside of her cheek to keep from laughing. "Fare thee well, Glenda."

Tears brimmed in the older woman's eyes. Despite her fear of the Scots and all the crazy notions she'd filled their heads with, Glenda meant well, and had been the only motherly figure Aliah had ever known. Dropping her satchel, she pulled her maid in for a hug, breathing in the scent of bread and rosemary that always seemed to cling to her. She would miss her.

"I shall return soon, Glenda." She wished to tell her maid of her promise to the church and that she intended to grace the sanctuary's threshold come the first day of spring, but word would get to her father who was certain not to agree. As much as she wanted to tell Glenda, she couldn't take the chance.

Glenda nodded, wiping a tear with her sleeve. "I shall pray for your safety."

"I thank you." Before she lost the courage she'd summoned to embark on this sudden journey, Aliah quit the room and the only home she'd ever known.

Chapter Two

Gritting his teeth, Blane helped the lithe and bonny lass climb onto her mount. Her curves were supple beneath his fingertips, reminding him in the most inopportune way that it'd been several weeks since his last encounter with a woman. And he loved his time with a willing, wicked lass or two.

Aliah de Mowbray was born to tempt a man. Long, golden locks plaited down her back with a few wisps fluttering free around her face. Her skin was flawless, creamy perfection and he wanted to drip honey over the curve of her shoulders and lick it clean.

But she was not for him. The lady was simply his latest mission. He never failed to complete a task. She didn't even realize who he really was, not that he would tell her. Disguise was his best cover—and for his own safety. Being discovered as a Scot dressed as an English knight in the midst of England when the English King Edward was trying to rid Scotland of Scots was not in his best interests.

Neither was meddling with an English maiden. Not when he had another agenda to tend to—one that he'd been bent on for over a decade. No lass, no matter how bonny, would get in the way of his objective and his retribution.

"Och," he grumbled, momentarily revealing his Scottish brogue and drawing her attention. *Damn!*

Crystal blue eyes flashed on him. Intelligence radiated in her gaze and he realized she'd heard him.

"Is aught amiss?" she asked. Her hands tightened on the reins, a small move, and ordinarily not something he would have noticed, but he'd been on high alert since entering enemy territory. One could never be too careful, and he'd slipped up.

He needed to be steadfast, another mistake could prove fatal. He cursed himself. Nothing like this had ever happened before. He was far too careful, so what was it about this golden haired lass that made him lose sense?

Blane was a master of disguise. He'd been traveling in and out of England under the guise of a merchant, farmer, lord or knight without anyone ever realizing he was Scots. He didn't make mistakes. And yet, being in her company for no more than an hour, he was reduced to a drooling pup.

He cleared his throat, hoping it would also help clear his mind. He was Blane Sutherland, brother to Laird Magnus Sutherland of the Highlands, and he was a master of deception. To Lady Aliah, he was Sir Blane of Yorkshire, her escort. If she found out the truth, she would never travel with him willingly. If his older brother Magnus or his younger brother Ronan found out about his misstep, they would tease him mercilessly.

"All is well, my lady," he said, making sure his English accent was strong. If she were to find out he was Scots now, she would run screaming. Likewise if she learned that the missive he carried was a forgery. Blane had never laid eyes on the Baron. He could be dead for all he knew, but Arbella had insisted on the ruse, stating that Aliah would never come otherwise.

He tilted his head to study her, seeing the bow and arrows strapped to her back. Nay. She would not run. Shoot him was more like it. Best he keep on his toes and not make another idiotic mistake. Blane wasn't sure if he was more worried about his brother's anger at not bringing him the English lass, or Aliah's sister Arbella's wrath if she found out that Blane had failed.

They shared a connection Aliah was not even aware of. His brother, Laird Magnus Sutherland, had stolen Arbella from her intended and married her. The match seemed perfect but Aliah would never believe it. Not until she saw them together. Blane had barely believed it himself.

"I thought I heard you mutter something."

Blane glanced toward his boots and made a pretense of wiping one vigorously on the barren ground of the courtyard. "Merely stepped in a bit of horse manure."

She wrinkled her nose, but asked no further questions.

Blane signaled for his men to mount and did so himself, adjusting his cloak from beneath him. His men didn't speak, under strict orders, unless they were with him in private. Grunts, nods and shakes of their heads were all they used to communicate. Lucky for them, it worked, leading most people to speak only with Blane. There was less chance of discovery that way.

From atop her horse, he spied Lady Aliah studying him. Her gaze made him feel hot, and he willed away any more thoughts of her, lest he speak to her in Gaelic and reveal his misrepresentation. Instead, he flicked his hand toward the wolfhound.

"The dog stays."

Aliah shook her head. "Nay."

Blane frowned, not understanding. "Nay?"

"He comes with me. As my personal guard, Sir Blane."

Blane raised a brow. The dog was no guard. Hell, Blane had stepped into the place and issued a few hand motions and the pup had fallen at his feet. "'Tis a long and arduous journey, my lady. I dare say your guard will not make it."

The woman lifted her chin and narrowed her eyes. What he'd thought to be a sweet natured woman quickly turned haughty. Stubborn.

"He goes or I stay."

There was no time to argue, and hell, Blane always lost when he argued with his own sisters, Heather and Lorna. He wasn't about to get into a match with a beautiful temptress. He'd probably offer to carry the massive dog upon his lap if he did. Blane shook his head in exasperation and sent a prayer up to the clouds that the dog made it all the way to Dunrobin Castle, his family's seat in the Highlands. "Very well, my lady."

He flicked his horse's reins, listening to Gunnar's snort of irritation. The horse had a mind of his own about who was in charge, although, he was an excellent companion in battle and upon the road.

They usually traveled to England for less dangerous purposes. Blane was in charge of delivering and generating wool sales for his clan—the thing that the Sutherland's thrived and prospered off of. Sutherland wool was thick, soft and kept anybody warm no matter how cold and frozen the earth might be or how barren their hearth. 'Twas a commodity that many paid heavy coin for—and none paid more highly than the English, as unfortunate as that was.

As they passed through the gates, Lady Aliah's men nodded to her from their guard posts. How easy it had been for him to come through their gates, to lie his way into their good graces and then to take their lady away. It astounded him. He was offended for her, and once they reached Scotland, and she knew who he was, he would let her know. Any liar with good acting skills could have conned their way through the gate and taken her away.

It'd been plain to see how worried she was over her father and sister, just as Arbella, his sister-by-marriage, had said the lady would be. He'd let Arbella tell Aliah why she'd married a Highlander instead of the English noble occupying a Scottish stronghold that she'd been promised to. Blane didn't want to get stuck in the middle of that one.

Crossing over the small bridge and onto the dirt-packed road, he increased his pace, and his men and Aliah followed. They traveled north along the road. If he had his way, they would travel through the woods, but the trees had already lost their leaves, their brown crust covering the forest floor in a dangerous blanket, hiding broken branches and raised roots. Best to stick to the road for now.

He glanced up at the sky, mostly white with clouds covering the sun, and a hint of grey in-between. The air smelled crisp as it always did in the fall. They'd ride for a few hours before stopping to rest, but then they'd continue on until nightfall. If the temperature dropped too much, he'd have to procure them a place to sleep, although he preferred for them to make camp in the woods, where no one would question Lady Aliah being in his company. Blane spurred Gunnar forward. He wanted out of this Godforsaken country as quickly as possible.

Several hours later, Aliah approached him, calling out to him over the sound of the horses' hooves. "My lord, there is a village just ahead. Might we stop to rest a moment, take a drink from their well?"

Blane was immediately on alert. Why would she want to stop in the village? Had she realized that he was not who he said he was? She'd asked for a drink, perhaps she was simply thirsty. He reached behind him and handed her his wineskin.

"What is it?"

He smiled crookedly. "The drink of the gods."

Her eyes crinkled up in a way he'd come to know as her questioning look, and he found it to be altogether adorable and disturbing. Not breaking their pace, she took the wineskin and drank deeply.

"'Tis naught but water," she said accusingly.

Blane laughed heartily. "Aye, and you took a rather generous gulp thinking it would be something else. Whisky perhaps? Did your father not let you have aught but watered wine?" he teased.

Lady Aliah frowned and thrust the wineskin back at him. "You're a cad, sir. I was simply thirsty."

"I see." He laughed some more and took the wineskin, securing it behind him.

"I was."

"And are you now?"

"Nay."

"You see, 'tis the drink of the gods, your thirst is miraculously cured."

She rolled her eyes and shook her head. "Aye, a miracle."

Blane chuckled all the more. "Now, if you had taken a drink from my men, I could not vouch for your lucidity after, for I do believe they have faith in the gods of liquor."

A couple of the men behind him chortled.

Blane winked at Lady Aliah. "You see? You are safer with me."

He couldn't tell if the becoming shade of pink coloring her cheeks was a blush or the chill air.

"Do you still need to rest, my lady?"

She glanced at him sheepishly. "I need but a few moments."

"Ah, I see." Having sisters he understood her need to stop and relieve herself. His sisters always seemed to have to stop every few hours whereas the men could go nearly all day without breaking their pace.

Lady Aliah's cheeks flamed redder, sending a flush down her neck. He imagined if he pushed back her cloak, even her dainty ears would be crimson, and he knew for certain her breasts would be strawberries and cream. Suppressing a groan, he held up his hand for his men to stop as he came to a stream. Dismounting, he walked over to her horse and reached up to grasp her around the waist.

Her gasp as his hands clasped her curves struck him, sending his blood pounding and straight to his groin. If they were alone... Well, if they were alone and she weren't a maiden, and he didn't fear the wrath of his laird and sister-by-marriage, he might... Nay, he could do nothing. No distractions.

Blane set her on the ground a little rougher than he intended, nearly shoving her away from him. He scowled at her, and she took a step back.

"Apologies, my lady," he said gruffly. "I...uh, lost my footing."

Lady Aliah's cheeks flamed all the more, and he resisted the urge to stroke her soft-looking flesh to find out if it truly was as silky as it appeared.

"'Tis nothing. I get tripped up myself sometimes." She whirled away from him, her cloak swirling around his ankles as she walked toward a clump of rather sad looking bushes.

Frowning, he realized he should have found a better place to stop, a place that would afford her more privacy. Glancing at his men, he noted that they were tending their horses and talking with one another in hushed tones. He nodded at them, then headed after Lady Aliah. The last thing he needed was for her to be accosted behind the scraggly brush. He remembered well the horror his brother Magnus went through when his wife had been attacked while they stopped to rest. Luckily, she'd come out relatively unscathed. But that wasn't always the case.

Little time could be afforded as it was. He felt unsafe in England. In fact, he would not feel at ease until they reached the

Highlands. Once they crossed northern England and into Scotland, he had friends who would help shelter them should they need it. But there was no one here he could trust, and they wouldn't be within reach of help for a few days. Although he was a master of disguise, he could not afford for anyone to ask questions—no one, including Lady Aliah could ever find out that Sir Blane of Yorkshire did not exist.

As he approached the bushes, Lady Aliah's faint voice called out, "Do not come any closer."

Blane had to keep himself from laughing. She was such a tough lass. And yet, he'd seen her vulnerabilities too.

"'Tis only, I, Sir Blane, my lady." He sought to reassure her, and stopped his steps within a few feet of the bushes. The shadow of her black cloak was visible through the bramble and so out of respect he turned his back.

"Stay where you are, Sir Blane."

"I dare not come any closer. I only wanted to make sure you were safe."

"I assure you, I am perfectly safe. Now, if you please, go back to the horses." Her voice sounded strained, as if she were in pain.

"Are you all right, my lady."

"Go away!" she shouted.

Blane was taken aback by her shout, and did indeed back away a few feet. What had gotten into the lass? Then he heard her retching.

"My lady, please, allow me to—" He stopped himself. What could he do for her? Water. She would want water he was sure. And a rag to wipe her mouth.

He rushed back to his horse, grabbed his wineskin, whipped open his bag, and sifted through in search of a cloth. But he had none, so he tore a strip from the closest thing he found. Damn, he'd have to figure out what it was, later. His men looked at him oddly.

28

"The lady is unwell."

A few of them grumbled their concern and others with their annoyance. Traveling with a female was cumbersome enough, but someone who was ill? Blane hoped it was only nerves.

Approaching the bushes again, he heard a rustling as she stepped out of her hiding place, face pale, and her eyes bloodshot from the exertion of purging.

"My lady, I thought you might like these." He thrust the wineskin and strip of white cloth toward her.

"I thank you." She grasped them, but used neither. Her gaze met his wearily. "I should like to wash my face in the stream."

He nodded. "Of course. This way."

"I can see it," she said rather haughtily. She was most likely embarrassed from her predicament and so he didn't mind her tone.

Blane was momentarily thankful for having grown up with sisters. They had certainly taught him many things about females and thus made him more patient—and it appeared patience would be what he needed in dealing with Aliah.

Keeping his distance, he followed her to the stream. His men kept to themselves, passing curious glances her way. She knelt before the water, scooping a healthy amount into her hands and splashing it onto her face. Aliah repeated the act several times before finally sitting back on her heels and using the cloth to wipe her face. Closing her eyes, she took a swig of his water, and then another. Then she sat there, unmoving, eyes still closed for the span of several heartbeats. He was compelled to ask her again if she was all right, but thought better of it.

Finally, she opened her eyes and glanced his way. Her lips were pressed firmly together in a frown, and her eyes looked weak. It was odd how much that weakness bothered him. Up until now—though he'd only met her that morning—she'd

Eliza Knight

appeared quite strong. Stronger than he would have ever expected an English lass to be.

"I suppose you will want an explanation."

"Aye," he said before thinking, then cursed himself for being so candid.

She pushed to her knees and he offered his hand to help her rise to her feet. Aliah took it, her small hand dwarfed by his own. Calluses marred the surface of her palms, just below her fingers. Probably from practicing with her bow. He found he rather liked the feel of a woman who did something with her hands. And then his mind traveled to what other things she could do with those slim fingers... Her calluses brushing over his shaft... Blane hissed and yanked his hand away as though burned, which once again had her nearly falling from his sudden disconnect.

"Apologies, my lady."

"I do not have the plague, Sir Blane. Seems each time you touch me, you think I might pass along some illness. I assure you, my being ill now has naught to do with something so perilous."

Blane wasn't sure how to respond. He admitted his actions certainly could be seen as such, but 'twas simply not the case.

"Apolo—"

She held up her hand, cutting him off. "I know, I know. 'Apologies, my lady,'" she mocked. "Listen, Sir Blane, 'tis simply a touch of sickness from riding."

Blane kept himself from blanching at her admission, and only uttered, "What?"

"The horse you procured for me is rather bouncy, and with trying to keep up with your rapid pace, it appears, I have a touch of motion sickness."

He'd never experienced motion sickness nor had he ever met anyone else who'd been sick from it, and he found the idea rather appalling. If he were to become afflicted with such an illness, his clan would suffer miserably from lack of funds. "That is awful, my lady. Is there anything I can do? Shall we trade mounts? Gunnar has a rather subtle gait."

She nodded. "That might work. Could we try?"

"Aye. I would not want you to be ill the entire journey." Already he imagined ways in which this would impede their return. It could be a month before they reached Dunrobin if she was ill every few hours.

Her eyes locked with his. "How long is the journey?"

"About two weeks."

Her face paled another shade, which could not be healthy considering her already vapid pallor. "I didn't realize 'twas so long."

"Do not fret, my lady. We shall trade mounts."

With that said, they returned to the horses and he introduced her to Gunnar, the latter acting like a besotted fool. Cursing his mount, he climbed atop her bouncy mare, and ordered his men to depart.

Satan's ballocks, the lass wasn't exaggerating. The mare had the gait of… Well, he didn't know what, but he jostled all around, and couldn't seem to get her to move correctly. 'Twas as if she walked with four left feet.

The journey to Dunrobin just grew unpleasant tenfold.

Chapter Three

Aliah bit her lips so hard she feared she'd break the skin. From the corner of her eye, she watched Sir Blane continuously try and fail to get Mad Maiden to correct her gait. The horse was a complete sweetheart, but also completely unrideable. Her sweetness was the only reason they kept her around. Distracted with thoughts of her journey while they were at Mowbray Manor, Aliah had not noticed the horse Sir Blane had chosen for her. It wasn't until they were through the gate and she was jostling about that recognition hit. By then, she was too embarrassed to say anything, and prayed the journey would be swift. She was also mildly surprised her groomsman allowed the horse to be taken. She was actually a little put out by that thought.

But, in any case, it was rather humorous to watch him jostling about. She'd never been sick riding, unless she was on Mad Maiden.

Mortification swept through her once more, making her cheeks burn despite the chill air. Had she really gotten sick in front of Sir Blane and all of his men? That might be the most embarrassing moment of her life. Well, that wasn't exactly true; she'd had many embarrassing moments. Perhaps this one could be classified as the most embarrassing moment in front of a man. A man she found she had particular interest in.

A man she should try to ignore for the remainder of her trip. He was no good for her, especially the feelings he stirred inside. Which was a major problem. She would have to seek a priest and confess her thoughts. She should be ashamed of how he made her feel, but instead intense curiosity filled her.

"My lady," Sir Blane interrupted her thoughts. "I see now why you were not feeling well. This mount is positively ridiculous."

Aliah tried not to smile. "You look as though you have her tamed somewhat."

The knight bounced to the left and then the right. "I do not think so."

"Will you be sick?" she asked, concerned. While it was funny to watch him on the horse, she didn't wish nausea on anyone, and certainly not a man she hardly knew and whom she hoped would bring her safely to her family.

"Nay. I have an iron stomach."

Judging by his pallor that was slowly turning a shade of green, Aliah thought otherwise.

"Would you like your mount back?"

Hope flashed in Sir Blane's eyes, but he shook his head. "Gunnar is pleased to have a lady ride him, I'm sure."

"Aye, he is a docile animal, isn't he?" Aliah leaned forward and stroked her hands over the horse's soft mane and patted his neck. His skin rippled beneath her fingers, warming them with his heat.

"He is only docile with you, my lady With me, he is every bit the warhorse."

She flashed Blane a teasing smile and nodded toward Mad Maiden. "Whatever you say. You are quite the master of any horse, I see. Mad Maiden is clearly taken by you." As if to confirm just that, the horse nickered.

Before they could continue on with their banter, Frosty let out a wicked howl and darted forward.

"What's gotten into him?" Aliah asked, leaning forward to watch him dash off.

"Must be something ahead. 'Twould appear your dear wolfhound is a good guard dog after all," Sir Blane muttered and spurred Mad Maiden jauntily forward.

Aliah tried to peer ahead, but saw nothing out of the ordinarily besides Frosty barreling into the woods.

"Frosty, wait!" she shouted, urging Gunnar forward.

"No, Aliah!" Blane called out. Veering toward her, he grasped her reins as she passed him. He pulled both their horses to a halt. His men fanned out, half staying behind with them and the others circling into the woods.

Panic seized her. Within the woods she could hear Frosty snarling madly. "We cannot let him go like that. He will be hurt!"

Using all the strength she possessed she wrenched the reins from Blane's hands and squeezed Gunnar' sides with her thighs. The horse flew forward, breaking through the trees. The force jolted her to the side, but she quickly righted herself, lowering close to the horse's neck so she wouldn't fall. Ignoring Blane's curse and subsequent shouts behind her, she blindly followed the sound of Frosty's growls. Pulling out her bow and nocking an arrow, she prepared to save him. When she came upon him, the animal was alone in a small clearing, surrounded by nothing but shadows. His silver coat was slick from his exertion and blood stained his snout.

Aliah hopped down from Gunnar and approached the dog. "'Tis me, sweet Frosty," she cooed.

Frosty turned wild eyes on her, his tongue rolling out of his mouth as he panted.

"What happened, boy?" she asked in a soothing tone.

Scanning the area, she saw no movement. The only thing out of place was the blood on her dog's face. He didn't appear to be injured, so the blood was not his. She returned her arrow to her quiver and her bow to her back.

At that moment, Sir Blane broke through the trees with his men, glaring daggers at her.

"Just what the bloody hell did you think you were doing? You're lucky we didn't find your body upon the forest floor." His voice was loud, threatening.

"I but wanted to make sure my dog was all right. You didn't seem inclined to fetch him."

Blane snarled. "That dog is trained to protect you. Did you not think he ran after a foe? Someone who intended you harm?"

She'd never been on a journey before, and since she didn't believe the things Glenda said, it'd never occurred to her that the dangers her maid preached about could be true.

"There was nothing." She twirled around indicating nothing but air. "There's no one here. What danger could there have been?"

"My lady," he said, sounding exasperated. "Surely you see the blood upon the hound's snout?"

"Aye." She'd thought Frosty simply banged it on a branch.

"There was someone here." He pointed to the ground. "See there? The ground is all disrupted. Looks like multiple people judging from the boot tracks."

Aliah glanced toward where he pointed. Sure enough the leaves and dirt were scattered, and deep impressions marred the earth as though a fight had occurred. Footprints and paw prints were pressed into the forest floor. And a piece of fabric.

She bent down to retrieve it. 'Twas dirty and stiff, with a few drops of blood.

"May I?" Blane asked, holding out his hand.

She nodded and stepped forward, handing him the scrap. Chills swept over her. Frosty had been trying to protect her, but from who?

Sir Blane frowned deeply, the scowl cutting creases into his forehead. "'Tis part of someone's tunic, is my guess. English."

"An outlaw?" she asked.

"Aye, most likely. 'Tis not safe for us to travel so openly it would appear. They may follow us."

The rest of his men melted from the shadows, shaking their heads.

"Damn," Blane muttered, his jaw muscles tightening. "They've found no one."

Aliah swallowed. "Are there many outlaws in these parts?"

Blane stared hard at her, a bit of surprise showing on his face. "Are you not aware of that already?"

"I'd been told but..."

"You did not listen."

She nodded, biting her lip and feeling as though she were a petulant child receiving a scolding.

"You are impulsive, Lady Aliah. 'Tis a flaw that could have gotten you killed this afternoon."

Mortification whirled through her. His words hurt. How many times had her father said those very same words? She could not argue, for she knew them to be true. Far too often she acted before thinking. And far too often she or someone else suffered from it.

Lowering her gaze to her dog, she patted him on top of his head. "Good boy," she whispered.

She refused to look at Sir Blane. So far, she had not made a very good go of this trip. Quite honestly, she wasn't sure the rest of their journey would be so uneventful either. Bad luck seemed to follow her in spades.

"My lady, if you will remount Gunnar, we must be on our way. I do not know how many were with the man your dog attacked and I don't want to wait around for an ambush."

Aliah shook her head. "You should be on Gunnar. Mad Maiden is no horse for a knight." Guilt riddled her for allowing him to ride the afflicted horse. Perhaps if he'd been upon his own mount he could have caught the outlaws who'd been stalking them in the first place.

Fire burned in his eyes as he stared at her. "Your horse's name is Mad Maiden?"

A flush crept over her neck and cheeks. "Aye."

Sir Blane just shook his head, then chuckled softly. "Fitting." He blew out a breath. "Mount up, we must depart."

"But your horse, surely he will be of more use to you."

"I shan't have you riding Mad Maiden, my lady. If we pass by an inn, I shall pay them for a new mount and have them return your mare to Mowbray Manor."

A thought occurred to her. "We could ride together. I did so many times with my brother Samuel. I wouldn't want Mad Maiden to slow us down."

"Eager to reach your father and sister?" He raised a brow.

"And keen to be away from danger." With Glenda telling her some things that were true and other things that weren't, Aliah suddenly felt a little lost. She appeared to know so little about the world. Certainly, she wasn't naïve enough to think that outlaws did not exist, but she also did not think they attacked just anyone. Looking around her party, she would have thought they were ordinary folks. None of them looked too rich, and what would an outlaw have to gain from robbing them?

Perhaps she should have spent more time exploring with Arbella and Samuel instead of staying behind to read the scriptures and volunteering her time at the abbey. At least she'd paid attention when Samuel snuck her outside with his bow and arrow. That was a skill she was glad to have, and one that she'd excelled at. Her father had even encouraged it, liking the fact that it took her out of doors when she would have rather stayed in. She missed her brother, but understood his duty to their country. Hopefully, he would be able to come home from France where he was currently serving King Edward in his royal quest to regain his lands.

So lost in her thoughts, she hadn't noticed Sir Blane dismounted Mad Maiden until his hand brushed her elbow.

"My lady?"

She jerked her gaze toward his and nearly drowned in the depths of his green eyes. They reminded her of a vast and fruitful meadow. Aliah licked her lips, her eyes traveling over his face until she settled on his mouth. What would it be like to feel his lips pressed to hers?

"Are you all right with riding behind?"

"Aye."

"I will mount and pull you up behind me."

"And what of Mad Maiden?"

"I will have one of my men lead her. We shan't leave her behind."

Aliah nodded, watching as Sir Blane turned toward his warhorse and gracefully mounted. She caught a healthy eyeful of his muscular calves and thighs, encased in hose, which sent her belly to quivering and her heart to pounding. He was exquisitely made and the urge to touch him was strong. Yet another sin she would have to confess.

He held out his hand to her. "Put your foot in my stirrup."

Taking his larger hand in hers, she put her foot in the stirrup and gasped as he easily swung her up behind him. Too late she realized what a bad idea it was.

Her thighs were spread wide, with his taut buttocks between them. Her knees touched the outside of his strong thighs and her breasts were pressed indecently to his broad back. Swallowing hard, she wrapped her arms around his waist and closed her eyes. Perhaps this was God's way of testing her. His way of finding out if she was suited for a life of serving only him. She would prove she was. This was a test she could pass, no matter how hot she felt of a sudden, or how her insides quivered. She could ignore the intense, dizzying need building within her. Couldn't she? She held her breath. What was happening to her? She'd never had these feelings before. It scared her. She didn't understand it, but knew somehow, Blane was at fault.

"Hold on, my lady, we shall set a grueling pace to reach camp by nightfall."

Aliah nodded, her chin bumping into his warm back. "Aye."

Holding on tight, her body lurched as Gunnar leapt into a gallop.

Aliah watched the countryside fly by as they rode hard over the dirt-packed road. Rolling hills and pastures were dotted with sheep and cows grazing lazily on the lush grass. Barren fields were cleared of their harvested crops, awaiting spring when farmer's would once again tend to them. Smoke spiraled from the roofs of cottages, its scent carrying on the light breeze. Aliah watched as the sun slowly sank, taking the day from bright to somber grey. Winter was coming soon. She was glad to make this journey now, knowing that if she did so within a few weeks' time snow would likely be falling impeding their progress.

By the time the horizon had turned pink and orange, and the moon and sun both showed low in the sky, Blane started to slow the horses. Aliah glanced around but did not see any inns or a village in sight.

"We shall make camp within the woods," he stated to his men, who moved as one into the trees.

They rode deeper into the forest for several minutes, and then stopped. She supposed Blane had found a spot he deemed a good campsite, however, Aliah could not tell the difference between this spot and any other.

A half-dozen of his men fanned out while Blane and another half-dozen stayed put, unmoving save for their hands resting on the hilts of their swords. Frosty sat down beside her, nuzzling her ankle.

"What are they doing?" Aliah whispered.

"They will make sure this spot is safe."

Visions of outlaws hiding in the shadows and leaping out at them had her heart beating fast, but soon the men returned and nodded to Blane.

"We shall stay here the night then."

He dismounted and helped her down. While his men prepared a fire, Blane made a makeshift tent for her using thick wool blankets.

"You didn't have to do that, Sir Blane."

"'Tis the least I could do. The tent will keep some of the chill air at bay. And you are a lady without a female companion to safeguard you."

"True enough, but I also have you to keep me safe."

His gaze darkened, and she didn't know why, but her skin started to tingle.

"Aye, my lady. I shall keep you safe. But you shall also have the tent."

He turned abruptly and started pulling the satchels, rolled blankets and saddle from his horse. Aliah couldn't help but wonder what had made him so cross. Perhaps he was having the same strange sensations that she was. If so, she could understand his attitude. 'Twas unnerving the way a simple gaze, a small touch, or just the thought of him, affected her.

Aliah followed Blane's example and went about unloading Mad Maiden. She dumped her satchels into the makeshift tent, and when she came back to give the mare a rub down, Blane was already doing it. He fed the mare some oats and cooed into her ear.

"I see you've taken a liking to my horse."

"What's not to like, other than her gait?" He chuckled and their eyes met once more.

She couldn't pull her gaze away. Lucky for her, Blane did. Flicking his eyes toward the fire he said, "Let us go warm ourselves. I have a meager supper, but I hope you will find it to your liking."

Aliah nodded and followed him to the fire. One of his men had placed a log on the ground for her to sit upon. She thanked him, happy to not sully her gown.

"Dinner of the gods," Blane said, handing her an oatcake and an apple.

"I should like to know what your favorite meal is," she replied, taking the proffered fare.

Blane bit into an apple, the crisp juice dribbling down his chin and making her hungry and uneasy. She bit into her own apple delighting in the sweet, tangy taste.

"Why?" he asked.

"Well, if oatcakes and apples are the meal of the gods, I should like to know what you consider to be heavenly."

A wicked glint flashed across his eyes. "There is only one meal I consider to be heavenly, but 'twould likely burn your delicate sensibilities."

"Oh, come now, I should think not."

"Pie."

"Pie?"

"Aye. Honey pie."

A few of his men snickered and when she glanced their way they averted their eyes.

"Sir Blane, why do I feel as though I am not part of some joke you all hold?"

"No reason, my lady."

"Hmm… Well, in any case, does your cook make you a good honey pie?"

At this Blane snorted, a bit of the water he'd just sipped spewing out. "Why no, my lady, never."

"Well, that is quite sad. If I were ever to visit you, perhaps I could bring you a honey pie."

At those words, his eyes locked on hers, darkening, his jaw tightening. He looked ready to devour her whole, and Aliah found she liked it all too much. She licked her lips, unable to turn away and unable to say anything. The air felt thick with tension, but she didn't understand why. Couldn't fathom why a tingle of something delicious wound its way over her back. This man did odd things to her just by looking at her.

"Eat your supper," he said, his voice low, stroking over her nerves in a way that sent a chill to pass over her.

Aliah swallowed hard and nodded. They did not speak again, and when she climbed beneath her tent to lie upon the hard earth, she found herself scandalously wishing that Sir Blane would crawl in beside her, to hold her the whole night through.

'Twas chilly. That was the only reason why. Not because she fantasized about kissing him, or because she wanted to know what he really meant by saying his favorite meal was a honey pie. As naïve as she was, she couldn't help but discern that such a thing had been wicked for him to say. If the hungry look he gave her was any indication, she might indeed be the meal he wished to feast upon.

Frosty lay down beside her, taking some of the night chill away. But her desire to kiss Blane did not disappear.

Chapter Four

Och, what was the matter with him?

Blane sat straight up on his bed roll, darkness surrounding him. The fire had burned down to embers, emitting little light. The moon was only a sliver, and what little light the orb emitted was blotted out by the towering trees of the forest. He couldn't sleep.

When his tossing and turning appeared to rouse some of his men, he tried hard to stay still. Flung his arm over his eyes, but even that did nothing to take the vision of Aliah from his mind. He was utterly spellbound.

He rested his arms on his knees and studied his men who slept peacefully around the dying fire. A lone man stood watch on the outside of their camp. Knowing he would not be falling back to sleep, Blane stoked the fire, and then offered to relieve his night watchman. The tired looking warrior nodded, grateful for an early reprieve. They'd traveled hard to reach Aliah quickly. With little time to rest and always on alert, sleep deprivation was a given.

Blane leaned against a tree, his gaze falling to the makeshift tent where his charge slept. Lady Aliah was beautiful and enigmatic. The way she pointed her arrow straight at his heart when he entered the great hall spoke of skill and protective instincts, yet when her wolfhound had charged into the woods, she'd gone after him without a thought.

In the dark he could just barely make out the silver tail of Frosty poking out from beneath the tent, and beside it, he could have sworn he saw a petite boot. But 'twas hard to tell. Pulling his dirk from his boot, Blane picked up a thick stick and began to carve it. The task always seemed to clear his mind, and sharpen his hearing. Tonight, he needed to unencumber his mind from thoughts of a certain woman. If not, she could be the death of him.

As if the devil tested him, the woman in question climbed from her tent. Her pale skin glowing in the dim moonlight, and her gown floating around her in a mystical way. If he wasn't completely aware that he was awake, Blane might have thought he was dreaming. He pushed off the tree, meaning to go toward her, but she looked around cautiously, before slinking around the opposite side of the tent, her dog in tow.

He narrowed his eyes. What was she about?

He didn't like that she was creeping away from camp. Perhaps Arbella wasn't aware that her sister worked as a spy for the king. Or maybe Aliah had figured out who he was and sought to run away.

Blane shook his head and walked stealthily toward the tent. The fact was, he'd been sent to England to collect a woman he knew nothing about. Continuing on her trail, he heard her let out a stream of unladylike words under her breath just beyond the next few trees. He had to stop himself from laughing. He always thought a woman should be allowed to speak her displeasure, if she was so inclined.

"My lady," he called out quietly.

"Sir Blane?" she whispered — very loudly.

"Aye."

"Give me but a moment of privacy?"

"Indeed."

He walked back several paces, now realizing her intent. Frosty ran over and nuzzled his palm. Blane patted the dog on the head, then flicked his hand for the dog to go back to camp. He smiled when the pet followed his direction.

Aliah emerged from behind the trees and sauntered forward.

"What are you doing awake?" she asked, her voice low, tantalizing.

"I am on watch. I saw you slink away and thought to find out what you were up to."

In the dim light he saw her push out her lower lip and he wanted to stroke it fervently with his thumb and then his tongue.

"I do not slink," she said.

He smiled and took a step nearer. Why, he didn't know. It was madness to be within inches of her. But she didn't back away. In fact, she took a step closer.

"Were you worried about me, Sir Blane, or did you fear I would alert your enemies that we made camp here?" Her head was tilted back, blonde locks flowing freely down her back. Her gaze met his, and the sliver of moon hit just right so that a sparkle shown in her eyes.

"Mayhap a bit of both."

She issued a throaty laugh. "At least you are honest. I do feel safer with you here."

Not the words he wanted to hear when he'd lied to her about who he was, but he found her trust in him gripped him tight. He wanted her to trust him.

"I would never let any harm come to you." His own voice had lowered, become husky, and the urge to take her in his arms grew. From this distance, he could smell the scent of wildflowers and herbs in her hair. Without thinking, he reached out and twirled a silky lock around his finger.

Aliah gasped and turned her head to the side, looking at his finger wrapped in her hair. He stepped closer, stroked her fair cheek, then rubbed his finger over her rosy lower lip as he'd desired to do. Her lip was soft, plush, kissable.

"Sir Blane," she whispered, her tongue flicking out to lick at her lips and catching the tip of his finger.

He hissed a breath, closed the distance between them so her body was flush to his. "Aye, my lady?"

"Will you kiss me?" Aliah's eyes were wide, and in her face he saw her trepidation as well as her passionate desire.

"If 'tis what you wish."

"And what of your wishes?"

"I would ver—" He cleared his throat, feeling the burr of his Scottish accent sneaking through his need to place his lips on hers. "I would very much like to kiss you."

She closed her eyes, tilted up on her tiptoes. Och, the lass would certainly be the death of him. Threading his fingers into her silken locks, he grasped her head and lowered his lips to hers. The moment their lips met, a strong jolt centered in his gut, spreading outward. 'Twas unlike anything he'd ever experienced with any other lass. And there had been many other lasses. He brushed his lips over hers, taking in the perfect softness and shape of her mouth. Although he wanted to thrust his tongue deep, to taste every inch of her, he kept his kiss sweet. He didn't want to scare her away with his carnality, even though his blood pumped straight to his shaft, which proudly stood at attention. He had to remember she was an innocent.

"Mmm," she murmured against his lips, and pressed closer, her arms encircling his neck and her hips pushing against his own.

Fire ignited in Blane's veins. Lady Aliah may have been an innocent, but her passionate nature and curiosity blended together into a sultry mix that he had a hard time fighting against. The way she pushed her hips against him, his shaft fit perfectly in the crux of her thighs. Gripping her hips, he pushed her a little away and begrudgingly took his mouth from hers.

He'd not take advantage of her. Even if his body demanded satisfaction. He wasn't in the habit of ruining noblewoman. Innocent noblewoman, at that. For one, his brother would kill him, and he shuddered to think what Arbella would do to him. Nay, he had to stop this. Now! He'd not be swayed from his true purpose.

"That was..." Slim fingers came up to delicately touch her lips and he wished with every fiber in his being to replace those digits with his mouth. To kiss her properly. "I enjoyed it." Shame filled her voice and he watched dejectedly as she looked toward the ground.

Guilt riddled him for having taken even that little piece of innocence from her. "My apologies, Lady Aliah."

She shook her head and then her sparkling gaze met his once again. "Nay, do not apologize."

"I must. You are a lady, and I should not have kissed you. 'Twas not my right."

"But I asked you to."

And he wished she'd ask him again. He curled his lips into a teasing smile. "Do you ask many knights to kiss your fair lips?"

Even in the dim light he sensed her blush. "Why, of course not."

"Am I the sole knight to have had the honor?" Blane didn't know why he asked, only that he wanted, needed the satisfaction of knowing that he'd been the only one to ever luxuriate in the decadence that was her kiss.

She nodded and a shock of lightning went through him. He had to step backward, else he'd take her into his arms again.

"We must return to camp," he murmured.

She nodded, then looked around. "Where is Frosty?"

"Most likely in your tent waiting for you."

"How do you know?"

"I sent him back to camp."

She narrowed her eyes and teased, "Why? Did you have hopes of kissing me and thought the hound might object?"

Blane chuckled. "If only I was so devious."

Her eyes widened and she gasped. Seeing his words shocked her, he immediately regretted admitting to his desire to be alone with her.

This was not good. He could not allow this to happen again. She was consuming his mind and making him go mad with passion. Such could make him forget his objective, a feat that would leave him with many regrets. Perhaps in future he would not send the dog away, but keep the massive wolfhound firmly planted between them.

Yanking his gaze from hers, he marched back to camp. Sleep would have better served him. Instead, he was kissing his charge in the woods, nearly overcome with the powerful need to take her on the forest floor. What in God's name was wrong with him? Her footsteps echoed behind him, crunching on leaves and snapping twigs. 'Twas a wonder she didn't wake all the guards when she'd gone off in the first place. 'Haps then he wouldn't have been tempted to kiss her. But knowing they were the only two awake and quite alone… Blane growled under his breath and turned back toward her.

"Do not leave your tent again until morning."

Aliah's brows furrowed together and she opened her mouth to argue when the snap of a twig echoed in the distance. He quickly scanned the camp noting that all of his men were there as was the dog. Instantly on alert, his first thought was of the outlaws who'd changed his life forever. The men he intended to put to death if he ever found them. Would today be that day?

"Someone comes," he whispered.

Aliah's eyes widened with fear and she froze in place. He softened his frown, hoping to comfort her. Blane grasped her hand in his and squeezed it gently.

"'Tis all right, no harm will come to you. Please, my lady, go into your tent."

She nodded and hurried to crawl beneath the coverings. Frosty stood at attention, the hairs on the back his neck stuck up on end, but he didn't bark. 'Twas as if the dog understood making a sound would call attention to the intruders, alerting them to their whereabouts. Smart hound. Satisfied that Frosty guarded his lady, Blane roused each of his men and put out the fire. While four of his men melted into the woods to surround their enemy, the rest formed a circle, weapons drawn, around Aliah's tent with Blane at the head.

They didn't have to wait long before a band of five shabby, dirt riddled outlaws emerged from the trees. Their clothes were torn and the stench of their bodies wafted even from a distance of ten feet away. Blane didn't recognize them.

The ringleader chuckled and stepped forward. "Well, what 'ave we here? Looks as though we've come upon a merry band of men and something they don't want us to see." He tried to peer between Blane and his men, hoping to see into the tent.

"I suggest you leave now, else we send you on your way," Blane said, keeping his tone purposefully bored.

The ringleader shook his head, eyes connecting with Frosty, who bared his teeth and growled. The man's eyes narrowed, and he grimaced, touching a grimy bandage on his hand. Blane was willing to bet these outlaws had been the ones Frosty encountered earlier in the day, which meant they were being followed. He guaranteed the man had the bite marks under the bandage to prove it.

49

Blane did not like being followed. This had to end, here and now. He couldn't be discovered. It would not only put Aliah in danger, but his entire clan. If they found out that he crossed the border dressed as an Englishman, he would never able to do so again, and his clan would lose their biggest source of revenue. He would never let that happen.

"We won't be leaving without a bit 'o coin," the man said, his beady eyes connecting with Blane's own gaze. The man fidgeted on his feet, his fingers gripping tightly to the hilt of his sword.

But still, the man didn't waver. He was either completely sotted or mad. Or both. In any case, Blane wasn't about to wait around to figure out which one. The crusty outlaw turned his gaze back toward the tent and licked his lips. His eyes widened a little. Blane didn't want to know why the man suddenly had a lecherous look in his eye—but he could guess one bonny blonde reason.

"We have no coin to give ye. Be on your way afore I slit ye from ear to ear," Blane growled.

The man jerked his gaze from the tent back to Blane, scrutinizing him, and a wide evil grin carved his features. His fidgeting stopped. Confidence suddenly bolstered the villain.

"What did you say, barbarian?"

Ballocks! In his anger a bit of his Scots dialect had slipped through. Blane hoped that no one had noticed. And now the maggot had the audacity to call him a barbarian… "I said, be on your way, before I slit your throat."

The outlaw shook his head, smirking as if he'd discovered a secret. "Nay, I do believe you said it slightly different."

What game was the man playing? It didn't matter, Blane was done with him. He took a threatening step toward the ringleader, and the man planted his feet in a battle stance, tossing his cheap sword from hand to hand.

"You want to fight?" he asked Blane.

Blane didn't say a word, he only nodded and took a step closer. His men who'd crept into the woods quickly pounced on the other four outlaws, while the remaining men surrounding Lady Aliah remained motionless. There was no need for them to intervene; he and the others could easily take on the outlaws. With a flick of his wrist and a twirl of his claymore, Blane disarmed his opponent within seconds. Untrained outlaws were no match for seasoned warriors. He kicked the man's legs out from under him causing him to sprawl backward with a harsh grunt. Blane placed the tip of his sword at the outlaw's neck.

He didn't intend to kill him. At least not in front of Lady Aliah. It could traumatize her for life. He'd clearly beaten the outlaw, and as he could see, his men had the other four on their backs as well.

"Do it," sneered the ringleader. His tone turned low and threatening. "My men will see that the English come crashing down on your black Scots' soul."

Coldness swept through Blane. Damn it all to hell, things were not going as planned, at all. There was no time to play games, now he had to deal with him. No loose ends.

"I'll not kill you if you agree to not follow us again." Blane pushed his sword further into his throat, just nicking the skin. "You must swear that you will not speak of our chance meeting to anyone. Or the next time I see you, I will have to put my sword through your heart."

The man shook his head. "You are a daft fool."

Why would the outlaw not just agree? 'Twas as if he wanted to taunt Blane into killing him. Did he want to die? Or did he believe Blane wouldn't do it? "You are lucky there is a lady here or else your blood would be seeping into the ground. Consider yourself saved."

The worm laughed, brown rotted teeth showing as his mouth opened wide. "I'll not be saved by the likes of you."

51

The outlaw jerked, knocking his arm against the sword, and cutting himself deeply in an effort to roll away.

"Bloody hell, what are you about?" Blane growled, moving to pin him down again.

For an untrained villain, he was wiry and fast. Most were when they saw their end was near. But he could still fall just as hard as any vermin. The man reached down and pulled a knife from his boot, about to throw it when an arrow pierced his arm, pinning his appendage to the ground. He cried out and dropped the knife, working on freeing his pinned and bloody arm.

Blane looked toward Aliah, who quickly cocked another arrow. Her gaze was steady, serious. None of the charming, soft lady he'd kissed moments ago. She called out, and let another arrow loose. Blane whirled back around, his eyes landing on the man as her arrow struck the blackguard in his heart. The villain's uninjured arm held another knife poised to kill him.

All speech left Blane. The lady had saved his life. Then again, she'd been the distraction that nearly caused him to be killed in the first place. He didn't know whether to thank her or curse his mission to retrieve her.

One of his men cleared his throat, and Blane returned his attention to the other four outlaws. "Tie them to the trees. Take their weapons and their clothes."

The maggots balked, but quickly quieted when Blane reminded them that while he took their belongings, he left their lives intact. "Do not attempt to follow us, or I shall see that each of you die painfully."

While his men saw to the prisoners and burying the dead outlaw, the others swiftly dismantled the camp and readied the horses. It was still dark and hours until dawn, but they were not safe in this spot. They had to move on quickly.

As he approached Aliah to help her onto Gunnar, he was taken aback by her stony mask and suspicious glare pointed in his direction. She raised her bow, and aimed it straight at his heart.

"Who are you? And this time, I'll have the truth."

Chapter Five

Aliah gripped her bow so tightly she was afraid the smooth wood would snap. But at least it kept her fingers from trembling. Every muscle in her body was tense and ached from fear of moving.

She kept her gaze steadily on the man who'd told her he was Sir Blane of Yorkshire, yet just spoke clearly with a Scots accent. Finding out his true identity was imperative—even if she had to fill him full of arrows. She tried to ease her breathing into a more normal pattern.

"My lady, please, would you put down the bow?" He held out his hands in supplication. "I am not your enemy."

His Scottish accent, while fleeting, had been evident when he spoke to the outlaws and threatened to slit them from ear to ear. Even if he held out his hands like that, even if his kiss had shaken her to the core and made her rethink for a moment her purpose in life, the truth was she had no idea who he was. For all she knew, he'd kidnapped her. Forged her father's letter.

Aliah glanced furtively at his men. None of them put a hand to their swords. She didn't know whether that scared her more or not. Did they think she'd put her weapon away? Did they believe she wouldn't put an arrow in this man's heart?

Mayhap they knew something she didn't. For she was not at all certain she could let her arrow fly to meet its mark.

"Who are you?" she demanded once more.

"I am Sir Blane."

"Of Scotland?"

He shook his head, his eyes searching hers. She felt compelled to believe him, to lower her weapon and sag into his arms. Aliah stiffened all the more.

"I am English, my lady."

"I heard you, when you were speaking to that dead man. Your voice changed."

Again his eyes searched hers. What was he looking for? Weakness. She worked to harden her gaze. Whatever it was he sought, she wouldn't back down.

He laughed a little, like she had made an assumption he found humorous. Again he shook his head, took a step forward.

"Don't come any closer or I shall let my arrow fly."

He held up his hands. "Nay, I do not want you to shoot me. I apologize for setting your heart to fear and for breaking your trust, my lady."

His accent was English personified. Confusion warred within her.

"I spent a lot of time in Scotland as a youth, my father was in the king's service. And then when I was fostered out, I served another English baron who also spent much time in Scotland. So, at times the accent pops out without my notice, but I assure you, I am one hundred percent English born and bred." His gaze that had been locked on hers scanned his men. "As are my men."

The knights nodded, grunted, but still none moved. She found their silence and stillness unnerving, but she supposed she'd rather have seasoned fierce warriors to protect her than weak ones—if she could count on them protecting her. Aliah still wasn't sure she believed Blane's story.

What choice did she have? If she left him to go home, she'd never make it. She'd either die of motion sickness from riding Mad Maiden or she'd be ravaged by outlaws. So far the only assault on her from Blane had been to her senses and her lips, and if she was completely honest, she enjoyed both.

Perhaps the best thing to do was to pretend she believed him and be ever more vigilant. Keep her own counsel and be prepared to defend herself if it should come to that. If this man had kidnapped her, the last thing she should do now was anger him into tying her up. She rather liked the freedom of walking about.

Decision made, Aliah nodded her head. "All right."

"All right?"

"I believe you," she said, her voice shaking slightly. She unnocked her arrow and slipped it back into the quiver filled with her custom-made arrows slung around her back. Her bow and arrows would remain on her person, she would not let go of her weapons. Her eating dagger was at her waist, and while she might not be able to land a killing blow with it, the blade was sharp enough to give a man an injury.

Blane clapped his hands and rubbed them together. "Well then, I am glad. And I am truly sorry for what has happened here. I should have been more vigilant while on watch. When next we make camp, several men will take watch at one time."

She wanted to add that perhaps if he hadn't followed her into the woods and kissed the sense from her that he would have heard the enemy approaching.

"For now, my lady, let us make haste."

Aliah nodded, and snapped for Frosty to come to her. How was it that the dog could trust this man? She supposed Frosty wasn't very smart. Then again, that was insulting herself since she too had fallen victim to his charms. Inside, she wanted to groan. This was not how a woman headed for the church behaved. Kissing aside, she should be forgiving Blane, accepting his word as truth for she had no reason to doubt him. He'd kept her safe—even if she'd had to save his life.

Killing a man was the last thing she wanted to do. She'd never done so before and the deed made her heart wrench. She had to remind herself that taking the man's life saved Blane's—the lesser of two evils.

"I um, need but a moment."

Aliah was aware that time was of the essence, but she could not leave here until she'd had a moment to say a prayer for the man's soul and to ask for God's forgiveness. She sought out the grave of the outlaw and knelt to the ground, her hands together in prayer, her rosary beads clasped in her fingers. Staring up through the trees she could make out a few stars in the sky and a sliver of moonlight. She closed her eyes and whispered the words. When she was done, she felt lighter, as if she'd unburdened a load, which in essence she had.

God forgave his children, she reminded herself. And she hadn't killed the man in cold blood; it had been to save the life of a man who was meant to protect her. A man she had grown...fond of since he'd banged on her manor door. Aliah pressed her lips together in a frown. Was she truly fond of him? She chanced a glance in his direction and the warm flip of her belly and buzz in her ears told her she certainly felt something for the man.

Saints! That was not the realization she was hoping for. She clung a little tighter to the straps of her bow and quiver and straightened her shoulders. 'Twas not in her nature to let a little thing like her feelings for a man get in the way of her dreams and her future. She was slated for the church. Looked forward to her service to God and his children — repaying the taint of her birth and the death of her mother. If her mother had to die while giving her life, then Aliah would see to it she did only good for others. She was going to make this world a better place, and spend her life in peace, solitude and reflection. Perhaps work in the sanctuary's herbal garden and hone her healing skills. Sew shirts for the poor. This little matter of a man interfering was nothing more than…a test. That was all it was and she'd best start realizing it.

No more kissing in darkened forests. No more drowning in the depths of his ivy-colored eyes. No more admiring his exquisite physique, or the way the light shined on his dark hair. This man was not what he appeared. She just couldn't figure out in what way.

Aliah marched to the horses, prepared to mount when she realized, yet again, she would be plastered to his back. 'Twould only make her newfound pledges all the more challenging. But she was up for the task. She could overcome this.

Aye, when she was riding behind Blane, she could also more easily study him, figure out his plans and keep herself safe.

Sir Blane mounted Gunnar and she avoided watching, instead she stared at Frosty to keep from swiveling her eyes in his direction. He offered his arm and she gripped it, gritting her teeth at the contact of his heat against her chilled limb. She swung up behind him and had to force herself not to purr when the warmth of his body seeped between her spread thighs.

Oh…stones! She wished to let out a string of curses but that wouldn't do, and while she sometimes forgot about her pledge to never take the Lord's name in vain, sometimes cursing at the sky did make one feel better.

Without asking if she was ready to depart, Blane urged his horse forward and his men followed suit. Frosty loped beside them, seemingly not noticing how little rest they'd been allowed. But Aliah was exhausted. They'd traveled hard all day, and slept little. They'd been ambushed. And now they were traveling again. She didn't want to ask when they would stop for fear of sounding too whiny, but she did hope it was soon. She needed a good night's rest, especially if she was going to keep on her toes.

The feel of Aliah's hands pressed to his abdomen had Blane gritting his teeth. It had his blood boiling and his cock raging with need.

Not good at all.

Putting aside such physical need was of the utmost importance. She'd had him so thoroughly distracted that he hadn't seen the ambush coming. That couldn't happen again. Even still, he couldn't get the memory of her kiss from his mind. Her soft lips, so willing and eager as he'd brushed against them. The way she'd plastered her body to his in blatant supplication to the pleasure he could give her. Blane had to remind himself that she was an innocent, that likely she was overwhelmed by the feelings he elicited in her. He wasn't arrogant, but he knew he was good at pleasuring women.

Normally he wouldn't hesitate to take a woman up on an offer of a carnal adventure, but Aliah was different—and he wasn't the type of man who took a woman's innocence. That was saved for her husband. Something Blane was not, and would never be. If only Aliah were a widow…

He shook his head, and grunted. This line of thinking would lead him nowhere and only provoked his need for the woman in question and his frustration at the fact that it could never happen.

Marriage wasn't in his future, no matter what his older brother Magnus said. Taking a bride was the last thing Blane wanted. He didn't want to be tied to any one woman, he loved all women... Except the thought of waking up to Aliah each morning did hold a certain appeal.

Satan's ballocks, where had that thought come from?

He had to concentrate on something else besides the warmth of her body pressed up against him, two particularly plush globes warming his back...

Wool. He would think about wool. They'd had a great run prior to his leaving to fetch the lass. Enough coin to pay for part of the castle's renovations and supplies for the clan. Even enough to upgrade their weapons and armor, with still more left for Sutherland coffers. Sutherland wool was unmatched.

When he returned to Dunrobin, he'd have to begin planning for their next trip, which might have to wait until spring depending on the weather. There were rumors of King Edward of England bringing his troops to Scotland in the spring — to retaliate against the Scots victory at Stirling. If that were true, Blane and his men would have an even tougher journey.

While on his travels, he'd passed through a town that held a monthly market. They garnered a lot of merchants and buyers which in turn increased other town profits. 'Twas an idea that held merit and one he'd have to speak with Magnus about. Their wool was in such high demand that they might be able to host their own wool market. During the winter months they could sell raw wool, yarn, and woven goods.

They kept off the main road, picking their way through the trees. Blane was careful not to let his horse trip on any fallen branches. They crept silently using only hand signals to communicate. Behind him, he could feel Aliah's body sag more with each passing hour. He held tight to her arms wrapped around his middle in case she fell asleep, fearing that she'd collapse.

Dawn approached and with it came the sounds of birds and insects chirping and buzzing their pleasure at another morning's arrival. Blane decided that it would be best to find shelter now, get a few hours of sleep and then continue on their way when the sun set that evening.

He'd found that traveling at night and sleeping during the day was the safest course of action to take. They'd already been followed by a band of outlaws, there was no telling what else would happen, and he wanted to arrive at Dunrobin unscathed and with all of his men — and Aliah — unharmed.

Ahead he spied what looked like the mouth of a cave set against a wall of solid stone. Moss and brush grew over the stones, and trees blocked his vision from discerning if it was indeed a place they could seek shelter.

"Go and see if that is a cave," he told two of his men. At the sound of his voice, Aliah jerked behind him.

She must have dozed off and he'd woken her. His men trotted up to the cave and turned back, signaling. They continued toward the cave as his men checked the surrounding area and the inside for the cave for danger.

Liam, his second in command, nodded that all was well within the cave, and the men who'd ridden around the area soon returned with news that it was all clear.

They dismounted from their horses, and while his men took care of their mounts, he led Aliah into the mouth of the cave. 'Twas dark inside, but warmer since they were now protected from the biting wind.

"Wait here while I make a torch." Blane met Aliah's gaze. Her eyes were red-rimmed from exhaustion, and she rubbed her arms as if against a chill. "I won't be long," he assured her.

The lass nodded, and gazed around the darkened cave, her face void of emotion. She hid her feelings well when she needed to he supposed. What he wouldn't give to get inside her mind and see exactly what she was thinking. Blane swiftly located a branch the size of his arm, cut slices into the end enough so he could fit some dry twigs and brush to create a makeshift torch. When he returned to the cave, Aliah was where he'd left her, still rubbing her arms.

He lit the torch with his flint. A golden glow lit up Aliah's face and provided a bit of light in the darkness of the cave. She looked pale, and dark circles smudged beneath her eyes. The cave was small, but big enough for everyone to sleep comfortably inside. Finding a crack in the stone, he wedged the torch into it then turned back to Aliah.

"I'm going to get the things to make your bedding. You look exhausted, my lady."

She nodded, her azure gaze catching his. For a moment, his breath ceased as he was caught up in her stare. The lass was beautiful to be sure, but there was something deeper that pulled him in. She was not a typical lady. He knew that she was different—special. If only he could be the one to explore her further, to unlock all of her secrets.

Wrenching his eyes away, he ducked out of the cave to retrieve their blankets and bags. When he returned, Aliah was no longer standing where he'd left her, instead she busily swept debris from the center of the cave floor with her feet.

"Will we build a fire?" she asked.

"I would like to, my lady, but alas, a fire would draw attention to us. Being so close to where we left some of our enemies alive, I'd rather keep our location as hidden as possible."

She frowned and her shoulders shook as another chill caught hold. Without thinking, Blane stepped up and stroked his hands over her arms. Through the fabric of her gown and cloak he could feel that her arms were well shaped. She jerked a little at the contact, but then sighed. He paused in his ministration, reminding himself that this was the last thing he should be doing right now. Reason warred with need.

Reason won.

Blane yanked his cloak from his back and wrapped it around her shoulders. "Since I cannot light a fire, this ought to help keep you warm."

"Thank you," she murmured. "'Tis still warm from your heat."

Desire sparked through his veins and his cock took a particular interest in another type of heat he could give her.

"Aye, 'tis a very good wool garment."

She nodded, glancing down at the shroud of cloth wrapping her in a cocoon. "Will you be cold?"

"Nay, my lady." Thoughts of her were sure to keep him warm the whole day through.

Unable to look at her any longer without giving in to his need to kiss her, Blane set about assembling her a makeshift bed. She lay upon it, Frosty curving his bulk against her back, while he dug through his bag to find her a bite to eat. By the time he found a few oatcakes and an apple, Aliah's breathing had evened out into a soft rhythmic pattern. The poor lass had been through a lot since he'd taken her from her manor. A whole new world, from what she'd told him. A sheltered life had not prepared her for the harsh realities of this world. Guilt ate at him for lying to her, for when they reached Dunrobin and the truth about his identity was revealed, she would never look at him the same way again. She would loathe him. He wasn't sure he could handle that.

They'd only known each other a short time, but in that time, he'd learned something about himself. He liked having a woman trust him, depend on him. What a sad mess that was. Shaking his head, he left the cave. He would take first watch with a few of his men.

And hopefully clear his head of thoughts of a certain blonde, enticingly beautiful and enigmatic lass.

Chapter Six

Aliah gasped, her eyes popping open as she sat straight up from the warm nest of wool blankets Sir Blane had made for her. Blinking rapidly, she took in her surroundings, trying to recall everything that had happened up to this point. Everything spiraled back in minute clips behind her mind's eye. Blane knocking on her door. Traveling into the unknown dangers of the forest. Frosty running away. Her first kiss. The outlaws. She'd killed a man.

Frosty shifted beside her, grumbling at her for moving. She patted his belly then pulled her knees toward her chest and stared out of the darkened cave to the light beyond. Within the cave several men slept. None of them snored, but all of them breathed as though they were in a deep sleep.

Closing her eyes, she said a prayer once more for the life she'd taken and for her own soul. The only consoling thought was that she'd killed a murderer and in turn saved a life. She hadn't killed him in cold blood, and she'd given him a warning by first shooting his arm, but the man had been stubborn and didn't want to back down. He'd pointed his knife at Blane and Lord only knew how swift he could be with his weapon. Blane had been shaken; she'd seen it in his eyes. He'd not expected her to save him, and he'd probably been disappointed in himself for not having noticed the outlaw's intent. She'd been stunned too, but the overpowering surge of protective instincts that barreled through her when she'd seen the outlaw reach for his concealed weapon had sealed his fate.

How did knights live with themselves when they had to go to war and take lives? Aliah knew they had no choice, didn't feel disdain for them because of it, she actually felt admiration. She took in a shuddering breath. How did they keep their sanity? Perhaps she should ask Blane what he did to cope. Part of her understood that she would be forgiven for taking a life, but for a simple woman headed for a life of peace within the church, having done such a deplorable deed weighed on her mind.

Her shoulders hunched and she pressed her chin to her knees. Blane was not among those sleeping in the cave. He'd told her he was taking first watch and if she wasn't afraid of going out into the forest alone, she would seek him out now and gain his opinion on her dilemma. As it was, she had Frosty, and trusted him to help her. Staying put would be best. She didn't want to bring any further complications onto the party who would strive to keep her safe until she reached her sister and father.

When she was about to force herself to sleep again, Blane appeared at the entrance to the cave. His intense gaze fell on her and immediately she felt tingly. He didn't just look at her, it was almost as if he absorbed her, memorized her, touched her with just his heated gaze. Blane broke their stare by scowling and motioning for her to join him outside the cave. Shucking her blankets, she was careful not to disturb anyone as she tiptoed out.

"My lady, why do you not rest?"

"I just woke." She handed him his cloak, now completely warmed.

He shook his head. "Keep it."

"I am warmed through, and my own cloak suffices just fine now."

Blane shrugged, taking the cloak from her. "Suit yourself. Why aren't you sleeping?" He swung the cloak around his broad shoulders.

Aliah did not like the way he stared at her as though she were keeping something from him.

She shrugged. "Mayhap 'tis because I am in a foreign place. Or 'haps 'tis even because I killed a man last night."

Blane's expression changed with her admission, softening. By the slight lift of his arm, she wondered if he'd thought about comforting her and then decided against it. Oddly, she was disappointed that he didn't. She rather liked the way he'd warmed her hours before by rubbing her arms. Objection would not pass her lips if he tried to do so again.

"Taking a man's life is no little thing, my lady. You were very brave to have done it, and you saved my life. I will be forever in your debt."

Aliah shook her head. "I don't want you to be in my debt forever."

"How can I repay you?"

Any number of ideas came to mind, most of them involving a sinful kiss, which made her blush and wish they'd already reached their destination so she could seek confession for such wanton thoughts. Good thing she would seek absolution from a priest in another country, for she feared what would happen if word were to get back to Mother Superior about her less than innocent behavior. Not that any priest was allowed to share what was confessed, but they could perhaps put a bug in Mother's ear that Aliah was not exactly what the church was looking for in a nun.

"There is no need. Simply get me to my sister and father quickly."

"That I can promise you."

She titled her head a little to the side, taking in his square jaw dusted with a day's growth of beard. Her fingers itched to touch him. "There is one other thing…"

"Anything, my lady."

"Is there anything…special that you do when you've taken a life? That helps you heal quickly from such a tragedy?"

He smiled and for the first time she noticed a slight dimple in his cheek when he did so. His smile was contagious and she found herself grinning despite the dark topic.

"Remembering the cause is always helpful. The man was an outlaw, intent on harming you if he got past me, which he was dead set on ending my life to do so. You saved my life and in essence saved your own. Trust me when I say he would not have been kind to you."

Aliah nodded. "That does make me feel a little better."

His grin deepened, taking on a roguish glint. "There is also…" He reached for the wineskin draped on his shoulder. "The drink of the angels."

"Water?"

"No, water is the drink of the gods. The gods keep us alive and thriving. The angels keep us sane." He took a long draw then passed it to her.

What game was he playing? She too took a long swig, only to regret it a moment later as the liquid burned a path down her throat. She spit out what was left in her mouth, the fire-filled liquid spewing from her lips—too late she realized—right at Blane.

Aliah's mouth fell open in mortification as she stared at him, his face covered in droplets of the liquor and the front of his cloak soaking wet.

"Well, that wasn't expected," he said dryly, wiping his face on the sleeve of his cloak.

Heat filled her face to flaming, and all Aliah wanted to do was seep into the leaf strewn forest floor.

"Oh, my…I'm so, so sorry," she managed to choke out.

Blane shook his head, merriment filling his eyes. Was he laughing at her? "No need to apologize, my lady. I should have warned you that 'twas a stronger drink than you might be used to."

"Stronger is an understatement…" She glanced nervously from the ground to his sparkling eyes.

He was laughing, and soon the sound escaped him. Deep, throaty, masculine and filled with humor.

Tears of embarrassment stung her eyes, but he shook his head vehemently. "I take it you've not had whisky before. Do not be upset, my lady. I but laugh at our situation. Look at me." He held his hands in front of him gesturing toward his wet cloak. "I am soaked in my own brew."

She nodded, not sure how she could not be upset when she'd been the one to spray the brew upon his person.

"'Tis funny. Come now, shall I do it to you?" he asked, looking quite serious.

Aliah narrowed her eyes, imagining Blane spitting whisky on her. She said with a shocked whisper, "No, sir."

Her response made him laugh all the harder. "Oh, Lady Aliah, I would never do such a thing. Your expression though upon hearing my question was priceless."

Aliah huffed a breath and crossed her arms over her chest. She was not used to being teased and wasn't sure how to feel about it. Irritation warred with humor. "Do you take pleasure in humiliating others? 'Tis a sin," she said with mock haughtiness.

His brows raised and he took a step toward her. "Do you lecture me, my lady?" His voice was low, underlined with a note of sensuality that worked its way up her spine. "'Tis a sin to be so tempting." The last of his words were said on a breath as he dipped low and captured her mouth with his.

She was taken aback at first and gasped. Her lips parted a little and Blane's tongue swiped for only a second at the small opening. He tasted of whisky, but this time it wasn't a fire that took her breath but rather a slow, sensual burn. He pulled back, abruptly in fact, and away from her, leaving her dazed and confused. Her legs shook, and she was in danger of collapsing. Her breaths came quick and her heart pounded in her ears. Not even a minute had passed since his lips brushed hers and his tongue slid enticingly over her parted mouth, but it rocked her to the core all the same. There was a blatant difference between their first kiss and this kiss.

Their first kiss had been sensual, slow and decadent. This was none of those things. It was hot, tantalizing and wicked. And Aliah wanted him to do it again.

Oh, Saint's toes… She ought to march herself to the nearest church and have the abbot send a missive straight away to Mother Superior, explaining that Aliah was not right for a life of servitude. She was a wicked, wanton woman, filled with a strong desire to taste the hot blooded man standing before her.

Aliah's face blazed with heat, that heat searing a path down her neck to her chest and to her breasts. Her nipples were hard, aching buds. And…she wanted Blane to touch them.

Thank goodness for her cloak, which she tugged closer, grasping it like a shield. But as much as she tried, she wasn't sure she would ever be completely shielded from this man.

Blane raked his hands through his hair and gazed into the forest beyond. "My lady, I apologize for taking liberties that are not my own." The way his voice was deep and hoarse with desire, licked its way along her wanton nerves.

What was it about this man that made her want to be wicked?

Was it a blessing in disguise? Was this her path? Was this God's way of showing her that she was meant for something different? For love?

Aliah shook her head. That couldn't be true. While her father wanted her to marry, she'd decided long ago she would go into the church. A place where she always felt comfortable, a place where she felt closer to the mother she'd never known. Arbella had fought against marriage for years and when she'd finally been coerced into an arrangement, Aliah had seen her sister's unhappiness, thus her own goal to join the church and never having to enter the bonds of marriage were fortified.

But according to Sir Blane, Arbella was happy in her marriage. Mayhap things could change. But could she? Would she ever be forgiven for having taken her mother's life?

"You had best get back to sleep. We shall pack up camp and resume our journey when dusk approaches." Blane's voice held an edge, as if he were on dangerous ground.

She supposed if he'd been as affected as she was by their kiss, that he was indeed facing a perilous precipice.

Aliah nodded. She opened her mouth to thank him for his advice, which had calmed her guilt, but he stopped her with a hard stare and the flexing muscle of his jaw.

"Sleep well, my lady."

Was it possible he still wanted to kiss her? Confusion filled her. She didn't understand men at all — often butting heads with her brother and father — and Blane was sending her one mixed signal after another. She frowned as she marched back toward the cave. He wasn't the only one sending mixed signals — Aliah was doing the same thing to herself.

Blane marched with purpose along the perimeter he'd marked out for their cave. The only intruders being the occasional rabbit, squirrel or deer. His mouth watered for a good meal. He was tempted to bring out his bow and arrows and catch them a hearty supper, but cooking the meat would require a fire and he'd already deemed one too dangerous to light.

Over the past few weeks, a succulent meaty dish had been few and far between. He was growing rather tired of jerky, oatcakes, apples, dried bread, hunks of moldy cheese and whatever else he could forage in the forest. Once they reached Scotland, he would stop at the inn he patronized whenever he went to market. He trusted the owners and knew the beds would be clean and the food ample.

Someone cleared his throat behind him and Blane whirled around, yanking his sword from its sheath and holding the blade at the man's throat. Too late he noticed it was his own man. "Liam, ballocks, man, I almost killed you."

"Ye are tense, Sir Blane." Liam pushed the blade away.

Blane looked around nervously. The rule was not to speak since his men had yet to perfect their English accents. He sheathed his sword when he was satisfied they were alone.

"The lass is fast asleep, buried in wool and dog." Liam chuckled. "Ye should get some rest now yourself. I'll wake ye when gloaming takes us."

Blane nodded. Sleep called to him. He would be no good to anyone if he continued on this path toward exhaustion. Moments ago he'd nearly taken his friend's head off. Cobwebs marred his thinking and his vision seemed a little blurred.

"I have seen nothing come to pass this way," he relayed. "While I sleep, make sure that no fires are lit. So far it appears we have entered here unnoticed and I want it to remain that way."

"I will see it done," Liam said.

The man scanned the forest then picked his way along his own imaginary path. Satisfied they were in capable hands, Blane headed toward the cave. With each step forward, sleep beckoned, drawing him closer. As he entered the cave, Frosty lifted his head and growled until he saw that it was Blane. Recognition dawning, his tail thumped on the floor, but he did not leave his spot beside his mistress. The other men were already settled in and sleeping. Blane tried not to look at Aliah, but his eyes disobeyed him.

She lay curled up on her side, some of her hair, loose from her plait, forming waves around the creamy skin of her face. Her lips were parted slightly, and when he listened intently, he could hear the faint sound of her breathing. Her lashes fluttered and he wondered what she might be dreaming of. His kisses?

Blane wrenched his gaze away. No more thoughts of kissing. She would never be his and he'd best get used to it. No doubt when they reached Scotland, Arbella would have located her father and the man would come to collect his youngest daughter. Blane did not want to be caught in the middle of that. The Englishman would be in a murderous rage if he lost two daughters to Scotsmen. Especially with the state of their two countries. A future with Aliah was impossible.

Blane's older brother and laird, Magnus, was lucky to have made it safely through his first battle alongside William Wallace when they took Stirling. During Blane's brief visit home after traveling to the fleece market and then agreeing to return to England to retrieve Lady Aliah, he'd come to learn much of the goings on between the two countries and his brothers' involvement. Even Ronan, his younger brother by a few years, had been invited to fight alongside William Wallace, and last he'd heard, was thinking of accepting. When Blane arrived at Dunrobin, would Ronan have already left? He hoped not.

Ronan was a true leader, an excellent warrior and very level headed. He was a lot like Magnus in that respect and Blane had no doubt his brother would make a great impression with Wallace and forge ahead with the war for Scottish Freedom.

Blane dropped to a free blanket, rolling another beneath his head. He made sure he faced away from Aliah. He didn't need to gaze at her as he drifted off. He was certain his dreams would be filled with her, even without looking. She captivated him with her beauty, intelligence, curiosity and her passion. When he was around her, common sense warred with need. Kissing her… Oh, God, when he'd tasted her lips, swiped his tongue inside to tease. The warmth of her mouth, sweetness of her lips, had nearly destroyed him. He would have plundered her mouth, pulled her to the ground and had his way with her.

'Haps when they traveled this eve he would have her ride with Liam. He wasn't sure if he could handle her breasts pressed to his back. 'Twas a sweet torture, one that only seemed to increase his need—a constant reminder of how he'd never have her.

Blane wasn't a glutton for punishment—not until yesterday when he'd met Aliah. Now it seemed he was in a constant state of arousal, which would forever go unsatisfied. The faster they got to Dunrobin the better. He'd drop her off and then leave. Beg off, making excuses about having to get word to someone. He didn't really care what excuse he gave Magnus; he just knew he wouldn't last being around her.

Chapter Seven

Blane woke on his own some time later. He sensed a change within the cave, and rolling over noted that Aliah was folding up her blankets. Frosty stood at attention by her side. Seeing Blane's movements, she turned her gaze in his direction and smiled.

He was mesmerized by her long slim fingers as she neatly and precisely worked the blanket.

The other men had already risen and taken their things. Blane felt lazy for having slept so long. But his body must have needed it. He felt refreshed.

"Did you get enough rest?" Blane asked. He stood and collected his own things, in not so neat a fashion.

"Yes, I did." She tucked the blankets under her arm and turned to fully face him. "Will we travel through the night now?"

"Aye, 'tis safer for us."

"I didn't realize how dangerous it was…everywhere." Her brow was creased with a frown he wished to smooth away with his thumb.

"'Tis not this way everywhere." Blane wanted to tell her of his own family's lands, of being able to ride freely, to walk the beaches without fear. But, was even that freedom changing? After all, Arbella had been attacked in the forest just an hour's ride south of the castle by men from the Ross clan. Ross land bordered their own and recently the laird's daughter Ina had married Arbella's original intended in a bizarre twist. Ina was supposed to have married his brother Magnus, and threatened all sorts of hell when she found out she'd been betrayed. Blane feared that with two of their enemies now united and living so close, the days of being carefree were coming to an end.

"I wonder why my father never told me of the dangers?"

"Did he not?"

She pursed her lips. "Mayhap he did. I knew that I must always be careful, but I would not have thought to be attacked within hours of having left my home. Glenda certainly did."

Blane chuckled. "Aye, she would. And even though she may have exaggerated most things, she was also right about a lot, it would seem."

"Truly?" Aliah's frown intensified and fear flickered over her features.

"Well, maybe not most, I don't know what she's told you."

Aliah waved her hand. "Mostly silly things, I'm sure." But she didn't look so certain.

"Perhaps your father thought Glenda was taking care of warning you. And as you must know, he probably did not expect you to leave home unescorted. Come, let us mount up. We'd best be on our way."

Blane was quite surprised that her father had not expounded more, but then again, she was excellent with a bow. 'Haps rather than telling her the horrors of the world he'd done what he deemed best and taught her how to take care of herself instead.

They exited the cave, stepping into the dimly lit forest. Fingers of orange and pink streaked across the sky. Soon the sky would be black, the moon and stars shining. The men had readied the horses and waited for Blane's cue.

"My lady, I was thinking that perhaps you'd like to ride with Liam this eve?"

Her sharp gaze told him his question was completely unexpected. "Why?"

How could he tell her he thought it best if they put some distance between them without coming off as a toad?

Blane shrugged. "Different perspective?"

She pursed her lips in a way that he'd come to notice meant she was questioning what he said. "What aren't you telling me? Do you not wish to ride with me? I am perfectly capable of riding Mad Maiden if you find my company to be so distasteful."

Blane groaned inside. She was a lot like his sisters, Lorna and Heather. Playing games with her words and confusing his meaning.

"My lady, I meant no offense. Your company is not distasteful, I but thought you might like to try another mount."

She shook her head and he picked up on the fear that snaked over her brow. "You are my escort. But mayhap you are right." She turned away from him and walked toward Liam.

Liam looked at her questioningly from his pale blue eyes, took the blankets she offered and tucked them onto his horse. He passed an odd look to Blane, and Blane realized he had not apprised Liam of his plans to have the lass ride with him. Jealousy socked him in the gut upon seeing Aliah take Liam's hand as he helped her to mount. Her warm body would be flush against Liam for hours…

Trying not to speak through gritted teeth he addressed his second in command. "The lady will ride with you this eve. I've a need to keep an eye on our surroundings, and I'd like to be able to weave in and out. Having her on the horse with me will make it difficult."

Liam nodded, but Blane noted that Aliah refused to look at him. He'd offended her. Part of him regretted that fact, but the other part of him was pleased. 'Twas best if she was irritated with him, they would speak less, and there would be less opportunities for kissing. They needed to keep their distance.

Blane handed the reins of Mad Maiden to another of his retainers and then mounted Gunnar. He felt the loss of her presence deeply and it bothered him. To forget about it—or rather to distract himself from knowing how she warmed Liam's back—he rode ahead of their group, backtracked and caught up with them again. Always on the lookout, he saw nothing out of the ordinary. They had to travel a little slower being that it was dark and they'd taken to riding just inside the forest rather than on the road.

Not once did they encounter anyone, a stroke of luck Blane was sure would end soon.

When the hurt of Blane's rejection hit her like a slap, Aliah knew then it was time to put distance between them. As much as his disinterest pained her pride, 'twould hurt more if they continued along the path they seemed to be barreling toward.

He made her question everything about her course, which to her seemed wrong. If a man could make her question her future was he the right one for her? Then again, he had not a clue as to what her future held. No one did besides her and Mother Superior. She'd been sure to keep her desire to join the church close to her heart, for she was certain her father would protest vehemently against it.

In his mind, he'd already given up one person he loved to God—Aliah's mother. The woman had lived long enough to bring Aliah into the world, but then she'd quickly passed. Baron de Mowbray had never made her feel as though she were to blame, but he'd stated loudly on occasion that God had taken his wife too early. The least she could do was to devote her life to Him. On one excited whim, Aliah had expressed that a life within the church would suit her fine. That exclamation had received a litany of curses from her father. She'd never said anything about it again.

While her father had his reasons, so did she.

But now, Sir Blane was ruining her plans. Making her want other things. So, while his dismissal hurt, it was also a blessing she would embrace.

"Have you served Sir Blane long?" she asked Liam as they rode through the darkened forest.

The man nodded.

"Are you also from Yorkshire?"

He grunted in reply.

"I wonder how Sir Blane was given direction to fetch me?"

The man grunted again.

His non-vocal responses were annoying, but what was more irksome was the realization that she'd never asked Sir Blane that question herself. He'd come into her home, relayed he was from Yorkshire. She'd never thought twice about it. Until now. Why had Blane come from Scotland where he'd been with her father and sister? What was a man from Yorkshire doing in Scotland and why would he agree to come back to England and then travel all the way back to Scotland with her? It didn't make sense. Why had her father not done that very thing himself?

Why not just come home?

Why not send a missive relaying that her father would be returning soon?

She'd been so consumed with worry that she hadn't thought about the details. Her mind was too focused on seeing her father and sister, that she didn't see what was right in front of her. The truth. His accent. The reason he said he grew up in Scotland... Something was off.

"When I am reunited with my family, will you and Sir Blane return to Yorkshire?"

The man nodded.

"Why did Sir Blane agree to this?"

The knight only shrugged.

Aliah wanted to throttle him. Why did he not speak? Was he being rude or maybe... She didn't want to think that perhaps he'd been injured in battle and was now mute. If she were to ask and that was the case, then she'd feel terrible for having brought up the subject. 'Twas best if she said nothing. Mayhap 'twas another test of her character, to see if she was worthy to serve God.

But even she was starting to doubt that. Instinct told her to be wary.

She watched the forest pass her by, growing darker with each lapsing hour. The branches reached out like long-limbed arms, ready to grab her at any moment. Owls screeched as they hunted, their prey screaming and then silent. Crickets chirped loudly. Above the moon shined its silver light down upon them.

Aliah kept her senses alert and watched as Blane weaved in and out of the trees, sometimes disappearing altogether. She held onto Liam, noting that he was not as thick with muscle as Sir Blane, but equally tall. He sat rigid on his horse, not at all relaxed and she hoped it wasn't from her riding with him. Her arms were wrapped around Liam's waist but he did not hold onto them as Blane had done. She was glad, for it seemed an intimate thing and she was just as uncomfortable on Liam's horse as he appeared to be.

"Might we be stopping soon?" she asked, her bladder screaming for relief. Liam gave no response. She looked up at him, letting go for a moment to poke him. "Did you hear me?"

He nodded, then whistled. The group came to a stop within moments. Liam dismounted and helped her down. He scanned the area then pointed toward a cluster of what looked like mulberry bushes.

Blane was nowhere in sight.

She would ask him about Liam. Although she really hated to be nosy, she was overwhelmed with curiosity at his affliction. She picked her way toward the bushes, tripping once on a lifted root. With only the light of the moon, she could barely see anything. She had to slide one foot in front of the other to keep from tripping again. Doing so in daylight would be so much easier — at that moment she was grateful that the sun rose at all and wished they could travel in the morning instead of at night.

When she finished, Aliah walked carefully back to the group, finding Blane now among their company. All of them stared up into the trees, mesmerized. No one made a sound. Aliah tried to look up, but saw nothing except empty branches, stars and the moon.

She gasped as someone took hold of her arm, but sighed when she realized it was Blane. His fingers were warm through the fabric of her gown. He pointed up into the branches and whispered, "See there? 'Tis an owl."

Aliah had never seen a wild owl — only those trained with the hawks and falcons at her manor home. She searched the branches to no avail. "I don't see it," she whispered.

"There." Blane spoke so quietly, 'twas almost indiscernible. "See his eyes, they glow in the moonlight. Like two flashing orange orbs."

Then she saw it—just barely making out the shape of the bird's body. They truly were like two flashing orange orbs as the bird turned its head first one way and then another. "Is it hunting?"

He shrugged. "Mayhap. Or he could have already eaten."

"Have you ever gone hawking?"

"Aye. We have a falconry at Dun—"

"Where?" What had made him cut off his own words.

"At my home."

"I have oft wanted to try it, but my father did not think 'twas a good idea. My mother used to have a falcon, but then the bird was spooked, nearly took off her finger he said."

Blane met her gaze, his own eyes seeming to shine in the moonlight. "Must have been very spooked. They are supposed to be extremely loyal birds."

"Enough so that my father feared them."

Blane smiled. "But you do not?"

Aliah shook her head. "Mayhap, when I return to England with my father and we pass by Yorkshire, we could visit your home and you could show me."

Shadows passed over his face, his lips curling downward somewhat. "I don't think your father would allow that."

That thought hadn't quite passed her mind and now she realized he was probably right. Her father would never allow it.

"I tell you what, when we reach Scotland, if they have a falconry, I will show you."

"Would you? Truly?" Excitement coursed a path through her veins. She imagined holding a bird upon her arm, safely protected with a thick leather gauntlet. Whispering a command and watching the falcon take flight, its golden wings spreading wide and a breath of air caressing her face as it flapped into the sky.

"Aye."

"I should like that very much." Although she felt like smiling wide, she was slowly reminded of her earlier vow to keep her distance from this man. But having a lesson in falconry could hardly lead to anything more sinful. They'd be accompanied by a falconer at the very least.

Blane's gaze pulled from hers back toward the perched owl. Aliah couldn't help but study his strong profile. If in another life, she was to have found a mate, she imagined she would have liked a man like Blane very much. He was strong, intelligent and a very skilled kisser. She jumped when the owl took flight, its silence and beautiful gliding power breaking whatever spell had held her mesmerized.

Blane quickly turned back toward her and placed a steadying hand on her elbow. She felt flustered for having jumped and from the heat of his touch.

"Are you all right?" he asked, his gaze a mix of concern and amusement.

"Aye," she said with a little laugh. "I was surprised, 'tis all."

"You are beautiful."

"What?" But she'd heard him, even if she was stunned by his compliment. Even he looked dumfounded.

He shook his head and let go of her arm. "'Tis true, you are, but I apologize for having said it."

"There is no need to apologize. A lady always likes to be told she is pleasing to the eye."

Blane smiled sadly. "Aye, but 'tis something reserved for your intended."

"I have no intended."

The interest that lit his eyes both tantalized and scared her. She had to tell him now, so that there could be no more kissing, no more admissions that could only lead to heartache.

Taking a step back and looking toward the ground, Aliah murmured, "I am to join the church."

"The church?" The shock in his voice saddened her.

Aliah could not face him and instead tried to piece together what type of trees the leaves at her feet might have fallen from—a difficult task considering how dark it was. "Aye. In the spring, I will take my vows."

"My lady, forgive me for asking, but why would you waste your beauty on the church?"

At that she did look up, and meeting his gaze she answered with all seriousness. "Beauty is only skin deep and fades with time. But my soul will last for eternity."

Blane didn't speak for the span of several moments. She supposed he was letting the heaviness of her words sink in. Had the man never met a woman intended for the church or had he, like she, fantasized about a life together?

"Then," he murmured, his voice no more than a croak, "I should ask you to pray for me, my lady."

With that, he extended his arm toward the horses and bowed. So formal he was, that she wished she could take back her words, wished she hadn't told him of her intentions, because he had made her think that perhaps a different life was possible. She opened her mouth to tell him just that, to tell him he was handsome and that she wanted him to kiss her again. But looking around she saw that his men stared, waiting. Sighing in frustration at the turn of events, Aliah marched briskly back toward Liam, tripping only once on a tree root in the process. She was thankful for the dark to hide her reddened face and even more thankful that not one of them blinked at her clumsiness.

As she settled atop Liam's horse, sitting behind his rigid figure, Blane approached with an apple in his hand.

"I thought you might want to have a bite to eat. We will stop in a few hours to eat a heartier fare than fruit, although I can't promise you more than an oatcake."

She took the proffered fruit, her fingers brushing his and a tingle raced up her arm. His eyes widened showing that he too felt their connection.

"Thank you, Sir Blane, for everything."

"'Tis my pleasure."

The way he said *pleasure* sent heat coursing through her. She watched him walk away, then, closed her eyes to try and steady her rapidly beating heart.

As much as Aliah hated to admit it, her eyes had been opened to a whole new realm of possibilities. One in which she did not enter the church. One in which she faced her fears, her demons and perhaps lived happily and with love.

Chapter Eight

Several hours later, when Aliah felt herself dozing in and out, her face pressed to Liam's hard back, the horses stopped. Thank the saints. She'd not ridden this much in her entire life. Every limb screamed for relief, to stretch muscles she didn't even know existed. Liam helped her dismount and when her feet hit the ground, her legs wobbled, feeling a lot like mushy berries. Even her arms trembled.

From what she could make out in the grey of predawn, they'd stopped in a small clearing near a creek. The sound of water burbling over rocks was calming. Crickets and other insects chirped, undisturbed by human appearance, which only unsettled her nerves. Was this area normally filled with traffic, hence the bugs not ceasing their calls?

Aliah stared hard into the darkness beyond. Trees were thick on the outskirts of the small clearing. She imagined all sorts of assailants waiting in the shadows for her to approach. Even imagined sets of glowing eyes—wolves, bears, wildcats.

"We shall stop here to rest a spell and to eat," Blane said from a few feet away, seemingly untouched by their location.

She'd been so out of it when they'd ridden she hadn't seen him or any of his men scout the area, but he must have, else he wouldn't have appeared so composed.

Aliah nodded and stretched out her back, hands on her hips. What she really wanted to do was lie upon the ground and stretch out her legs. A small smile touched her lips at the reaction that would garner from Blane and his reserved men. "Thank you. I find my body grows weary of riding."

"Aye, and we've hardly had solid rest."

Aliah nodded. Her head felt a little fuzzy too.

"My men will take themselves in that direction for relief, if you'd like to go this way." He pointed toward a cluster of thick trees and brush that looked almost like a curtain.

"Thank you, Sir Blane."

Blane nodded. "I shall accompany you."

"What? No. Go with the men." What could he possibly be thinking? 'Twas not a moment she wished to share with anyone.

Blane chuckled. "I won't watch you, my lady. Promise."

She didn't move. "What is your purpose then?"

"I must keep an eye on you. You are my charge and I promised to get you safely to Lady Arbella."

"And my father."

He hesitated a moment. "Aye."

"What aren't you telling me?" She was sorry for the accusatory tone in her voice, but over the hours her mind had tumbled with a hundred questions.

"See to your business and then we shall speak."

Muttering under her breath at his underhanded tone, she stalked toward the trees with the sounds of his footsteps almost inaudible behind her. She whipped around when she reached the covering.

"Stay there."

In the faint moonlight, she saw the flash of his teeth and a slight nod of his head. Satisfied he wouldn't see her take care of herself, she slipped behind a fir tree, making sure to check for animals, snakes or spiders before lifting her skirts. When she'd completed her business, she found Blane standing in the same spot, scanning the sky.

"Looking for more birds of prey?"

He chuckled quietly. "Aye. I do like birds."

"See anything?"

"Nay. Most likely they've gone to rest with morning soon to come. Let us return."

Blane spread out a blanket upon the ground for her sit on. Aliah sank to the ground, her muscles protesting and yet, the simple way she sat with her legs tucked up under her helped to stretch them with an aching pleasure.

"Might I offer you our best fare?" Blane said, a teasing note in his voice.

"And what might that be, kind sir?"

With a flourish, he handed her two oatcakes and a thick strip of jerky.

"Never have I seen a finer meal," she teased.

"At the House of Blane we aim to please, my lady."

The men sat far enough away to seem distant. Blane stood beside her blanket, munching on jerky and staring down at her.

Aliah bit into the thick leathery piece of dried meat. 'Twas dry and chewy, and she had to work the bit for an agonizingly long time. Her jaw became tired and she noted to herself that she would not accept the jerky again. She felt like she was expending more energy than it was worth.

"You eat meat," Blane noted.

"Aye."

"Your sister does not."

Her ears perked up. "No, she doesn't." There was proof enough he knew her sister well.

He chuckled. "She does eat quite a range of interesting foods though."

A man who was up to sinister objectives wouldn't know so much, would he? Would he even care? Would he have noticed? The only answer she could come up with was, no. Blane knew something intimate about her sister and from his tone, appeared to look on the notion with fondness.

"Aye."

"Her husband has enjoyed her cooking and I must say those who've had it, find it to be quite a treat."

"Her cooking," Aliah drawled out, not understanding. "She has cooked for you?"

Father would be appalled to no end…

"Well, not exactly. I believe she advised cook."

"Ah." Aliah nodded, that made more sense.

"Father does not eat meat either."

Blane looked taken aback at that, although he quickly recovered, taking a bite of his jerky. Even still, she'd taken notice of his expression. How could he not have noticed that fact about her father, but he did notice it about Arbella?

"How did you come to meet my father?"

Blane stopped chewing for a moment, his gaze flicking away from her. "What do you mean?"

"You were sent to England at the request of my father. Why did he not join me himself?"

Aliah hadn't meant to confront Blane just yet, but the words came forth before she could stop them. She tensed, waiting for his reaction. What he did next shocked her more than anything. The man dropped to her blanket, sitting close. He took her hand in his, rubbing his thumb enticingly over her knuckles.

A shiver passed up her arm and then settled warmly in her chest. She tried to yank away, disliking her instant interest and excitement. Blane held fast, and his mesmerizing eyes latched onto hers.

"The truth, my lady..."

"Aye, tell me."

"The truth is, your father was injured in the battle. Your sister requested your presence straight away. When she learned that I knew the area well and would be able to locate you, she asked me to go. I am...close with her husband, and would have done whatever she requested."

The shock of his words hit Aliah like an arrow to the chest. Father. He was injured. Even now it could be too late. Her breath hitched and she was able to yank her hands from Blane's to cover her face as hot tears stung her eyes. Arbella would only send for her if the situation was dire. She knew her sister well, knew that this situation was not quite right and now she knew why.

"My lady." Blane's voice was filled with regret. No doubt he'd tried to keep the truth from her to protect her and keep her in good spirits on their journey, but still she wished he'd told her the truth from the start.

Aliah shook her head, wishing to be alone. She jumped to her feet and ran into the trees. Realizing where she'd gone and how scary it was in the darkened forest, she stopped and leaned her back against a tree, her arms encircling herself for consolation. Tears fell. Tears of fear, frustration, the inability to control the world around her.

Blane's soft tread sounded beside her.

Without asking, he pulled her into his embrace and she melted against him, finding instant comfort in his warmth and strength. Aliah wrapped her arms around his waist and rested her head against the cool leather of his armor. Through his armor she could hear the sound of his steady heartbeat.

"Why did you not tell me sooner?" She hiccupped from her sobs.

"I am sorry... I didn't think it was necessary."

"Necessary?"

"To upset you."

She shook her head, bumping her cheek into his chest. "You didn't think I should know that my father could be dying?"

"Nobody knows for sure, my lady. I thought not to worry you."

Aliah supposed she should be grateful for his obvious concern of her wellbeing. And in fact, she did feel a measure of comfort knowing Blane was looking out for her. "The truth from now on," she demanded.

Blane did not respond.

"Sir Blane." She tilted her head back, meeting his gaze. "Will you tell me the truth from now on?"

Even in the near darkness she could see that his gaze had changed from one of concern to one filled with longing. Whether it was the knowledge that he cared somewhat for her feelings, or a basic instinct to respond to the attraction growing between them — or both — her own passion answered, leaping up to take control. Her breathing accelerated along with her heart beat. Aliah's insides curled and flexed, warming and need flooded her. Her treacherous nipples pebbled and she found herself running her tongue over her teeth.

In that moment, gazing into the eyes of a man filled with passion just for her, Aliah made a decision that any other day prior would have horrified her. She would acquiesce to her curiosity. When she joined the church, she wanted to do so without reserve and the only way to do that was to let her passion go with the man holding her so deliciously in his arms. To float away from the reality and fear of her injured father.

Swallowing back the last vestiges of her reluctance, Aliah stood on tiptoe, pursed her lips and pressed them to Blane's chin — as she couldn't quite reach his lips. Blane reacted by a shakily indrawn breath.

"What are you doing?" he asked, his voice raspy with the same need pulsing through her veins.

"Kissing you."

"Kissing me," he repeated.

"Aye. Will you not kiss me back?"

"Oh, aye," he said in a tone that made her breathless.

With an arm encircling her waist, he pulled her flush against him. Every inch of his hard body touched hers, sending a jolt of awareness straight to her core. Aliah gasped, but did not pull away. Blane stroked his free hand over her cheek, grasped the back of her head and lowered his face to within an inch of hers.

"I'm going to kiss you properly this time, Aliah."

Her heart skipped a beat at his promise and at the way her name rolled off his tongue. She nodded. "Please."

Blane closed the distance between their lips, settling his mouth on hers. At first it was subtle, like the first brush of their mouths had been. Within moments, when she sighed, he deepened the kiss, his tongue running over the seam of her lips. She gasped, and when her lips parted he glided his tongue inside. The man had not lied; he was kissing her—although she would not have called it proper at all. It was carnal, wicked and utterly satisfying.

Aliah whimpered as his tongue stroked over hers and tentatively moved to mimic his caress. Blane let out an encouraging groan, tightening his hold on her body as he completely took ownership of her mouth.

Never in her wildest imaginings would she have thought a man and woman could kiss this way. It was intoxicating. Glorious. Sensual. Made her ache for something that seemed out of reach. Her insides coiled tight as though they waited for some signal to release and she found herself rubbing her body wantonly against his. Along the plains of her belly, his hardened shaft pressed against her with obvious desire.

Aliah was both frightened and enticed.

If this was what he considered a proper kiss... What did he consider scandalous?

Blane's blood rushed through his body at the pace of a river rapid. Swirling, churning this way and that, upsetting the natural course. And yet, he couldn't stop, he wanted more. His tongue delved into the heated, sweet velvet that was Lady Aliah's mouth. He craved the soft whimpers coming from her dainty throat, and reveled in the tight grip she had around his waist.

When she rubbed her body against his, he nearly doubled over from the pleasure of it. Did she realize how passionate she was? How she stirred his blood? The church was not the right place for her. No, within his arms, kissing him like this was where she needed to stay.

Massaging the back of her head, he deepened the kiss, taking complete ownership of her mouth the way he wanted to take possession of her body. With a hand at her waist, he kneaded her curvy hip, daring to move a little lower and place his hand upon one rounded globe of her bottom. When she didn't protest, he gripped it. Not hard, but enough that he could tug her pelvis more snuggly against his own. The deep moan that escaped her was pure seduction. He answered her moan with one of his own and pinned her against the tree, grinding his throbbing cock against the heat emanating from between her thighs.

"Oh, Aliah," he murmured, trailing his mouth to her chin and neck. He savored her flesh, tonguing the spot where her pulse beat rapidly.

Aliah sighed, her fingers roaming over his lower back, and she tilted her neck to the side. He continued to tease her flesh, soaking in her gasps and whimpers.

"You are so beautiful," he murmured, his mouth moving to the base of her throat. He pushed back her cloak so he could rub his lips over the length of her collarbone. "How could you want to spend your life in the church, when you could spend it…" He trailed off, realizing what he'd been about to utter.

He would have asked her to spend her life with him. To enjoy the pleasures of the flesh instead of doing what her heart had been set upon. The only reasonable answer for such a foolish notion was that he was undone by desire. Placing both hands beside her, he braced himself on the thick width of the tree and pulled his mouth from her skin.

Aliah's eyes were wide, her mouth forming a perfect, plush and thoroughly kissed O.

"Ballocks," he growled under his breath. "I am a boar."

Shoving off the tree, he turned from her, raking his hands through his hair. What had he done? He'd nearly taken her against the tree. Thrust his cock against the sweet innocence between her thighs. Thrust his tongue deep into her mouth… Good God, he was a total licentious monster. He'd nearly taken one of the Lord's own maidens. 'Twas a sin. Or was it? He didn't truly know.

"Blane," came her soft call from behind him. He turned around. She still leaned up against the tree, her face twisted into a jumble of confusing emotions which he himself felt keenly. "You're not a boar. I…"

He waited, wanted desperately for her to say she never wanted him to touch her again. That would make his own choices easier—he'd honor her decision, wouldn't have to war with his own conscience. For what did he have to offer a woman? Especially a woman as precious as Aliah?

When she didn't say anything, seemed to have lost her voice in fact, as she continued to stare at him with wide eyes, he felt the need to prompt her. "You…"

"I wanted you to kiss me. I asked you to kiss me. And I'm not sorry for it."

Damn. That was not what he wanted to hear.

"I shan't do so again," he replied. *Agree with me*, he begged silently.

But she didn't agree, she only nodded, all the while her eyes held desire for more. She wouldn't utter words she didn't mean, he knew that much from having spent time with her. That could only mean one thing—she wanted him to kiss her. *Mo creach*!

He was a fool. An utter fool.

Taking a deep breath, he stepped closer to her, gazed with all seriousness into her eyes. "My lady, I have been a complete cad since we first met. I wasn't truthful with you and I've taken liberties that are not mine to take. I've apologized for it and then gone back on my word and continued. I hope that you can find it in your heart to forgive me, and although I make assurances that it won't happen again, I know you have no cause to believe me."

The woman had the nerve to smile. Her lip curled up on one side, a teasing lift to it. "You have done so several times now haven't you?"

How could she tease him when he tried to apologize? What game was she playing?

Aliah stepped closer to him, her eyes crinkling a little with her merriment. "I want to thank you, Sir Blane." She reached up, cupped his cheek, her fingers running delicately over his stubble. He had to hold his breath to keep from issuing a pleased murmur. "You've shown me what I would have missed had I never met you."

With those words she turned away from him and walked back toward camp. All he could do was stare after the delicate sway of her hips, her touch still burning his cheek.

Chapter Nine

A whistle rent the air as Aliah stepped from the shadows of the trees into the moonlit clearing. Liam hissed and gestured fiercely for her to come closer. Behind her Blane rushed from the trees and let out a whistle of his own.

"We have company, my lady. We must ride."

Her escort did not wait for her to respond. Blane threw her up on his horse and quickly ordered Liam to watch their backs. Liam nodded, and Aliah couldn't help noticing the pure look of relief on his face. She wasn't that bad of a riding partner. Was she?

Blane squeezed Gunner's flanks and they took off at a dangerous pace. To her relief, he guided the horse out of the darkened woods and onto the main road where the light of the moon and stars lit their path. Blane once more increased their pace. Her bottom bounced painfully against the horse, and her already protesting muscles screeched. Fear of those who followed won out and she squeezed her arms around Blane's middle, and pressed her face to his broad, warm back — so much different from Liam's. Her heart surged as she watched one of Blane's men gather Frosty up onto his mount. She laughed a little at the sight of the enormous dog draped over the knight's lap, nearly dwarfing the man.

"There are only a few types of people who travel before the light of dawn," he called to her, the wind making his voice sound as though it were far away. "Those who might have an emergency. Those who run. And those who give chase. The whistle from my man meant it was a group of the latter, which makes us the runners."

Once again.

How did Arbella ever make it to Scotland and to her husband unscathed? Well, she supposed her sister had been in the midst of a battle. Dear God, Aliah didn't want to be in a battle!

They raced at a grueling pace until dawn breached the darkness with purplish pink light on the horizon and then the sun became blinding. The horses were covered in thick lather, and foam formed at their mouths.

"We will stop now," Blane said, his voice a low rumble that tickled her cheek resting against his back.

A short whistle had her jerking her head around to see who'd issued it.

"Why is Liam whistling?" she asked.

"He must have found a place for us to rest." Blane urged his horse along a thin path off the main road, leading over a field of abandoned crops.

The path was made of worn down vegetation by horses or feet, and Aliah wondered when the last person had crossed over it. She peeked around his side to see they were headed toward a cottage.

"Is it safe to stay with someone?" she asked, worry lacing her tone.

"Looks abandoned," he answered.

That would explain the untamed crops and gardens. The thatched roof was caving in the middle and the entire place looked sad and forlorn. But that didn't mean it was abandoned. Perhaps the inhabitants were too ill to tend the fields or too old. Or perhaps they'd been called away somewhere and would return soon.

"Sir Blane," she said quietly. "I don't know…"

"I will keep you safe from harm."

But could she keep him safe from herself?

They came to stop in front of the cottage, several of his men were already inside. One of those tending the horses offered her a hand down but Blane shook his head, taking her down himself. She didn't even bother to think on what that could mean. The knight smirked, then took Gunnar to join the other horses in a small roofed, wall-less shed, with several posts and hooks. Mayhap the previous home of the farmer's own mount or mule.

"Come inside," Blane said, holding her elbow.

They entered into a small main room with a dirt-packed floor, another room fanned off to the side and a ladder led up to a loft straight ahead. 'Twas quaint and cozy.

The main room was furnished with a table and several stools and even a cauldron sat in the hearth. A taller table held a few bowls and spoons. Cobwebs laced the ceiling and every nook and cranny — including the stools and handle of the cauldron. The cottage was truly abandoned. What had happened to the inhabitants to make them up and leave all their possessions behind?

Blane climbed the ladder, peeking into the loft. "There's a mattress up here, my lady. Seems fairly clean, if not a bit dusty. You shall sleep comfortably."

The thought of sleeping on a mattress excited her. Although she'd not been traveling long, the way her muscles ached, she was sure if she spent another day of rest on the ground, she wouldn't be able to move.

Frosty sidled up beside her, rubbing his ribs over her legs. She bent down and patted his head. Having gained her affection, he found a corner to curl up in and was promptly snoring loudly. Poor hound. The ride had probably been hard on him.

"What of Frosty? Will you carry him up the ladder for me?" She kept her face serious, even though she jested.

Blane turned around and winged a brow at her. "If you insist."

"I might."

Blane shook his head. "I've two sisters, my lady. Nothing you ask will surprise me."

She had her doubts, especially if she were to ask if he'd like to warm her back instead of the dog. Where had that thought come from? Oh, who was she jesting? After their kiss... She was willing to go a little further for curiosity's sake. To kiss him some more. Although he'd begged her forgiveness, she wasn't naïve enough to believe he didn't want her, that he wasn't as unaffected by their kiss as he pretended. The hardness of his body pressed against hers was evidence enough, if his growls and licks weren't. Glenda, her maid, lamented the act was disgusting, painful and embarrassing, but if he could make her body come alive by connecting his lips to hers, massaging her hips and gripping her buttocks, she was willing to bet lovemaking was one thing her maid was wrong about.

"I shall endeavor to surprise you then, Sir Blane."

She turned away to hide her smile as he faltered on the ladder. A secret part of her liked that she'd flustered him. Blane hopped down the last few rungs and came to stand beside her as his men slowly filed into the cottage. The room quickly became smaller as the men took up a large expanse. They brought in all the satchels.

Blane's men were odd to her, in that they kept to themselves. Several pulled food and drinks from their packs, then meandered into the second room, leaving the main room not as crowded. They all kept silent, which Aliah found completely unnerving. They nodded as they passed her. The men were never rude, quite the opposite, but nevertheless, they made her feel awkward.

"Why do your men never speak?" she asked, turning to Blane who'd taken one of the satchels and began shuffling through it.

"They speak to me all the time," he answered. "Do you like stew?"

She nodded. Did he have the ingredients for a stew in his pack? "Why is it, they don't speak to me?"

"You are a lady."

"What difference does that make?"

Blane shrugged, seemingly uncommitted or uninterested in her line of questioning. "Are you offended?"

She pursed her lips, put her hands to her hips and tapped. "No."

"Then is something amiss?"

Aliah narrowed her eyes. How had he turned this completely around? "No."

He broke out into a wide grin, the little dimple in his cheek creasing. "Then we are in agreement."

"About what?"

"Stew?" He hooked his thumb to the cauldron.

Exhaustion must be eating away her ability to think straight. Blane tossed a small packet of barley, a few onions and carrots onto the table. "Let us go and hunt. I'm hungry for a warm and hearty meal."

Aliah couldn't agree more. "I am ready."

Blane grinned, his energy contagious. She felt her sleepiness ebb as excitement coursed a path within her. He called to his men telling of their plans to hunt, and while he and Aliah walked off into the trees to the left, several others went right, apparently liking the idea of a meaty meal as well.

They walked side by side, and every few feet a hand or arm brushed against one another, sending thrills racing along her limbs. "Have you ever hunted before?" he asked.

"Aye."

"Did you catch anything?" Blane's tone was teasing, and Aliah raised a brow in his direction.

"Perhaps."

"A wee squirrel?"

"Many a squirrel."

"Any rabbit?"

"Aye, but only once."

"Only once?"

"'Tis a long story..." She still recalled the look of horror on Arbella's face as she'd come home with the bloody hare, excited about her accomplishment. Her sister—a devout lover of all things cute and furry—had lamented over Aliah's treachery for weeks.

"I'm intrigued. Will you tell me about it as we sup? For now, we must be silent in order to catch our dinner."

She nodded. "Rabbit?"

Blane chuckled. "'Tis a second chance for you."

Aliah's heart constricted. She wasn't sure she could go through with it. Even still, she followed in Blane's footsteps, crouching low and nocking her bow. She held her arms steady as she gazed at the newly lit forest from the dawn.

They stayed motionless and silent for some time, and then Blane picked up a small rock. He threw it against a tree some twenty feet away. Within seconds a rabbit bounded out from the brush and Blane let his arrow fly, hitting its mark. She was glad for him to have done it, because when it came down to it, she'd hesitated. Moments later a squirrel came into view and this time, she did let loose her arrow.

Blane smiled, his eyes sparkling with humor. Aliah rolled her eyes, almost hearing what sort of jest was running through his mind. Another squirrel scored for Aliah. An hour later they returned to the cottage with three rabbits and four squirrels — and Aliah could lay claim to having shot one of the hares. Blane skinned the animals, and while Aliah cut up the rabbits and vegetables to put in the stew, he roasted the squirrels, then tossed two to Frosty.

The other two, he held on a long stick toward her. "Should you like a little snack?"

She wrinkled her nose. "I don't know."

"Frosty is devouring the squirrels you brought him."

"Perhaps he'd like the two you brought?"

Blane chuckled. He took a large bite, closing his eyes and emitting a soft moan. "Mmm. These are actually quite delectable after days of jerky and oatcakes."

Moments later the other hunting party returned with a half dozen pheasant that they'd already cleaned.

They gestured to Blane, who gave them some of the long sticks he'd gathered for roasting. Aliah noted the lack of speaking, and shook her head. There was something he wasn't telling her, but she didn't want to ask. Mayhap his men had taken a vow of silence. Such things weren't uncommon.

Dumping the meat and vegetables into the boiling cauldron, she checked around for any herbs and was lucky enough to find a tied bunch of dried thyme. She flavored the water, the scents emanating from the stew already making her mouth water. Aliah had never cooked before. She'd spent plenty of time in the kitchens swiping rolls and sweets. Enough to have gotten stuck hiding under a table, her only option was to watch those at work in the kitchen. She was surprised at how easy cooking was.

She cleaned up her mess and watched as the men finished cooking their pheasants and then took hearty bites. Liam offered her one and she shook her head. "Will you all be eating stew as well?"

The men nodded emphatically, walking into the other room and a few outside. She was left quite alone in the main room with the one man she knew she should stay away from.

"Can I offer you a drink?" Blane asked, his voice soothing.

She turned to see him lounging on one of the stools, his back against the wall, his long, muscular legs spread out before him. He held out his wineskin to her.

"What is it?" she asked with narrowed eyes, remembering the last time he'd offered her a drink.

"'Tis watered wine, I promise."

That sounded heavenly. She nodded, and sat on one of the stools, arranging her skirts properly and sitting with her back as stiff as the wall he leaned against. She took a nice long sip. Even though it was watered, the wine soothed her nerves, making her feel more at ease. She was surprised at the flavor and quality.

"How do you like it?" he asked.

Aliah glanced at him. He looked so comfortable sitting there, relaxed. His eyes were slightly hooded as he gazed at her and her flesh started to heat, remembering how she'd seen desire flash within their green depths hours before.

"'Tis very nice."

A slow, sensual smile curled his lips. "I'm glad. I was afraid you'd spit it on me."

Aliah frowned, then laughed, finding humor in a situation that had mortified her before. "I promise not to spit on you ever again, so long as you don't give me anymore of that — what did you call it? The drink of the angels?"

"Aye, and next time, should I happen to give it to you, I'll make sure to stand far away." That smile still touched his lips making her want to reach out and run her fingers around the edges.

Shaking her head she said, "Oh no, I won't be needing the angel's drink. This suits me fine." She held up his wineskin and took another sip. A small drop dribbled over her chin and she swiped it away with her thumb. Her eyes flicked to Blane, wondering if he'd seen her mishap, but what she saw made her wish she'd not looked at all.

Desire blazed in his eyes as he roved his gaze up and down her length.

Trying to lighten the intensity, Aliah handed him the wineskin, ignoring the spark when his fingers brushed hers.

"What do you call this drink?"

Blane let out a chuckle that was both sensuous and wicked. "I had not a name for it before, but now I think I've come up with one."

His voice stroked over her body, just as his hands had in the darkened woods. "What?" she said, her voice not sounding like her own, but a tighter, strained version. She desperately wanted him to kiss her again, to take away the aching pulse that seemed to center in her middle when he paid attention to her.

Blane sat forward, his knee brushing hers. Her immediate reaction was to pull away, but her stubborn knee wouldn't move. Blane's heat seared a path from that spot, up her thigh to parts she didn't even know she possessed.

Aliah's breath hitched as Blane seemed to come even closer, his face inches from hers. His intense stare bored into her as though he would see inside her soul. What did her own eyes reveal? For his showed a promise of pleasure, merriment and warmth. How deeply she wished to close the distance between them, to sink into his lap and let him take her away, at least for a little while before she had to return to the harsh realities of life and the loneliness of her future.

Loneliness had never been how she thought of it before now… Not until she'd met Blane had her choice to join the church seemed a dreary existence.

"I would call it…" Closer he came, until his breath stroked over her cheek and his hand slid a tentative path up her arm. "Temptation."

With that decadent word uttered, his lips claimed hers. 'Twas like she'd been dying of thirst and even with a drink placed at her lips, she could not quench her craving. She could not get enough of him, she let herself come undone, becoming lost in the pleasure of his kiss.

Somehow she ended up on his lap, wrapping her arms around his neck, her fingers threading into his hair. Her hip was pressed to his rock-hard stomach, and she felt each hitch of his breath against her. Their tongues dueled, stroked, teased, tasted, sucked. Saint's ears, she was wicked and she didn't even care. She wanted this. Wanted all of him.

"Blane," she murmured against his lips. Her body moved in a wiggly, rhythmic motion of its own volition, trying to acquire something. She wasn't sure what.

"Oh, Aliah…" he answered. "You're so filled with passion."

Was that the word? Passion. Yes…and she wanted…

His hands skimmed over her breasts, her hardened nipples instantly sparking with undefined pleasure.

"Oh," she breathed, her head falling back as his mouth sizzled a path down the side of her neck.

"You like when I touch you." He didn't ask, he stated, and he was right.

"Aye."

"When I kiss you."

"Aye."

"What about this?" His mouth trailed from her neck over her chest to rest at the valley between her breasts.

Aliah whimpered, thinking she might just lose consciousness from the sensations he sent careening through her, and from the sheer excitement of it. Her breaths came fast and shallow. Her heart beat so loud she felt as though it echoed off the cottage walls.

"Aye," she managed.

He nuzzled around her collarbone. With one hand holding onto the side of her ribs, the other massaged the swells of her breasts. And then, she cried out as his mouth captured a turgid nipple through the fabric of her clothing.

"Shh..." he murmured against her, sending even more wonderful sensations along her flesh.

She squeezed her thighs together as frissons of pleasure shot from her breasts to her core and the curls between her legs grew damp.

What was happening?

How could this man make her feel...so delicious?

A thump against the wall had them scrambling apart. Aliah jumped to her feet, feeling completely mussed and her body still yearning for Blane's touch and the satisfaction he could give her. Blane looked as filled with longing as she felt, his hair too was mussed and his eyes were heavily lidded.

There was no one in the room, and no shouts of warnings from the guards, but it was just as well. She'd vowed not to kiss the man again and then, with one touch, she'd fallen into his arms, let him touch her, put his mouth to her breasts. Oh, just the thought of it had her heating up for more.

"I...um...need to−" She didn't bother finishing, she quickly left the cottage to find peace in the woods, to breathe in the fresh air and put some distance between them. Frosty followed, an ever present guard. If only the hound could help guard her heart.

Aliah felt as though her entire world was crashing down around her. Confusion filled her. Her entire future was in question. And with Blane…she was starting to feel more for him than the fire of his touch. Nay, her feelings for him went deeper than that. A realization she was not willing to explore.

When she returned to the cottage, Blane was not in sight. She ladled herself some stew and took it to the loft, eating alone and contemplating all that had happened. Aliah fell into a dreamless, restless sleep. When she was nudged awake to leave, 'twas by Liam. Although, she rode with Blane, they spoke little beyond the necessities. They remained like that, distant and quiet for the next several days.

Although they kept away from each other, Aliah still burned from their last encounter and had to fight the growing attraction every minute. 'Twas obvious she wasn't the only one affected by what happened, as every time Blane looked at her, the intensity of his stare made her want to melt into the forest floor. He kept his expression well-guarded so she couldn't decipher whether he stared at her with disdain or desire.

Since he didn't speak to her, she rather thought it was the former. Aye, it must have been for she'd hardly acted like a woman meant for the church.

Blane exposed her to another side of life she'd never thought existed—a realization she'd had more than once. Aliah had struggled with that awareness from the moment she met him. She wasn't quite sure how to come to terms with her newfound knowledge. Ignoring it would leave her without worry for now, but with her future hanging in the balance…she was lost. When she reached Father and Arbella, she would have a hearty talk with herself to figure things out.

Chapter Ten

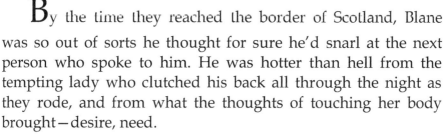

By the time they reached the border of Scotland, Blane was so out of sorts he thought for sure he'd snarl at the next person who spoke to him. He was hotter than hell from the tempting lady who clutched his back all through the night as they rode, and from what the thoughts of touching her body brought—desire, need.

At least now they'd stepped onto Scottish soil and he could breathe again. In fact, he was intent on heading to the Fir Tree Inn, so named for its location amidst a grove of firs. 'Twas owned by a loyal couple who'd kept his identity secret on many an occasion and whom he could trust without reserve. He stopped at the Fir every trip to and from the wool market.

The inn was located at an inconspicuous location that many Scots used crossing the border, hence their reputation for discretion and many repeat visitors. They were far enough away from Berwick upon Tweed and Dumfries, which was where the English tended to congregate on the border.

Once they were settled in the inn, he would bathe the grime of over a week's travel and savor a hearty, warm meal.

As Fir was his base of sorts, he and his men had stashed their plaids there. Blane could almost feel the freeness of his plaid. He couldn't wait to take off the constrictive hose the English insisted upon wearing. To be able to speak naturally again… To no longer pretend to be someone else.

He would once again be Blane Sutherland.

And his men would likely cheer for joy when they were allowed to once again speak.

"We've reached Scotland, my lady," he muttered to her in the same dull tone he'd made sure to use since nearly devouring her whole and stealing her innocence. He'd hoped to push her away by acting harsh and disinterested, but she only returned his attitude with one of her own, and it stung. Blane was actually surprised how much it hurt to feel her rejecting him in the same way he'd rejected her.

Conquering her innocence was one triumph—although he'd die a happy man doing it—that he'd never lay claim to. Especially after he revealed who he truly was.

"'Tis beautiful," she murmured back, just as noncommittally.

His homeland *was* beautiful, not that crossing the border changed things much, but the open fields here, the trees and the air just felt different. Once they reached the Highlands though—then Aliah would see true beauty. Vast rolling hills with snowcapped mountains in winter, and in the spring, fields and valleys of wildflowers and meadows dotted with sheep.

A chill wind swept over the group as they continued on. Aliah shivered behind him and he resisted the urge to reach around and rub her in an effort to warm her up.

"We shall stop soon, at an inn."

"An inn?" Her voice was filled with quiet pleasure.

"Aye." He found he liked pleasing her. She'd been surprisingly well spirited on their journey. They'd been chased by madmen—and they were indeed madmen for having stepped into their midst. She used her bow to end one's life. Hunting for food, sleeping in places a lady did not normally lay her head. He was proud of her.

And that was a feeling he didn't want to partake in. Having pride in her was dangerous. It only led to all the other feelings he had for her…made their relationship one of intimacy.

Pushing aside the dangerous path his thoughts were taking, Blane scanned the area to make sure all was well. Dawn was nearly upon them, and the landscape was cloaked in grey. The clouds kissed the earth leaving an eerie fog rolling across the lush plains. He followed a route he'd taken more times than he could count. They entered into the woods toward a path hidden from view, unless you knew it was there. They traveled for several minutes more before coming to a clearing, wherein sat the Fir Tree Inn. The main building was large and built of cut stone with a thatched roof. The ground floor boasted a main room, a private dining room and the kitchens. The main room hosted a tavern of sorts, and a few locals imbibed on brew and Mistress Kerr's scrumptious, savory venison stew and buttery baked bread. Which he could smell from the clearing. The second floor had several rooms for rent, although Blane had only ever stayed in one. The Kerrs knew his schedule and tended to keep it free when the time grew near for him to travel.

To the right of the inn was a wooden stables and to the left was their cottage, a small and homey looking building nearly identical to the inn, save for being much smaller.

As they approached, several children stopped playing and ran, disappearing inside the inn. He'd lost track of how many children the Kerrs had. They seemed to be in a constant state of breeding. Blane supposed that meant they were happy.

"Ah, Sir Blane, we've been expecting ye." The large form of Master Kerr appeared from within the stables. The man was like a thick oak—nearly as tall and as round as one. His long red hair was thinning on top, and indeed he boasted more hair on his chin than the top of his head. His arms were thick with muscle and if Blane had met him when he was a child he would have sworn the earth moved when the man marched over it, for he did not walk.

"Master Kerr," Blane drawled, still using his English accent. "I have returned and brought with me the Lady Aliah, who will require a room."

Master Kerr met his eyes, understanding the situation. He nodded. "Mistress Kerr will be happy to house a lady. We dinna get verra many. 'Tis a pleasure to meet ye, my lady." The innkeeper bowed low, a feat Blane wasn't sure the man did very often if the stiffness of his body was any indication.

Blane felt Aliah tense behind him as Master Kerr returned to his full height and studied her. What could she be nervous about? Although doing so warred with everything he'd been fighting against over the last couple of days, he placed his hand over hers at his waist and squeezed gently. It worked. He felt her relax a little and let out a breath.

"Why dinna your men get the horses into the stables and I'll take ye and Lady Aliah inside to see about a room and a hearty meal."

"My thanks," Blane said, glad that Master Kerr did not ask about his English accent or the fact that he had an English noblewoman on his horse. Master Kerr was the epitome of discretion and Blane was only further impressed with the man he chose to trust and the safe haven he provided.

Dismounting, he took Aliah down, and she didn't resist when he placed her hand at his elbow. She was nervous, that much was obvious, and even though she'd relaxed somewhat he could still feel that she was on high alert. Her knuckles were nearly white from clutching the straps of her bow and quiver.

"You will be safe here," he said under his breath. "I stay here often."

She glanced up at him with wide, questioning eyes.

"Whenever I return home, I prefer a road less traveled by, and the quiet, peace of the Kerr's inn."

Aliah nodded, but still didn't utter a word. She was probably exhausted as they all were. A warm bed and a hot meal would surely put her at peace.

They entered the inn, and Blane had to duck through the door as did Master Kerr. He'd never asked the man, but he wondered why he hadn't built the doorway taller? Perhaps the Kerr's weren't the original owners.

"Your things…" Master Kerr started, but Blane shook his head, stopping him.

He was sure the innkeeper would tell him his things were stowed beneath the floorboards within the man's cottage — a favor for which Blane paid him handsomely.

"My men will be happy to see about my things," he said quickly. Sooner rather than later, he would reveal his true self to Aliah, but he had to think of a way to do it. Mayhap he would simply change and then reintroduce himself, tell her it was for her own safety and that he was in fact the brother of her sister's husband. His stomach tightened. 'Twould not be a pretty scene, he was sure, when he did tell her the truth, however necessary. Being in Scotland, 'twas safer to travel as himself with the Sutherland name and might behind him.

"Well, Sir Blane, we are so pleased to see ye again." Mistress Kerr scurried from one of the back rooms toward him. "And I see ye've brought a companion with ye."

Blane and Aliah shook their heads at the same time. "Not a companion, Mistress Kerr. I simply provide Lady Aliah with an escort to her sister's home."

"Oh, well, in that case my apologies for having assumed…" She studied them both, her voice trailing off and Blane could only imagine what was going through her mind. Worse, he felt his cheeks heating and he never blushed. Never. From the corner of his eye, he noted Aliah's face had also turned a particular shade of crimson. "Would ye like a bath, dear, before I serve supper?" Mistress Kerr did not wait for Aliah to respond, but instead ushered her toward the stairs. She did turn around once, her narrowed gaze on Blane. "I will put her in your usual room. The hound can go in the stables. Will ye bed down with your men tonight?"

He nodded, rubbing Frosty's head, trying not to laugh at Mistress Kerr's meddling. Although, he was pleased that the woman had taken a liking to Aliah. His charge would be safe with the innkeeper's wife, and no doubt spoiled by her too. He hoped once she'd had a bath and a steaming bowl full of Mistress Kerr's famous stew she'd get some rest and when they were ready to depart, she'd be in the best of moods.

For then she would learn who he really was. And most likely she'd try to put an arrow through his heart.

Aliah allowed the older woman to lead her to a comfortable looking room with a large bed, a chest at its foot, table and chairs beneath a small window covered by a fur, and a wooden bath tub sitting before a modest hearth. As Mistress Kerr chatted about the fall and the coming of Yuletide, she stoked the hearth, setting a fire to blazing. Aliah sat dazed in a chair as a few servants bustled in, filling the wooden tub with steaming buckets of water and then a few colder ones to decrease the boiling temperature.

Without asking if she needed assistance, Mistress Kerr grasped Aliah's hands and pulled her to standing, taking her gown and chemise off and then her hose and shoes. She continued to ramble on about the weather, drying flowers and herbs for winter, and that Aliah seemed like a nice lass despite her heritage. The older woman left no pause for Aliah to respond, which was fine with her as she had nothing to say.

The innkeeper led her to the tub and Aliah sighed with gratitude as the heat seeped into her weary bones and aching muscles. She sank down into the water, allowing its warmth to take away the stress of their journey. Leaning her head against the back, she allowed the woman to tenderly wash her hair.

"My oldest used to let me wash her hair, but she's long gone now, married off and the little ones dinna appreciate a nice hair washing. Did your Ma wash your hair, my lady?"

Aliah startled from being asked a direct question. Opening her eyes for a moment, she stared up at the ceiling, then simply shook her head. She didn't wish to answer. Couldn't bear to tell this stranger that she'd never felt the loving arms of her mother wrapped around her. That she would rather join the church than subject a child of her own to such loneliness. That Blane made her want to take a chance…

Perhaps noting that Aliah was not in a talkative mood, Mistress Kerr eventually quieted, going about the rest of the bath, and then handing Aliah a linen warmed by the fire. She dried herself as the innkeeper pulled a new chemise and gown from her satchel and laid them out.

"Should ye like me to brush out your hair?"

Aliah decided that she would indeed like to indulge in such a nicety. Her maid Glenda had brushed her hair but was always a little rough. She donned her chemise, tying the ribbons at her chest, then allowed Mistress Kerr to help her into her gown, tying the bodice tight at her sides.

"'Tis a nice fabric, this," Mistress Kerr said.

Aliah nodded. Then sat as the woman instructed in a chair before the fire as she brushed her hair until it crackled.

"Shall I plait it for you?"

Aliah shook her head. In the quietness of her room, she wanted to leave it down. "Not now. Could you have my meal sent up?"

"Aye, my lady. My stew ought to renew your strength."

The woman left the room quickly, promising the heartiness and robustness of her stew would please Aliah immensely. Her mouth watered at the thought. It'd only been a couple days since she'd eaten a real home cooked meal, but even still, she felt as though it'd been ages.

A slight knock at the door turned her attention from staring into the hearth. She walked to the door and cracked it, hoping it was Blane. A couple of servants stood in the hallway.

"If ye're done with your bath, my lady, we would clean it up for ye."

She nodded and allowed the servants entrance. Taking a seat before the window, she pulled back the covering and stared out into the clearing at the children who played a game of chase. Vivid memories from her childhood flooded her mind. She and her sister and brother used to play similar games between studies. The baron had approved of games, unlike most of the aristocracy who coached restraint and order. Aliah and her siblings were lucky in that way. They'd been allowed a childhood. Part of her guessed that it was their father's guilt at them having lost their mother. No matter that it wasn't his fault, the baron had always carried some of the blame upon his shoulders.

The servants left and a few moments later, Mistress Kerr returned with a tray. She set the tray and its contents on the table. A bowl filled with steamy, thyme scented stew, a thick piece of brown bread with a hunk of butter melting at its center, and a cup of ale.

"Mmm. This smells divine, Mistress Kerr." Aliah closed her eyes, allowing a few moments to take in the scents of the various herbs, vegetables and venison.

"I do hope ye enjoy it, my lady."

"I'm certain I will."

Mistress Kerr curtsied and quit the room, leaving Aliah to savor the stew. Her first bite was pure decadence. She was convinced she'd never tasted anything so glorious in her life. Following the savory stew with a bite of warm buttered bread, she moaned at the flavors and the warm feeling settling in her belly.

Aliah polished off the stew, swiping the last bite of bread through the bowl and popping it into her mouth when a loud, single knock rattled the door.

That had to be Blane. She smiled and turned her attention to the door. "Enter."

But it wasn't Blane who entered. No, it was a Highlander, dressed in a plaid, his naked knees shouting at her sensibilities. A silver dirk gleamed at his hip, and a white *leine* shirt covered the bulk of his expansive chest and shoulders, over which the end of his plaid had been tossed and pinned. Her stomach plummeted and every bite of her delicious dinner backtracked up her throat. They found her and would kill her now.

Who *they* were, she didn't know. But she couldn't look into his eyes. Fear held her still, and her gaze settled on the dirk at his hip.

"Lady Aliah." Blane was here!

She tried to glance around the Highlander, to shout for Blane that an intruder had come, but her words died on her lips... Blane's grassy-green eyes stared out at her from the Highlander's face. Aliah's mouth went dry as it fell open in shock. Blane was a...

Saints above. Glenda had been right. Highlanders were a treacherous lot to be feared. The man had tricked her. She'd willingly left her home with him. Traveled to his country. And now… And now she was his prisoner.

Oh, dear God, did that mean Glenda was right about other things? Aliah chewed her lip, praying desperately the maid wasn't correct in her warnings that sneaking honeyed buns from Cook would result in a woman being barren later in life. That one had to be false — for her sister's sake.

She shook her head. Now was not the time to ponder Glenda's ramblings. Now she needed to escape. Thankful for her foresight, she yanked her bow and quiver from beneath her chair, nocking an arrow within seconds, and for the third time, pointed it straight at her escort's heart.

All the odd feelings and trepidation she had, had not been for naught. Her gut knew this man was not who he said he was.

She was not going to let him take advantage of her again.

"Get out," she demanded. "Else I am forced to follow through and put an arrow deep inside your lying heart."

Chapter Eleven

Blane held out his hands, his eyes locked with Aliah's. He couldn't shake the pierce of her accusing gaze. He'd known she would react to his appearing before her this way.

'Twas essential to show her who he really was, as he couldn't very well travel through Scotland as an Englishman. That was more likely to get him killed than the gentle warrior standing before him.

"My lady, please, put down the arrow. I have no intention of harming ye." He didn't hold back his burr now. "I am still Blane, I am still taking ye to Arbella and your father." He took the dirk from his hip and kicked it across the floor.

She scoffed. "Why should I believe you? You've obviously lied to me up to this point, *Scot*."

"Aye, but 'twas for your own protection."

"I was perfectly safe inside my home."

"Aye, but ye weren't with your sister and father."

"And you aim to take me there?" Her eyes narrowed further.

Blane had to figure out a way to disarm her. If she were startled in any way, even from a noise outside the window, her arrow would fly and he'd be a dead man—or at the very least an injured one.

"Might I entreat ye to put the bow down?"

She laughed. "So you can subdue me? Make me your prisoner?"

Blane shook his head. "Nay, simply so ye dinna shoot me."

"Mayhap 'twould be best if I did." She lifted her chin and Blane did not like the challenge in her gaze.

"I pray ye dinna, my lady."

"A liar such as yourself is no better than the outlaws in the forest." She winced and he had to keep his hands fisted at his side so as not to reach out and comfort her.

"I am no outlaw. I swear to the Lord, strike me now, if I am not Blane your escort, come to take ye to your sister."

Aliah's eyes widened and she stared up at the ceiling, perhaps half expecting to see a diving hand reach down to strike him.

"Ye see, I am still here, 'tis as I say."

She narrowed her eyes, the arrow still pointed with deadly accuracy at his chest. "Aye, you are still here, but your words mean little. You could be taking me to the graves of my family. And you the one who took their lives."

Frustration whipped an angry chord through him. Blane snarled. "I am no devil."

"Then who are you?"

With a deep exasperated breath through his flared nostrils, Blane pressed his lips together. The urge to throttle her was becoming strong. "I am Blane Sutherland."

"Of?"

"Of Sutherland."

"What is that?"

"Ye truly are sheltered."

Her face flamed at his comment. "I refuse to take offense."

"Good, because I meant no offense, only stating a fact."

"Well, you might be stating a fact, but you still haven't told me where or what Sutherland is."

"'Tis my family name and the place where I am from."

He watched her grit her teeth at his watery answer.

"Blane of Sutherland, where is your homeland and don't you dare say Sutherland else I strike you down here and now."

Blane was impressed with her show of bravado and irritated with the way it warmed his blood. "Sutherland is a large holding in the Highlands. My brother is the chief of Clan Sutherland. Our leader."

"And where is my sister being held?"

"She is not being held, Aliah," he said with annoyance.

"What do you mean?"

"Your sister is Lady Sutherland."

"How is that possible?"

"I'll let her explain that to ye."

At his words a myriad of emotions flitted across her face, some of which he could recognize—anger, denial, question. But she settled her features into a mask of non-emotion that sent a chill down his spine. As naïve as Lady Aliah was, she knew how to play the game well.

Lowering her bow and arrow, she again lifted her chin, her cool blue eyes meeting his. "Very well. I should like some time alone to think about all you have revealed to me."

Blane sighed with relief and bowed low to her. "As ye wish, my lady."

As soon as Blane shut the door behind him, Aliah leapt into action. Gathering her satchel she quickly shoved her belongings inside it and threw on her cloak. She strapped the satchel to her back, making sure she still had access to her arrows. Without looking back, she flung back the fur covering the window and looked down. 'Twas a steep drop, but not unmanageable. If she placed her feet just right, she could land without hurting herself too badly. Luckily the children had gone somewhere, mayhap inside to eat or nap. The only witnesses to her escape would be a few sheep and chickens.

Aliah swung her leg through the opening of the window, praying that savage Blane would not return to the room to tell her more of his lies. Wind swept up the inside of her gown, making her shiver as it touched hidden places. Before she could deliver an excuse as to why she shouldn't escape, she swung her other leg out the opening, and turned so her belly rested on the ledge of the window. It was now or never. Slowly she lowered her body, her arm muscles straining from her own weight as she dangled in the air.

Trying to find purchase with her feet, she was able to slip her toes between a couple of rocks giving her arms a moment's rest as she gathered the nerve to jump. Scrambling down these walls was not an option, most of the stones were smooth, and Master Kerr obviously kept up with the mortar as she could find barely a spot to grab between the stones.

"You must jump, Aliah. 'Tis the only way," she said to herself.

Closing her eyes, she took a deep breath and let go of the window, falling through the air eight or ten feet to the ground. The drop was quick, and she landed with an, "Oof," onto her bottom. She rubbed the spot, then quickly jumped to her feet and turned in a circle. Still appearing to be alone, she took a step toward the stables when the sound of clapping stopped her.

"Well done, my lady. I didna figure ye for a woman mad enough to jump from a window."

Blane.

She whipped around to see him at the corner of the building. He stood leaning casually against the stone, a crooked grin on his face. Aliah refused to let his charm and sensuality waver her decision to escape.

"But glad I am, that I caught your wee foot poking from the window and stood back to see what ye'd do. Are ye hurt?"

Seething, Aliah whipped out her arrow and nocked her bow. "I told you I wouldn't hesitate to shoot you."

He shook his head, annoyance in his gaze. "Ye still dinna believe me, lass?"

"Nay. Never."

When he stepped toward her, Aliah only reacted. She let her arrow fly, not looking to see where it landed and ran toward the stables. Blane let out a shout of pain. She'd hit him. Her heart hammered, thundering blood through her ears. Never having missed a mark, she replayed in her mind where she'd aimed and she couldn't recall. Guilt made her hesitate, but self-preservation moved her feet forward. Storming into the stables, she didn't bother to saddle Gunnar, but instead simply put the reins on him and hopped up onto his bare back. With a shout to Frosty, she was through the doors of the stables, just as Blane hobbled toward her, gripping an arrow protruding from his thigh. At first she was relieved to see him, but then realized he meant to stay her from her task. He shouted at her to stop. His men looking confused until they spotted her atop the horse.

Well, at least he wasn't dead. Blood ran down his thigh, over his naked knee. She shivered as the memory of his touch, his kiss invaded her mind. And she met his gaze. His fiery, livid gaze. The man would murder her if he caught her.

A loud whistle pierced the air, and beneath her, Gunnar stopped his progress toward the woods. She yanked on the reins, her hands trembling, stomach knotted. "Gunnar!" she shouted, trying to get the horse to pay attention, but he simply refused to move.

Blane came closer, clutching at his thigh, the broken shaft of the arrow protruding from his flesh.

"Get off that horse, ye mad woman!" he said through gritted teeth.

Liam ran toward her, and she attempted to jump, but her own cloak caught her legs and instead she felt herself falling; only she didn't land on the hard earth, but into the rigid, outstretched arms of Liam. She would have preferred the earth as he glared at her as though he wished she were dead.

"Put her down," Blane said, his voice gruff with pain.

Liam set her on her feet, her knees knocking together, heart beating so rapidly she thought it would surely burst.

"Please," she pleaded. "Please let me go."

Blane stopped within inches of her, the heat of his fury lashing off onto her body. "I will do no such thing, Lady Aliah. I have been charged with bringing ye to my brother and to his wife. If I should have to do so with your hands tied and mouth gagged, I will."

Aliah swallowed hard at the unpleasantness of his threats and the realization that he was deadly serious. She couldn't even think about what his brother wanted with her. Only that it couldn't be good.

"Ye will come inside the inn now, and ye will take this arrow from my leg."

"No," she said weakly.

"Dinna deny me, Aliah." His breath fanned over her face, and she dared to look up into his stormy eyes. "Ye shot me. Ye shot the man who was meant to protect ye."

Something in his words, the conviction in them struck her. Was it possible he didn't mean her harm?

"Take her bow," he ordered Liam. "Now come with me."

But her feet would not follow his command as Liam disarmed her. She felt naked without her own protection.

"Now, lass. My leg bloody hurts and 'tis your doing. Ye'll undo it. And if I've a mind, I may tell ye the whole of it."

Her lips parted slightly. There was more to tell. She wanted to hear, even if meant she had to take care of the barbarian. Hope renewed her energy somewhat and she was able to put one foot in front of the other.

When they entered the inn, Mistress Kerr gasped and called out for water and linens.

"Whisky, Mistress Kerr. I'll need more than a wee dram of it."

The woman nodded and shouted for whisky. Liam took Blane's arm over his shoulder and helped him up the stairs to the bedroom that had been Aliah's. Blane's grunts of pain reached her ears, increasing her guilt at having hurt someone who meant to protect her.

The problem was, she wasn't sure who he was protecting her from. And shouldn't she protect herself from him?

Once inside the room, Blane laid down on the bed, his face pinched with pain and turning ashen in color. His eyes met hers, but surprisingly they did not hold any of the hatred she expected to see.

Mistress Kerr hurried into the room with a jug of whisky and passed it to Blane, eying Aliah with question.

"What happened to Sir Blane?" she asked.

Aliah swallowed, not prepared to tell the woman who'd been so kind to her that she'd been the one to shoot him.

"An accident," Blane answered, his voice laced with agony.

He took a large swallow of whisky and then dumped a healthy portion on his leg. With a growl, he flung the bottle down on the bed and grabbed at his thigh. Mistress Kerr grasped the bottle before it spilled. Aliah couldn't take her eyes from the wound, the protruding arrow. Ghastly. Her stomach roiled, and she felt very near to passing out.

"Take it out," he ground out.

"I...I don't know how," she managed.

"I'll do it," Liam said, shouldering his way to the bed.

Aliah shouldn't have been shocked by the burr of Liam's Scottish accent, but she was. Now everything made sense – the reason his men did not speak. They couldn't for fear of their accents being revealed, but what of Blane? He perfected the most flawless English tongue, and yet his Scots brogue was thick and she found...she liked it.

Liam tied a thick strip of linen around Blane's thigh, then took hold of the arrow shaft. Shaking her head, she turned away as Liam methodically took the arrow from Blane's leg. Blane shouted, cursed, and growled. Mistress Kerr thrust the whisky bottle at him which he greedily slurped before dumping more onto his wound.

"'Tis out. Ye can sew him up," Liam said to Aliah.

Aliah nodded, then looked down at her shaking hands. She had to steady them. This was her fault. She'd shot him, and thank goodness she'd aimed for his thigh, else he could be dead by now or worse – maimed for life. Just the thought of nearly killing him made her head spin. An outlaw in the forest had been one thing. He'd been intent on killing the lot of them. But Blane was different. She could see that now, even if she hadn't understood it when she'd climbed from the window and dropped to the ground. Even if she didn't see it when he'd smiled at her from the corner of the inn and clapped at her courage to escape. He'd only been amused, not intent on brutalizing her for trying to escape. Impetuousness had once again marked Aliah.

Mistress Kerr handed her a long needle and horsehair thread. She nodded encouragingly, and Aliah somehow found the will to still her hands and settle her stomach. Sitting on the bed beside Blane, she threaded the needle, tying off the end. His pain-filled eyes followed her movements. She placed her hand on his thigh, acutely aware of its corded muscle and warmth, then she stuck the needle into the edge of his torn flesh, ignoring the ooze of blood on her fingers. Thankfully, Mistress Kerr wiped away the blood with a piece of linen. Concentrating on her task and not on his moans and groans helped to keep her from completely losing her mind and the contents of her stomach.

As much as she abhorred the task, part of her felt better for having taken care of him, even if she was the one who harmed him in the first place.

When she completed sewing up the wound, she cleaned off the blood on his thigh, then wrapped another piece of clean linen around as a bandage.

"Leave us." Blane's voice was noticeably less filled with pain and more filled with drink. His eyes met hers. "Ye stay."

Aliah glanced up to see the room empty. They were alone. Noticing she was still sitting next to him, she quickly hopped up from his bed.

"Sit back down, lass." His voice was low, drawing her in.

She obeyed, feeling the warmth of his thigh pressed to hers.

"Ye will know the truth of it."

Aliah nodded. She did want to know.

"I am brother to Laird Sutherland—your sister's husband. As I know it, when she arrived in Scotland to marry her intended a battle broke out. She fought valiantly, but 'twas not enough. The heathens were upon her."

Aliah shuddered to imagine what he was telling her. Arbella struggling for her life amongst a bunch of savages... 'Twas a nightmare come to life.

"Magnus, my brother, saw her. He thought of nothing save her safety, and so he took her away from the battle. Away from the danger."

A savior.

"But then she was attacked by one of Magnus' own men. He determined the only way to truly keep her safe was to marry her. Your sister agreed to the marriage for her safety. At first they thought to be married in name only, but…"

Aliah could hear no more. She held up her hand. Emotion overwhelmed her. She'd shot this man. This man who'd kept her out of danger thus far and sought only to bring her to her sister.

"How is your leg?" she asked, trying valiantly to change the subject.

"'Tis fine, now let me finish."

She shook her head. "Not now."

"Aliah, I must. 'Tis imperative ye believe I was not sent to harm ye." His eyes, bloodshot from the whisky and pain, pleaded with her.

"I believe you."

Chapter Twelve

Shock radiated through Aliah. Had she really just uttered those words?

But what was more shocking was that she meant them. She believed him. He was not sent to harm her. Although, she wasn't certain she could believe her sister had willingly married a Scot. That was so unlike Arbella as to be almost blasphemous. Somehow Blane was connected to her sister and her father — *how* was the question she'd get an answer to when she came face to face with them.

Arbella had lamented of marriage. Their father had nearly dragged her kicking and screaming from the house to marry an Englishman housed at Stirling. The idea of living in Scotland scared the daylights out of her sister. Marrying a Scot and being doomed to a lifetime of Scottish living was the very last thing her sister would do. Unless coerced.

Aliah couldn't let that bother her now. She had to stay alert. Stay alive. When she met up with her sister in Scotland she would make sure Arbella was safe and offer her a chance to go home with her to England. As to her father, she prayed he healed from whatever injuries he'd suffered soon so they could make their escape before winter.

Blane's eyes slowly slipped closed, his thick lashes fanning over his chiseled cheeks. 'Twas a sin for a man to have lashes so thick. His breathing deepened, and she watched the slow rise and fall of his chest. A soft puff of breath escaped his lips as he fell deeper into sleep induced both by pain and whisky. A pang of guilt rippled through her at having been the cause, especially when he'd only ever been kind to her. Too kind if she thought of his kisses.

Aliah's gaze traveled over his full lips. Perfect for kissing. Without thinking, she traced her fingers along the outline of his mouth. Blane's tongue darted out—by instinct she was sure—but she yanked her arm back before he could touch her flesh. 'Twas as if her appendages had minds of their own, and as though in sleep he meant to seduce her.

Chewing on her lower lip, she continued to absently stare at him, wondering what would happen when he woke. She prayed he wouldn't catch a fever from his injury. They were meant to leave in the morning. Their journey would now most likely be postponed by several days. All because of her.

Arbella could be in danger and Aliah played with her own sister's safety.

Doing the only thing she knew how, Aliah knelt on the floor beside the bed. Her hands coming together in prayer, she stared up at the ceiling, then closed her eyes.

"Dear Father, I pray to thee that you will see this man healed. That our journey will not be too long extended. That we make it safely to the Highlands and my sister and father. That you shall guide me, for I fear I know not the way. My actions have caused…" She swallowed, wanting to give excuses for the way she'd reacted but knowing God would already know. The excuses were for herself. To make herself feel better. But how often had her impulsive actions resulted in someone getting hurt. Was coming into this world before her mother was ready, causing her own mother's death, the start of her disastrous reputation for impulsivity? "So much pain," she ended in a whisper.

Opening her eyes, she glared at the bandage, tinged with a small stain of red, that covered Blane's wound. Tears stung her eyes and she swiped angrily at the large drops gathering in the corners. Crying would solve nothing. She straightened her shoulders, preparing to harden her heart and to stand when Blane's fingers skimmed her cheek.

She jerked her gaze toward him, his bleary eyes connecting with hers.

"Do ye pray for me, lass?"

'Twas hard not to lean into the subtle stroke of his fingers, to let him comfort her. Aliah opened her mouth to answer, but his eyes slipped closed again. He wasn't even awake.

"Aye," she answered anyway, knowing he wouldn't remember.

"So sweet," he murmured, a slight smile touching his lips. His hand fell from her face, landing with a plop by his side.

Where his hand had last touched her was cold. She missed the feel of his fingers tracing over her jaw and cheekbone. With a sigh of longing, she stood from the bed, gazing down at his prone figure. In sleep, he seemed so peaceful. Not at all the robust, confident man he was when awake. On impulse she bent down and brushed her lips over his. But as she attempted to lift up, his hands skimmed through her hair, keeping her lips locked on his.

Blane's tongue swiped over her lips then slipped between them to stroke lazily over her own. A shudder of need passed through her, and she sank against him, letting herself have this one last kiss. He tasted of whisky and his flesh smelled clean as though he'd also had a bath. The stubble had been shaved from his face and no longer scratched her sensitive skin. Aliah braced herself against his shoulders, feeling the muscles flex and roll beneath her. The urge to climb into the bed beside him, to let the world melt away, was strong. Too overpowering.

Enough so that she fought to control her desire, and pushed away. The force of her movement had her stumbling backward and her booted heel caught on the rug.

"Oh!" she cried as she tripped. Her arms flailed to and fro in the air as she tried to catch her balance. She took a number of staggered steps backward on her heels, until finally her rear met with the table. Clutching the surface, she stared wide-eyed at Blane to assess his reaction.

The frustrating man appeared to doze once more. Aliah didn't know whether to be grateful or to shake her fist in the air and shout for him to wake up. She supposed it was a blessing in disguise, for her cheeks already felt aflame at having kissed him in his state and from falling when trying to get away.

Aliah swallowed several times, trying to get around the lump in her throat so she could breathe normally. She smoothed her skirts, stood up straight and decided it was best for her to get some fresh air. Silently she left the room and descended the stairs into the main room of the inn. A few of Blane's men sat around a table drinking ale and eating stew. None of them appeared to have noticed her, and she was glad. She was too embarrassed to greet them or to have them engage her in conversation.

When she reached for the handle of the front door, Mistress Kerr's voice sounded behind her.

"Where are ye going, my lady? Not that ye have to tell me, I'm just curious 'tis all."

Aliah turned around to see the woman looking nonchalant, but her acting skills weren't polished enough for Aliah not to see that she'd been asked to keep an eye on her.

"I need some air."

"Would ye like some company?"

"Nay."

"If 'tis all the same to ye, I'd like some air as well. I'll walk behind ye if ye've a mind not to indulge an older woman."

Aliah abhorred when Glenda made similar remarks. They were meant for her to acquiesce and she always felt obligated. She supposed she should be grateful that the woman even asked. She could have just trailed her like a spy, but was instead offering companionship.

Nodding, Aliah opened the door. "Come then."

"'Tis awfully nice for ye to allow me on a walk with ye, my lady. I've never met a real lady afore. Especially one who knew how to use arrows."

There it was. The taunt. The barb. As if Aliah needed any more reminders of her blunder. She ignored it. The woman was only trying to be friendly, and probably didn't realize how her words affected Aliah.

"I'm happy to make your acquaintance, Mistress Kerr. You've a lovely inn."

"Thank ye."

Several children ran around once more and the women had to dodge their path.

"Are they your children?" Aliah asked.

"Aye, mostly."

"Mostly?"

Mistress Kerr nodded, a shadow coming over her eyes. "Four are my sister's. She passed some time ago."

"I'm so sorry." Aliah felt genuine sadness for the woman at having lost a sister. She couldn't imagine what it would be like to lose Arbella. Heartbroken was the only thing she was sure to feel.

"'Tis the way of things. God felt good to call her up to Heaven. But in doing so, he gave us a special gift." Mistress

Kerr nodded to the youngest child running around. A girl with a mop of golden curls who couldn't be more than three or four summers.

"Your sister died in childbirth."

"Aye. We named Sarah after her mother."

A pang of sorrow clenched at Aliah's heart. Without knowing little Sarah, she felt a kinship to her. "My mother passed the same way," she muttered, not realizing she'd said the words aloud until Mistress Kerr responded.

"Then we should be so lucky God bestowed an angel upon us."

Aliah's gaze met Mistress Kerr's. The older woman's brown eyes held warmth. "Thank you."

"For what, my lady?"

"Trying to make me feel as though I did not do something wrong."

"Ye didna."

Aliah gave her a weary smile. "I fear that I have. Many times."

"No one is perfect, my lady. We can only work with what we have, and try to do our best."

Aliah laughed. "Aye. I do."

"Then why be so hard on yourself? Ye seem like a good lass to me. Ye even have a bit of courage most of us dinna."

Aliah bent to pick up a small stone upon the ground. A habit she'd formed years ago, if she ever spotted a stone that could be carved into an arrow, she collected it.

"Mistress Kerr, I'm afraid that courage was not what hastened me to fire my arrow upon Sir Blane."

The innkeeper smiled. "Aye. But 'twas courage that had ye coming back inside to sew him up."

"Do you think he'll forgive me?"

"He already has."

"How do you know?" She rubbed her thumb over the stone, gathering comfort from its solid mass.

"Because if he hadna, he wouldna let ye sew him up. Men are stubborn as mules, my lady. I've known Sir Blane for a few years now. He strikes me as a man with a clever head on his shoulders. I dinna think he would allow ye into the room if he didna forgive ye, or if he feared ye'd hurt him more."

A slight weight was lifted from Aliah's shoulders and she continued walking around the perimeter of the small courtyard. "That is good to hear."

"Besides, I saw the way he looked at ye."

Aliah's eyes widened and she tucked the stone into the small pouch at her waist. "How did he look at me?"

"When ye first arrived, he looked at ye... I'd say besotted but I'm not sure Sir Blane would appreciate it. 'Twas the look of a man in lo —"

Aliah shook her head, held up her hands. "No, please. Don't say it."

Mistress Kerr tilted her head and stopped walking. "Why do ye say that? Are ye married? Betrothed? Is it wrong?"

"Nay... Aye..." She shook her head and looked up at the sky, grey clouds starting to gather, blocking some of the sunlight. The air smelled of rain. "'Tis not a thing that can ever happen. I am spoken for."

"Ah. I see. That explains it then."

Why did Aliah have the feeling the woman thought she meant something else? Curiosity got the better of her. "What do you mean?"

"That explains why ye return his gazes, then your face falls, flaming with guilt."

Was she that obvious? Aliah felt her face flaming even now. She whirled on her heels and started to walk away briskly.

"Apologies, my lady, I overstepped," Mistress Kerr called behind her.

Aliah didn't stop. She couldn't face the woman, for she'd seen right through her. To the need in her heart. And the guilt that came each time she allowed herself to dream.

Pain radiated from the middle of Blane's thigh outward. He resisted the urge to clutch at his leg, to rub away the pain, afraid he'd tear the stitches or cause his wound to bleed again.

The room was silent, too silent. He wished for Aliah to return. To listen to the sound of her breathing. When she'd been there before, he'd not truly fallen asleep. Although he wanted to. The whisky made him feel warm, and her fingers touching his thigh hotter. As she'd sewn him up, the pain had dulled. Then to hear her prayers...

She'd prayed for him. Prayed for him to heal. Prayed for their safety.

But the end of her prayer had seemed more internalized. A feeling he knew well.

Guilt. Pain.

Aliah wasn't just talking about shooting him. There was something more. Something deeper.

What could it be?

Blane blinked his eyes open, trying to stay awake, to mull over what he'd discovered. Everyone had secrets and he wanted so badly to discover what hers were. He wanted her to open her heart to him, to share what was hidden beneath. To comfort her. His head rolled toward the door, willing her to come back so he could ask her, but the door remained firmly shut. Closing his eyes, he tried to listen, willing his ears to pick up the sound of her voice.

He thought he could hear her outside. Was she leaving? She might try, but he'd given strict orders that she was not to leave the inn or the grounds. Blane trusted his men, trusted the Kerrs. Aliah would be there when he woke.

Still, he willed himself to remain conscious. Even tried to sit up, but the loss of blood, the pain and the surge of overpowering energy that had forced its way through his body as soon as he was hit with the arrow had made him weak. Blane hated to be weak. Hated to be out of control. *Stay awake, ye bastard!*

However, the edges of his mind were growing fuzzy, whisking him back to a time he'd rather never remember. To relive a moment in his history that was better left hidden within the graves of those he loved…

A history that no one, not even his brothers and sisters were fully aware of.

He was a lad of twelve summers. 'Twas the day after May Day, and the sun shone over the hills. Gleeful that his parents had decided to take just him on their ride through the countryside, he'd packed his new iron sword and stuck his tongue out at his brothers and sister Lorna who'd begged to come — the only one not asking was Heather, his youngest sister, a wee babe at the time. Even Magnus, a great lad of fourteen, had wished to partake in the afternoon's ride. But today was Blane's special day. 'Twas his day of birth and he'd been out fostering at a neighboring clan when his father called him home, gifting him with the sword and declaring that it was time for Blane to return to Sutherland, a man now.

Blane had missed his family so much, his parents most of all, and the fact that they'd decided to give him a day all to himself made him soar.

They'd ridden out, his father waving away the men who wanted to provide escort, saying his son Blane would be enough of a guard. Blane's pride had gone through the roof. His father believed in him. With Blane growing up a second son, his older brother Magnus had gotten most of the attention. Magnus was, after all, being groomed as the next laird.

How sad it was that none of them could have predicted how soon that would be. That at the age of fourteen, such responsibility would be thrust upon his brother's shoulders. Thank the Lord for the help of the clan elders, or the lot of them would have suffered greatly. And thank the Lord for the training Magnus received, for he was an excellent leader, even at a young age. If he could go back in time, Blane would have begged his father to bring an escort. To stay home behind the thick walls of Dunrobin.

But instead he'd been cocky, full of himself, and selfish.

Not an hour passed when they were ambushed by a mass of outlaws—some of whom he could have sworn spoke with an English accent while others spoke Gaelic. Playing dead was the only way he'd survived. His father and mother had both fought valiantly... Blane had fought, even injuring a man with his new sword. Until he'd fallen and remained painfully still as he bled into the grass.

Their deaths were on his shoulders.

How he wished he'd been killed that day instead of his parents. He never found out who the perpetrators were. But he'd sworn that day, to himself and to God, that he would never stop looking for them.

It was a huge part of why he'd taken on the duties of traveling with the wool—so he could search each and every face he passed. To find those who'd murdered his family. To bring them to justice at the end of his sword. His fingers itched to run them through. Although they'd felled him, cut him clear through the ribs, he'd been lucky enough that the blade did not hit any vital marks. He bore an ugly, jagged scar as a reminder, not that he needed it.

Each day was filled with emptiness and guilt. Each day he saw the faces of the dozen or so warriors who'd attacked.

Who'd jeered at his father and mother. Laughed with each cut of their swords.

Blane's throat closed, his eyes burned with unshed tears. He searched for the jug of whisky. Anything to take away the awful memories. Grappling with the jug on the bedside table, he pulled it to his lips and drank greedily.

Liquid burned down his throat and he coughed once as he swallowed, letting the warmth of the liquor fill him.

At last, blissful sleep came to take him away, to dull the pain in his heart and make the memories fade.

Chapter Thirteen

Two days later, exhausted from barely getting any sleep, Aliah stood in the main room of the inn waiting for Blane. She'd been given another room to sleep in as he recovered from the arrow wound in hers. But having gotten used to sleeping during the day and riding at night, she found it hard to fall asleep, despite the extreme tiredness that made her body ache.

Yestermorn, Blane had claimed he was ready to leave. But Mistress Kerr had insisted he stay at least one more night to be sure his wound would not become infected. Aliah had agreed. One more day wouldn't hurt—at least she prayed it wouldn't. Her sister was most likely fine, as Blane did not seem at all worried about her. If his brother Magnus was anything like him, then she was sure Arbella was in good hands. Besides, her father was with her, even if he was injured. Highlanders weren't all barbarians—at least she prayed as much. Magnus wouldn't harm her sister while her father was there. Would he?

Ugh. So many questions, without answers. She didn't even know what was going on with her sister and trying to figure it all out was simply frustrating. Frowning, she folded her hands in front of her. She should have allowed Blane to tell her the whole story when he wanted to, instead of insisting that he wait. Then she wouldn't be standing here worrying over it. She could be doing something productive such as… Oh, she didn't know what.

Stomping her foot she headed toward the stairs. She had to move, it was the only thing that would keep her sane.

"I will go and see if he needs help," she mumbled to the room at large.

She felt a bit like her father, coming to see if she was ready to greet guests. What was taking the man so long?

When she arrived at the door, she found out, when his raised voice called out from beyond the door. He was speaking to Master Kerr who'd gone up to relay some news.

"I dinna expect…" his voice trailed off and then there was a garbled response from Master Kerr. But then Blane's words, harshly spoken, did come through the door, "Spoken for? By whom?"

Her throat closed up, hands grew clammy. Mistress Kerr must have relayed Aliah's conversation with her to her husband, who promptly decided to warn Blane off. A trickle of betrayal crawled up her spine. She attempted to chase that feeling away. 'Twas for the best. She was spoken for — by the church. All of the tempting that Blane was doing had led her down a path of an unvirtuous nature and doubt. She'd even been contemplating not following through with her promise to Mother Superior.

Not wanting to listen to the rest of the conversation, she hurried downstairs. Mistress Kerr had inadvertently solved a major issue for her. Aliah would no longer have to worry about Blane's steamy kisses, for they were sure to never grace her lips again. He would think her a wanton for having engaged in such sensuous embraces anyway, given that she was promised to another.

As her foot touched the bottom stair, a realization occurred to her. She'd told him that she was promised to the church. Would he now think her a liar?

Saint's big toe! She didn't want him to think ill of her.

But why did it matter what he thought of her at all? Once she was reunited with her family, she'd be on her way. Blane would be nothing more than a man from her past. And he'd stay that way.

Taking a few breaths to calm herself and her flipping stomach, she returned to the main room and found Liam.

"I wish to wait outside."

He studied her hard, never having fully given her his trust again after she'd shot Blane. She didn't blame him, but the way he studied her made her just a little irritated. Finally, he nodded.

"Dinna run off, Lady Aliah."

Aliah didn't honor him with a response and instead simply whirled around. She hadn't asked for his permission, simply told him out of courtesy. Outside it was cold, the temperature having dropped significantly in the two days they'd been at the Fir Tree Inn.

Clutching her cloak tighter and moving her cowl over her head, she proceeded toward the barn. Aliah snatched an apple from a bucket outside the wide double doors and brought it inside. The scent of hay and animals was strong, but not offensive. Mad Maiden stood docilely in her stall and nickered as Aliah approached her. They would leave her here. The Kerrs had agreed to keep her well until Blane's next trip to England when he would return her to Mowbray Manor. In the meantime, they would allow her to use one of the mounts they owned. The innkeepers had been more than gracious toward

Aliah. As a thank you, she had left a small token upon the table in her room.

'Twasn't much, simply a few silver coins and a note. She'd known that Mistress Kerr wouldn't accept any extra payment from her out of respect. Stubbornness was a flaw they both had in common. Aliah wasn't going to let that get in the way of her saying thank you to the woman who'd befriended her, supported her, comforted her and opened her eyes to a new way of thinking.

A little blonde girl ran by the barn door, reminding Aliah so much of herself. The child was happy, a smile wide on her cherubic face as she chased after the family's dog. Frosty, beside Aliah, let out a little growl, leaning into Aliah's thigh.

"You are a good pup, Frosty," she murmured patting his head.

From outside, the child screamed with fear. Frosty took off running as Aliah leapt to see what was happening. Before she could see anything, Blane grabbed ahold of her, lifting her into the air.

"Shh," he said urgently. He raced, limping slightly, to the ladder leading up to the loft, carrying her over his shoulder like a sack of grain. His shoulder pressed uncomfortably into her belly, jabbing her with each of his jerky movements. Even still, he held her tight and she did not fear falling, only feared losing her breakfast. The crying from outside ceased, but the shouts of unknown men remained.

"What are you doing?" she hissed.

"Dinna say a word," he whispered harshly. When he reached the top, he tossed her gently onto a pile of hay, moving quickly to pull the ladder into the loft behind them. He pointed toward the corner behind a stack of hay and mouthed, "Hide there."

Her first instinct was to argue but the pinched look about Blane's eyes had her obeying. Aliah's stomach plummeted and her mind conjured up all sorts of horrid things that could be happening. The band of outlaws had followed them... But they were in Scotland. Any English outlaw with a worm's brain wouldn't venture into this heathen land where they'd be quickly turned to dirt by the Scots. So who was it?

Shouts came from outside the barn—and they sounded English.

Bloody hell! She crossed herself for having blasphemed.

Blane dove beside her after making sure the ladder was pulled up and well out of sight. Hay fluttered into the air with his movements, and his face registered pain. His leg must be hurting him immensely. Carrying her extra weight on his shoulders, diving. 'Twas all too much for a man in his state and she meant to tell him so when the danger was gone. And 'twould be gone soon, she prayed.

The heat of Blane's body beside her made her all too aware of their closeness.

Boots thudded on the ground below and a few of the horses let out warning snorts and neighs. Even the animals could sense the danger.

"What can I do for ye, sir?" Master Kerr's voice sounded from beneath the loft. Miraculously, he didn't sound in the least concerned.

"'Tis Lord Surrey, you Scottish swine." The man's voice was harsh, priggish, and Aliah immediately disliked him. "We would like rooms for the night. And boarding for our horses. A hot meal. In the name of King Edward of England, you shall give us what we demand and not expect to be paid. 'Tis the will of the king, and should you deny me, you will be punished."

"Of course, my lord," Master Kerr said amiably.

Bless his heart. Aliah wanted to reach out and hug the innkeeper for being so cordial to an English lord who'd just insulted him and theoretically robbed him. She prayed that

Mistress Kerr had taken all the children to safety. This lord seemed cruel enough to flay one alive.

"Get these nags out of here. Our horses should not reside with Scots rubbish."

There was some shuffling and Master Kerr gave a soft command, she guessed to one of the stable hands.

"Any Scots rebels come through here, innkeeper?" Lord Surrey's voice held a dangerous note.

"Nay, my lord."

"This is an awfully nice destrier to reside at an inn," he drawled.

"Aye. 'Tis not mine."

Aliah chewed her bottom lip raw. They were caught now. Master Kerr had a family to protect; it was understandable that he would give them up in the face of their danger.

"Then whose is it?" Lord Surrey asked.

"'Tis a knight's. The horse was injured and he left it here to heal."

The earl grunted. "Mayhap I'll take it off your hands. Seems to be plenty healed to me."

Beside her, Blane stiffened. She wanted to reach out to comfort him, but feared moving would give away their position.

"I dinna think 'tis a good idea. He said he'd be back afore winter, and well, that is anytime now."

Aliah closed her eyes, sure the lord below would react viciously at Master Kerr for having denied him.

But the man only grunted again. "I think if the man were merely a knight he wouldn't mind offering up such a beautiful beast to a man superior to him."

"Agreed, my lord, save he wasn't any old knight."

"What do you mean by that, Scot?"

Every muscle in Aliah's body burned from holding perfectly still. The hay itched her nose and she thought she'd sneeze. She held her breath, praying the men would leave. Placing her hands over her mouth and nose, she willed the itch in her nose to go away.

"'Twas the king's own man."

"Percy?"

"Aye, that's the name."

"Well, then. I'd best keep the horse where he left it."

There was a shuffling of feet, and the voices receded. Yet, still she and Blane remained motionless. Below, she could hear the stable hands moving the horses around. She prayed they had the good sense to take the saddles and reins for her party's mounts aside so they could easily escape.

When at last there was silence, Blane sat up and she too rose beside him. Her sneeze had luckily abated.

"We must leave now," Blane said, his voice hushed but urgent.

Aliah nodded. "What of our things?"

"The Kerrs know the drill. Our horses will be ready and our bags already fastened. We need but climb down and mount."

"Then, let us depart. That man makes me nervous."

"He should make ye more than nervous. The Sassenachs are a vile, malicious lot."

Longshanks was definitely a harsh king, but that did not make all the English so horrid. Aliah raised a brow, and Blane curled one side of his mouth in a teasing smile.

"Well, my lady, most of them are. At least those in league with Longshanks."

She nodded, although she didn't know much about the war between the English and Scots, she'd heard from Arbella the horrid things the English king was doing, and it wasn't something she believed in. The Scots were their own people, their own nation and they should be allowed as much freedom as the English.

As they moved to stand, the loud obnoxious voice of Lord Surrey sounded below once more. He shouted to one of the groomsmen about his horse. At the same time, Blane silently moved over her, flattening her to the wooden, hay-strewn floor with his body.

Aliah's breath caught at the danger and at the feel of his hard length covering every inch of her. Eyes wide, she gazed up into Blane's face. His own eyes had darkened into the color of pine needles. Their gazes locked, breaths coming hard and ragged as one. He didn't have to tell her to keep quiet, she knew the danger they were in should they be discovered.

Even the position they were in literally would change both of their futures, but that didn't stop her body from heating at his touch. A slow, warm ache built up from her toes and fingers and slowly made its way to her breasts and her core. Aliah licked her lips, wanting to feel his mouth on hers. Desiring his hands on her breasts. Needing him to take that aching pulse that sat between her thighs and…and…

Blane must have seen her thoughts mirrored in her eyes, as his lids became heavy with desire and he shifted his weight so the hardness of his shaft pressed to the apex of her thighs. Aliah tried hard not to buck at the intimate touch and what it meant. She could not, however, keep her body from shuddering.

A wicked smile curled tantalizingly on Blane's lips as she shivered and he leaned down, she thought to kiss her. The voices and sounds from below faded into the background and all she could hear now was the thudding of her heart and the shallow breaths she took. But he didn't kiss her lips. His mouth skimmed her cheek, his warm breath sending tingles of pleasure throughout her body. She closed her eyes, letting her senses come alive. The scent of outdoors, leather and fresh soap covered his flesh. There was another scent too…one she couldn't quite put her finger on, other than to say it was the scent of desire.

Blane's lips brushed the lobe of her ear, and he took that sensitive flap of skin between his teeth. Aliah bit down hard on her lip to keep from crying out. Of their own volition, her hips rocked, sending lightning to pass through her thighs and into that sheath her wicked body begged for him to plant himself inside of.

"Ye lied, my lady," he said so quietly she could barely make out his words.

She shook her head. No lies had passed her lips.

"Oy, aye, ye did." As if his purpose was to distract her from the words he uttered, his tongue came out to trace the shell of her ear. "Ye told Mistress Kerr ye were spoken for."

Now, *that* she had done. But she was. How could he say she was lying?

As if reading her thoughts, he went on, his lips brushing back over her cheek, settling a mere breath over her mouth. His words were not so much whispered as breathed, "No one's claimed ye yet."

With those words uttered, his lips came down hard on hers—claiming her. There was such power in his kiss. Such sensuality, Aliah thought she'd drown from it. Her entire body was a boneless mass of pleasurable sensations. She couldn't think straight, didn't want to. Never wanted this kiss to end.

Blane's tongue slipped between her willing lips to stroke over hers, and she met him with a fierceness of her own. Wanted to claim this man as he'd done to her. Refused to be intimidated by his power, his prowess. She was a daring woman herself. A woman with desires and passion, which only this man seemed to bring out. Aliah wanted him to feel everything she felt. She wanted him to become as undone as she was, to soar within the heights of passion. Unbidden, her hands stroked over his strong back, feeling the muscles ripple, over his spine, his neck, burying in his thick hair.

Her fingers tangled between his locks, softer than she'd expected, and an altogether delicious sensation for her fingertips.

Beyond touch though, were the sensations whipping through the rest of her body. Her nipples were taut, straining for his touch. Between her thighs was damp, and she couldn't stop herself from squirming. Only the firm grip of his hands on her hips kept her still. He broke their kiss only for a moment to tease her ear again and whisper, "Shh..."

'Twas then she realized they were not alone, but still in the loft. Oh, what a wicked woman she'd become, but she didn't care. She wanted this. Needed this. If anything, her sensual adventures with Blane would last her a lifetime in the cold and loneliness of the church. His kiss only served to remind her of what solitary existence awaited her—and that dulled her passion.

Refusing to think about it at all now, Aliah threw herself back into the kiss, tasting, licking, nibbling, exploring. Blane's hands tightened on her hips as he too devoured her lips. Slowly, his fingers traveled up over her ribs, before stopping at the sides of her breasts. She waited, praying he would touch her soon, but he stilled his movements. If she could speak she would beg him to touch her, but voicing her desires would only get them caught. Instead she arched her back, hoping that movement would give him the permission he waited for.

The move worked. Aliah sighed into his mouth as his thumbs brushed over her turgid nipples, and his palms massaged the roundness of her breasts. This was heaven. This was decadence.

This was sin.

A sin she'd gladly take punishment for.

'Twas then she noticed her right wayward leg, slipping up around his hips, allowing him to settle deeper between her thighs.

The pleasure was almost too much as Blane removed his hand from her breast to slip up her calf, beneath her gown and massage her bare thigh. At the same time, his hips pressed back and forth at the juncture of her thighs. Aliah couldn't breathe. She gasped into his mouth, sucked at his tongue.

"My lady?" came an urgent whisper.

With a silent cry, Aliah jerked her mouth from Blane's and tried to scramble from beneath him.

"My lady? Are ye up there?"

"*Mo creach!*" Blane whispered.

"Aye," Aliah said back quietly.

"They've gone inside to sup, ye had best fly now."

Aliah attempted to smooth her hair, but it was impossible to remove all of the hay that seemed to have become a permanent feature.

Blane smiled at her roguishly, as if he were proud to see her so mussed. Even with a flaming face, Aliah rolled her eyes, and descended the ladder he replaced. Mistress Kerr met them at the bottom, her shrewd eyes scanning them both.

"Ye'd best make haste. 'Tis a nasty lot. They made no qualms about running down one of my sister's babes."

"What?" Aliah gasped. "Is the child all right?"

"Aye, she'll live. A few scrapes and bruises, nothing broken."

"Bastards," Blane seethed.

"Oh, aye. And they've a band of outlaws with them."

"Sassenachs?" Blane asked.

Mistress Kerr shook her head. "Nay. Scots."

Blane's features darkened into a scowl that made Aliah shiver. She never wanted to be on the end of that anger. His jaw twitched and he glanced in the opposite direction Mistress Kerr wanted them to go.

"Ye must go, Sir Blane. They willna hesitate to run ye through and there are a lot of them. Ye must take care of Lady Aliah."

Those words seemed to draw him from his intent of heading back to the inn. Aliah couldn't understand why, but she felt the pull from him, the need to see who those men were. She shivered, and let Mistress Kerr usher her to the back door of the stables.

"Will you not get in trouble when they notice all the horses gone?"

The innkeeper shook her head. "Never ye mind, we'll take care. We've dealt with them afore."

Aliah couldn't help giving the woman a last minute hug, before Blane hoisted her onto her own borrowed mount. His men already waited, having come out from their own hiding places. Within seconds, they were riding briskly away from the Fir Tree Inn.

Chapter Fourteen

They rode hard through the afternoon, avoiding roadways when possible and staying hidden in the shadows whenever the noise of an approaching rider sounded. When they were crossing through a valley or over a ridge, completely exposed, Aliah tried to keep herself from trembling, to ward off the imaginative foe that ambushed them from every possible hiding place. She even imagined men camouflaged in grass rising up from the fields to strike them with deadly blows. The sky was grey, threatening either a cold rain or snow, she wasn't sure which, only knew she wished for neither.

Blane whispered explanations of the ongoing war between the Scots and English. The rulings of King Edward and how they oppressed the people—Blane's people. He spoke of his family's close ties to Wallace, the Scots freedom fighter who led the battle at Stirling Bridge to victory—the place Arbella had been saved by his brother. Of his clan, his siblings. The

151

importance of wool trade and how it had increased their income over recent years.

Aliah found herself feeling sympathetic toward the Scottish people's fight for freedom, which felt like a betrayal to her own country. But to feel otherwise in itself seemed a sin. Perhaps this was why her sister had agreed to marry a Scot. Arbella was known to be compassionate too. She would not have been able to abide an English noble occupying Scotland, especially if that man had been anything like Lord Surrey. Just thinking of her near brush with the man, Aliah shivered.

"Blane," Aliah cried out as they passed yet another burned out village and miles of smoking fields. The crisp crops were blackened to soot, and the once standing buildings completely demolished into piles of ruin. This fire had only occurred within the last day or so.

Blane and his men looked alert, surrounding her in a cocoon of warrior flesh as they surveyed the area.

"The Sassenachs have burned yet another village," Liam muttered.

"Aye. I see no survivors," Blane replied.

"Where could the people have gone?" Aliah asked.

"Hopefully they ran when they heard the approach of the English bastards," said Blane. "Even still, we must tread carefully. These fields are still smoking, there is no way to tell which way or when the Sassenachs left here."

"Why would they burn the fields? Couldn't they use the resources?" she asked.

Blane shook his head. "The fields are mostly harvested now. They took what they could find and burned the rest because they could, because it hurts a man where it counts when his sole ability to provide for his family is literally burned to ash." His voice was bitter acid and his words a harsh dose of reality.

Men and war... She couldn't fathom why some felt the need to oppress others. Why could not everyone live peacefully? To not only take their lives, but their homes, their *everything*.

Passing the burned village, Blane led them onto a path in the trees, giving them some cover from any enemy that might linger.

They slowed their pace so the men could meander in and out of the woods, checking on any hidden forces and to keep themselves from notice. Eventually they found a burn, the sound of the water trickling gave Aliah a sense of peace. They took a brief moment of rest. Once more Aliah's body cried out from stiffness, her rear completely numb. She was at least grateful for having a horse without a shifty gate, and for the distance her own mount provided her from Blane. Having a stiff body that also burned with a heated desire she barely understood would only make riding with him more difficult.

"How much farther to our destination?" Aliah asked, hoping she didn't sound like she was grumbling. "I've lost track now."

Blane gave her a charismatic smile that reminded her of every single kiss, touch, stroke, smile and whispered word. "Not much longer 'til we reach my sister Lorna's castle. She married Laird Montgomery a few months back. We shall stay there the night and then continue to Stirling, where we'll cross the bridge and be ever closer to the Highlands."

Aliah nodded. "'Tis colder here," she observed. "Did you say Stirling? Isn't that where the battle occurred?"

"Aye. Snow will be coming soon." It appeared he would ignore her second question but then he answered her. "Ye've nothing to fear from those who hold Stirling, but we will have to be careful. I've word that King Edward has spies keeping their sights on the castle. They're likely spoiling for a fight. Mayhap Mother Nature will be on our side and allow a snow fall to distract the English spies."

Aliah shook her head. She did not want to travel in the snow. "I hope we've reached your home by then. I don't like to be cold..."

Blane moved his horse closer, and she swore she could feel the heat of his body emanating from him.

"There are ways to keep warm," he said quiet enough for her ears alone.

Her cheeks heated and she looked down at her horse's mane. "'Tis not possible for us to be together, Blane."

"Aye, I know it." His voice sounded dejected and she chanced a glance upward.

His jaw muscle ticked as he looked off in the distance. Without her permission, words fell from her lips. "But I wouldn't mind if we were to keep each other warm in other ways." What in all the heavens had she just said?

With a brow raised, he swung his eyes back toward hers, raking his hot gaze up and down her form. She meant they could *innocently* share each other's heat.

"That didn't come out the way I wanted," she said in a whisper, hands tightening on the reins.

Blane shifted even closer, his uninjured thigh brushing hers. She was a little unnerved that Frosty, trotting beside them, didn't even bother to push them apart.

"I think it came out exactly the way ye wanted it, my lady." Then he leaned, slowing his gait, and whispered, "Ye might say ye're for the church, but we both know ye've too passionate a nature for that."

A call from one of his men meant they had to ride a little harder, and that she couldn't reply to his scandalous — but true — statement. Aliah would never survive the strict rules of the church, and now that she'd tasted passion, she wasn't likely to forget or not ever desire it again. However, what did he mean by his words? Was he offering for her? Surely not...

Blane took a moment to glance at her, raked his hands through his hair.

"My father would see me married," she said, wondering if Blane would make his intentions or lack of intentions known.

"Then the baron probably has a man in mind for ye." Regret flashed in his eyes, but the words were uttered, and she fully understood his meaning.

Despite steamy kisses, he would not ask her to join him on the subsequent journeys through life. She was left bereft, and numbly prodded her horse into a faster gait with the rest of the group.

The church, which she'd once found haven in, seemed to be her only option. Had she truly thought there could be a future between her and Blane? Aliah felt more naïve than ever. Her life had been so sheltered and now she'd been thrust into reality. A dangerous reality, where people were intent on harming her and a certain man had already done more damage to her soul than all the outlaws had done to her sense of safety.

Blane wanted to run headlong into the next tree he passed. To smash his thick skull again and again.

Why did he bother to trifle with the girl if he was only going to turn around and tell her she was on her own? He felt like an utter cad. Lower than low.

He should have left well enough alone. But he couldn't. Blane was drawn to her. Her essence, her smile, her very nature. And those lips... He couldn't get enough of them. Every time she glanced at him, her blue eyes wide with curiosity and their depths filled with a passion he'd only just begun to tap, he lost all sense of what was right and what was wrong. Being in her arms *felt* right.

But it wasn't.

Aliah would never be his. He himself wouldn't allow it. Her father would certainly never condone it.

Blane was not good enough for Aliah. She deserved to marry a man with a title, his own home, land. A man who would be there, not one that would spend most of his time disguised as someone else. Not someone who was bent on revenge and could spare no more.

Glancing her way, he wanted to tell her that. How did one say they were attracted to a person, wanted to be with them, but it just wasn't meant to be? Was it even worth the telling? Dejected. That's how she appeared when he'd said her father would likely have someone in mind for her to wed. That forlorn, lost expression ripped at his heart. As tough as he was, Blane wasn't the type of man who blatantly went around breaking women's hearts. All the same, 'twas an instance that kept repeating itself.

Not only did she deserve someone better than himself, she deserved a man with a clear conscience, and right now, Blane's conscience carried a wagon full of demons.

He couldn't shake Mistress Kerr's words either. The Sassenach lord had traveled with a band of Scots outlaws. If only he'd been able to take a look at just one of them… His gut told him that those men were the one's he'd spent over a decade looking for. But the innkeeper was right. His mission was to take Aliah to her sister. Aliah didn't deserve to be thrust into the midst of a battle. As soon as he saw her to Dunrobin, he would head out and find Lord Surrey himself. Then he could determine whether his intuition was right, or if he was simply going mad with grief and guilt.

He'd never broken down and told his brothers, or anyone else for that matter, what'd happened all those years ago. The shame of it was too much. Even when he did dispatch the men, he wasn't sure if he'd share the news with anyone other than his parents' graves.

Of course his men knew he hunted a band of outlaws, but they believed the group had stolen something valuable from him — they knew not that the priceless stolen goods were his parents' lives.

"Sir Blane?"

Shaking himself from his thoughts, Blane realized he was still staring at Lady Aliah and she looked back, a questioning expression on her beautiful face.

"Is aught amiss?" she asked, a note of irritation in her voice. He couldn't blame her, she'd been led on a merry, confusing chase by him, one that had abruptly ended when he'd pushed her away.

"Nay, my lady, I was only…" He trailed off, unsure of what to say. The master of disguise, always with a quick reply was suddenly speechless. He swallowed against the dryness in his throat. "I was going to ask if ye were hungry?"

Aliah shook her head, disappointment crinkling the corners of her eyes. She looked away and slowed her horse just a little so she was no longer beside him. Blane should be grateful for the distance, but he wasn't. Not having her by his side felt off somehow.

'Twas for the best though. The more distance they put between them, the easier it would be to move on.

Blane squeezed Gunnar's sides, intent on getting to Glasgow Castle quicker. Montgomery — his sister Lorna's husband — would be glad to have them as guests, but only if they arrived at an appropriate hour. In order to get there before dusk, they needed to increase their pace. No more stops.

Gunnar was only too happy to oblige as were the rest of their party.

Once settled into the castle, Blane would make sure to find a distraction from Lady Aliah. Lorna would surely like to visit with another lady, and would most likely keep Aliah entertained. Meanwhile, he could tempt himself with a large cup of ale, a dram or three or six of whisky, and not thoughts of Aliah.

For several miles they'd seen the towers of Glasgow Castle looming in the distance. Stone touching grey clouds, where it seemed to mingle with the sky. They rode out in the open, but Blane seemed more relaxed then he had before.

The set of his shoulders did not look as tight. Seeing this helped Aliah relax too. She supposed Blane felt safe near an ally. They rode over an open plain of green and brown grass, and soon came within shouting distance of the tower gates. Several men stood atop, gazing over the battlements when they saw Blane, ordered the gates open.

"Welcome back, Sir Blane," one shouted down.

Blane nodded. The wooden gates opened and in they rode, greeted by a number of stable hands who took their reins and a few servants who took their baggage.

"Ye shall have a real bed to sleep in tonight." Blane's words were lost in the flurry as a beautiful young woman rushed toward them.

She had light colored hair, brilliant green eyes and a belly rounded with child. While her features were beautiful and feminine, there was a hint of Blane on her face—somewhere around the eyes.

"Blane!" The woman thrust herself into his arms.

"I see marriage does ye well," he said to her, kissing her on the cheek.

"'Twould do ye well the same, brother." She playfully punched him in the arm and then caught sight of Aliah. "And who is this?" She gave her brother a pointed look as if to ask if he was indeed married, making Aliah's face heat to burning.

Aliah slid from her mount and then stepped forward. "I am Lady Aliah de Mowbray."

"De Mowbray? Sounds familiar..." The woman glanced off into the distance as if trying to recall, then said, "Ah, yes, your sister is married to my brother, Magnus."

Aliah nodded curtly, whatever hopes she'd had of finding her sister not married to the man dashed.

"I am Lady Montgomery, but ye must call me Lorna." She held out her hand. "Come inside, I'll show ye to a chamber where ye can freshen up afore we sup."

Aliah let herself be ushered along, turning back to see where Blane was, but he was in the middle of what looked like an arm gripping fight with a man close to his own size. Both men possessed a strength she found vastly awe-inspiring.

"'Tis my husband, Laird Montgomery," Lorna said with a tilt of her head in Blane's direction. "He and my brothers have sort of a...love-hate relationship."

Aliah smiled, deciding she liked Lorna already. "Why?"

Lorna waved her hand in the air, "Oh, 'tis naught but men wanting to best each other." She pursed her lips and then smiled, lost in her own thoughts. "Ye look positively famished. Let us get ye cleaned up so we can eat."

Aliah thought it was more like Lorna was famished, the woman continuously rubbed a tender hand on her thick belly.

"When is the babe due?" Aliah asked.

Lorna glanced at her, her eyes glowing. "I suspect late February. 'Tis a strong and healthy bairn."

"You look well," Aliah said. She'd only ever seen a few pregnant servants, and Lorna most definitely looked in better health then the overworked women of her household.

"'Tis true, I am. Jamie doesna allow me to do a thing. I have to beg him to go for walks, but he's hard pressed not to give in."

Aliah smiled. They were in love. She wondered if it had been a love match or if they'd fallen in love after marrying.

The scents of roasting meat and freshly baked bread filled the castle, as did the sounds of laughter. Glasgow Castle was a happy place, as it should be given their lady and laird were happy leaders.

Aliah was unprepared for the lavishness of the chamber Lorna presented her with. An ornate, feminine four-poster bed graced the side wall, complete with a canopy and embroidered, soft looking curtains. The coverlet matched the bed curtains, and plush pillows enticed Aliah to sink onto its surface. Dainty chairs and a table sat before a hearth and the floor was covered in several tapestried rugs. It looked to be a room fit for a queen or duchess in the least, not for Aliah.

"This is too much."

"Och, dinna be modest, my lady, ye are deserving of some beauty. I can only imagine the filth ye've had to endure on your journey. I know my brothers well. They think nothing of sleeping on the ground when a lady's sensibilities require a much more pleasant locality." Lorna swept past her into the room. "Here's a basin with fresh water and some linens. Cook is ready to serve supper, so would ye be offended if I asked ye to wait for a bath until after we eat?"

Aliah shook her head vigorously. "Nay, my lady, this will do fine. I shall freshen up and come down directly."

"Ah, good," Lorna said, patting her belly. "I was prepared to allow ye to have your way and wait, but the bairn is mighty hungry."

Aliah laughed. "You are too kind."

"I am glad for the company." Lorna left her in peace and Aliah took a few quiet moments to sink onto the feather mattress and let her bones relax.

If only she could have refused to dine with the rest in the great hall. She wasn't sure she could face Blane after today's humiliation. Her heart still lurched and her fingers trembled whenever he glanced her way. Thank the heavens they were halfway through with their journey. Only a few more days and then she could avoid him indefinitely.

Chapter Fifteen

Patience was a virtue. And not one Blane possessed at the current moment.

He stood just inside the great hall, shifting from foot to foot like a nervous lad awaiting the girl he'd dreamed of every night. Only thing was, he was a man, and he waited for the woman whose image refused to leave his mind. His thigh pulsed with a dull ache but nothing seemed to relieve the pain.

Making his mood worse was the odd looks Lorna kept throwing him, and the knowing smile Montgomery kept flashing his way. Bastard. Did the Lowlander really think he knew him so well?

Damn if the man wasn't right.

Blane stalked toward the hearth, letting the heat of the fire sink into his bones and hoping it would help to relax the stiff muscles of his neck, ease the pain in his leg. He rolled his head from side to side, rested his elbow on the oak mantelpiece and stared into the blaze. Blue flames licked between the few dozen logs, growing from red, then orange until fading completely to whitish-yellow. The logs snapped, popped, and sent sparks flying to sizzle right out of the hearth, landing too close to his boots.

Mayhap his own heat was the same—right now it was blue, hotter than hell. But soon, the warmth that claimed him would grow weaker until it was nothing more than a little ball that would snap and turn to ash—cold to the touch.

Blane rested his head on his arm, seemingly mesmerized by the flames, but truly his mind was trying to work around the attraction he held for Aliah and the impossibilities of them being together.

'Twas ludicrous. Not only was she the daughter of an English baron—damn Sassenachs—she wanted to join the church. To live her life forever in innocence and peace. Already he'd taken away a bit of that purity. Dashed some of her naivety to the flames before him. He was a wicked man for having done that.

But *mo creach*, he couldn't help it. And, honestly, he didn't regret kissing her either. He savored it. 'Twas as if every time she was around his sense of decency depleted and all he could think about was her, kissing her, touching her, breathing in her scent.

He'd nearly ruined her in the hayloft. And every other time he'd touched her.

Blane could think of no other reason save for he was a debauched man. If he cared about her, he'd encourage her to go into the church, to follow her dreams. He couldn't help wondering though, if that was what she really wanted.

If she was set on the church would she have let him kiss her time and again? Touch her so intimately? Would the passion that filled her eyes have been so prominent? Blane shook his head. No, she wouldn't have. And she wouldn't have told him that her father would rather she marry. To him, it seemed clear she was giving him an invitation. That she was open to possibilities.

Blane pushed back from the fire, slamming his hand on the mantelpiece and cursing softly under his breath.

No matter how she enticed him, or how she invited him to take her, she was not his and never could be. That was the plain truth of it, and he'd better —

All thought left him as she entered the great hall.

Aliah glided into the room, every bit the lady. Her hair had been fixed, pulled into a fresh plait, and her skin seemed to glow. Lips curled into a subtle smile, she inclined her head to those who greeted her, although her gaze searched the room. Until she found him.

From where he stood, some fifty feet away, he sensed the tension thickening as their gazes connected. Aliah's eyes widened, her hands clasped each other at her waist and she licked her lips. Her throat bobbed as she swallowed. And he didn't miss a movement. Blane realized he scowled fiercely and tried to calm his features. He took a step forward, intent on greeting her as a proper lady deserved. He would bow, take her hand, kiss the air above her knuckles. He'd be the epitome of propriety. Something totally foreign to him. But as he approached, Lorna, who'd been eyeing the both of them, swept in front of him and led Aliah away.

Blane gritted his teeth, wanting to shout at his sister for having done such a thing, but the clap of Montgomery's hand on his shoulder stopped him.

"Women. They genuinely baffle me. I pray the wee bairn is a boy, only for the reason I've yet to come to understand the fairer sex. I canna have them outnumbering me."

Blane eyed the man he'd detested for the last several months with weariness. "Aye. Even growing up with sisters I find I am still mystified."

Montgomery laughed. "'Tis even different with women we are not related to, but instead wish to bed."

Blane let out an involuntarily growl. "Dinna remind me of how ye stole my sister, Montgomery."

The man's grin widened. "Ye know I love her, Blane. She is my world. I canna breathe when she is away from me. Ye'll find that, if ye havena already, and then ye won't be hating me so much."

"Och, I dinna hate ye, man. I merely loathe what ye did to my wee sister."

Montgomery laughed. "As Arbella will when she finds out about ye and her sister."

Blane turned the full force of his glare on Montgomery. "Now ye listen, Montgomery. There is nothing between the lass and me. I am merely her escort."

The man grinned and nodded in the most annoying way possible. "As ye say. As ye say..." Then he sauntered away, leaving Blane without closure, and with the need to hit something—someone.

Lorna clapped her hands for everyone to take their seats before he could chase after her husband and demand satisfaction. Blane trudged to the dais table. His sister had decided that it was best for him to sit beside Aliah—of course she did. Little meddler. And Montgomery just kept giving him that dumb grin. Blane frowned, but did as any gentleman would and pulled out the chair for Aliah, albeit a little rough. He tucked her in quickly, ignoring her look of annoyance as he'd pushed her too close to the table. He didn't mean to do it, but he wanted to get the act out of the way so he could sit down and proceed to fill himself with a barrel of ale. 'Twas the only way he was bound to get through the evening having to be so close to her heat, her scent.

"You do realize I'm not a child, do you not, Blane? You pushed me clear into the table," she grumbled. Despite her ladylike appearance, her tongue was just as sour as ever.

His leg throbbed where she'd shot him, and he put a hand under the table to rub it.

"Apologies, my lady."

She didn't speak for several moments and then said, "Accepted. Do you not like it here? I find it absolutely cheerful and your sister and Laird Montgomery quite accommodating. But you've been growling since we arrived."

Finally, a maid put a mug of ale in front of him. He picked it up and winked at the maid. "Stay close, I'm in need of a full cup at all times."

The maid blushed and scurried away.

Aliah had grown still beside him. He realized it was not a nice move he'd just pulled, flirting with the maid so openly, but it was best if Aliah understood there was nothing between them.

"I like it here just fine, Lady Aliah," he finally answered. "'Tis simply that my leg pains me." He said it to hurt her. Knowing that it would sting. And he was right.

Aliah gasped, and from the corner of his eyes he watched her put her trembling hands into her lap.

'Haps he'd gone too far. He didn't have to be a complete arse to her. Blane turned to apologize, but Aliah had engaged herself in conversation with Lorna on her right. Not wanting to interrupt, he instead nursed his ale, pleased when the maid rushed over to refill it. A few people approached to speak with him, he answered in grunts and nods, still too spun up in his thoughts of Aliah.

She, on the other hand, managed to ignore him throughout the meal, which only served to increase his ire and the pain in his leg.

Despite outward appearances, Aliah was all too aware of the man sitting to her left. She tried beyond might to ignore him. With every ounce of willpower she possessed, she refused to look at him, acknowledge him. When his arm accidently brushed hers, she simply leaned closer to Lorna.

Thank goodness his sister was in the mood to chat, else Aliah would have settled for talking to herself over having to speak with him.

Blane's manner was simply atrocious. She'd not witnessed him in so callous a mood before—even when he'd been cursing as the arrow protruded from his thigh. Things between them had irrevocably changed. There was no going back. They'd crossed a line that altered who they were to one another. Kissing, touching. They were intimate encounters—encounters she'd never forget. His lips were forever burned to hers. Her hips still tingled where his fingers had massaged her. Breasts ached for him to cup them once more and her nipples were nearly always hard as rubies, waiting for his attention. Her body was no longer her own.

She wasn't sure she could ever forgive him for that. For tempting her with the forbidden and showing her what passion could be had.

Taking a sip of the wine she was offered, she let the tangy drink roll over her tongue and down her throat. If she were to be fair, she was in just as irritable a mood as Blane. Mayhap it wasn't that he wanted to be rude to her, but that he didn't know how else to behave. He wanted to push her away.

His feelings for her... Were what? She had no idea. He wasn't likely to share and she wasn't going to ask.

Lorna tapped her on the arm and leaned close to speak with her. In low tones she said, "I believe my brother is taken with ye."

Aliah shook her head and looked into Lorna's bright green eyes. "Nay, you're mistaken about that."

Lorna smiled knowingly. "He suffers much. Ye shot him?"

Guilt curdled the wine in her belly. "Aye... But I thought he was..."

Lorna squeezed her hand. "Nay need to explain, my brother has already told me the story. I say he should have told ye the truth sooner, but then again, if I were ye, I wouldna have gone with him."

Aliah gave a brief smile. "Aye. I still have reservations," she said wryly.

"Ye'd best tread with care, lass. When a man falls, he falls hard."

"I'll not be there to pick him up, Lorna. He doesn't want me in that way. He said as much himself."

"They all do."

Lorna's words mystified Aliah, but before she could ask her to explain, the feast was presented and the mistress of Glasgow Castle called out with excitement upon seeing her favorite venison pie.

An hour or more later, Aliah wasn't sure how much time had passed since her belly was now warm with wine and her head buzzed a little, Lorna clapped her hands for music. Several musicians sat before the hearth strumming and blowing a beautiful melody. Aliah felt the music invade her limbs, making her sway.

"Come dance," Lorna said, pure joy in her voice.

She grabbed Aliah by the hand and tugged her to the dance floor, where they twirled and laughed, joined by several other clanswomen. Not wanting to be left out, Laird Montgomery bowed before the ladies and begged a dance from his wife.

"Only if my brother should dance with our guest," Lorna answered.

From his perch at the dais, Blane glowered at them all. Aliah felt almost felt sorry for him. His leg probably hurt like the devil. Dancing was not what he needed, but a good solid sleep in a comfortable bed.

She started to shake her head when he stood and stalked toward her.

He bowed stiffly before her. Aliah's heart stopped. He meant to dance with her? She curtsied in turn, and then allowed him to take her hand. Blane twirled her about, his face a mask she could not decipher. Was he angry? Tired? Bored? Then his greenish eyes gazed into hers and her breath caught.

His stare was intense, hot, and she felt her insides start to melt. Knees grew weak. Even her arms seemed to lose all their power. She licked her lips, wishing instead that it was his tongue running over her sensitive flesh. What was she thinking? Distance was what she needed. But his body was hard and flush against her. Every plane and dip of muscle and sinew branded her.

Troubling that being in his arms felt so right and so wrong at the same time.

"Why would ye think I didna like it here?" he asked quietly.

"I told you, you haven't stopped grumbling." She was quick to continue, "But you made it clear 'twas because of your leg."

He nodded, his eyes never leaving hers. "That was part of it."

Dare she ask? "What is the other part?"

"Ye."

"Me?"

"Aye. Whenever I'm around ye, I canna seem to…"

"Breathe?"

Blane looked at her with a bit of awe. "Aye."

Aliah's face flamed and she pulled her eyes from his to look over his shoulder. She couldn't believe she'd essentially admitted to the same thing—that he'd agreed.

Blane took her subtle cue of silence, and twirled her for several more minutes. The music did not stop. 'Twas as if Lorna had commanded one long continuous song. Aliah did not mind so much. Being in his arms was the first time she'd started to relax all evening.

He leaned close, his breath fanning her face, his lips brushing the shell of her ear. "I dinna know what it is about ye, lass. I shouldna want what I want. Shouldna desire the taste of your lips, but I canna help myself."

Aliah swallowed hard. "Aye," she murmured.

"What are we to do?" he asked.

She shook her head. "I don't know."

"I canna kiss ye anymore, even if every muscle in my body strains to tuck ye tight against me, and ravish your sweet taste."

Why did he have to talk like that? Put such visions in her mind. Her head swam with too much wine, desire and the remembrances of the last time he'd touched her.

"Nay," she answered, agreeing with him, despite her body's desire to do the opposite.

"Dinna say nay…" he murmured against her ear again.

"Why?" she whispered back.

"I want ye..."

Saint's knees! Blane had admitted it, but he'd also drowned in an entire cask of ale before taking her hand to dance. He didn't mean it—and he said he wanted her, desired her, as in her body, not her soul.

"You cannot have me," she said through her teeth, angry at herself for having even played into his games. "I am a woman of virtue, not a woman to be tussled with. I deserve more than a bedding, Sir Blane."

She yanked away from him and without a backward glance headed from the great hall. The winding stairs seemed steeper than when she'd descended them earlier. Perhaps because earlier there had been hope left in her heart, now she knew for

170

sure that hope was dead, and she'd a long climb to where she needed to go.

Behind her, footsteps pounded on the floor, and someone gripped her elbow, whipping her around. Aliah lost her footing, falling against Blane's hard chest.

"I dinna want just to bed ye, lass. I want much more than that," he spat, his chest heaved with his breaths, nostrils flared, eyes blazed with emotion. "But I've naught to offer ye but a lifetime of loneliness. I've no home and my soul is black. An angel such as yourself deserves better."

"No one is perfect, Blane. Not even I." She dare not tell him that whether he had a home or not wasn't important to her. His soul however was another matter. "You leave too much inside here." She flattened her hand to his chest. "I'd have had you for my own, but only if you were to unburden yourself with whatever demons you fight."

"Even then I'd still be damaged."

Aliah started to shake her head, but his hands came up to clasp her face and she barely had time to take a breath before his lips descended on hers.

Chapter Sixteen

Out of control. Unequivocally mad. 'Twas the only thing to describe the sensations whipping through Blane's body and the thoughts tumbling through his mind. Aliah's lips were pliant, warm and all too luscious. He crushed his mouth to hers, tasting the wine she'd drunk mingled with the ale he'd imbibed too much of. Beyond that was her own sweet essence that drove him wild. How could he possibly think he could ever get away from her?

With both hands he hauled her closer, fitting her body perfectly to his. She whimpered in the back of her throat and he answered with a feral growl. Not caring who saw, or what the consequences would be, he lifted her into his arms, never losing the connection with her mouth. On pure instinct he climbed the circular stone stairs as he continued to pleasure them both with his kiss.

"Chamber?" he said gruffly, between sucking on her lower lip and licking at her tongue.

"There," she panted, her breaths as ragged and shallow as his own.

Blane stopped moving a moment to further explore her mouth. The ache in his leg was gone, replaced by a pulsing throb throughout his whole body — the only thing that could cease that ache was to bury himself deep inside her.

He nudged open the door and shut it with the heel of his boot in one fluid motion. Setting her down on her feet, he pressed her back against the door, held her arms above her head, keeping her captive to his kiss. Aliah didn't seem to mind, and instead moaned against his lips, pressing her hips against him. Her passion ignited his own. Blane slid his lips from her mouth, down along her chin to her ear, teasing the lobe as she squirmed against him. He pinned her hips to his, pressing her hard against the aged oak.

His cock throbbed, thick with need and begging for the warmth of her slick channel. Heat emanated from the apex of her thighs and he knew to take her, to slide inside her, would be sweet heaven indeed. He continued his path of kisses over her collarbone, moving lower to kiss the center of her chest, just above the plush globes of her breasts. She smelled so sweet, tasted even better. Never in his wildest encounters had he come across a woman as worthy of the name goddess as she.

Letting go of her hands, he slid his fingers with feather-light touch up her ribs until he reached her breasts. He itched to touch her with a power he wasn't able to control. Slowly he cupped her breasts, weighing them, kneading them, brushing his thumbs over the turgid peaks.

"Blane," she murmured, her hands coming to rest on his shoulders, then snaking into his hair, massaging his scalp.

Hearing her say his name sent a whirl of fresh desire blasting through his chest and straight to his groin. His cock strained with the need for him to remove his plaid, to get ever closer to the velvet flesh she offered. But he couldn't do that…

He had to pleasure her, make her quiver. And he was an expert when it came to making a woman's thighs twinge.

Trailing his lips from the center of her chest, he brushed over the silkiness of the tops of her breasts, breathing hotly on her flesh. Gasps came from her mouth in quick fashion, parting the hair on his head, egging him on. Skimming his nails gently over her skin, he yanked her gown down, revealing one rose-colored nipple and then the other.

"Ye're more beautiful than I imagined," he said, his voice husky with need.

"Thank...you," she managed.

"Nay, thank *ye*," he answered, dipping to swirl his tongue over one nipple.

"Oh!" she cried, her back arching.

"Aye," he said with a little chuckle, kneading both of her breasts as he suckled her.

Aliah's response was hot, swift. She moaned, yanked at his hair, and then pulled him closer. Her hips ground against his, seeking, searching.

Blane wasn't sure how much more he could take... He slid a hand down over her ribs to her hip, bunching her skirts up until his fingers skimmed the bare flesh of her leg. He stroked over her inner thigh, feeling her tremble.

Knowing she desired him pumped something primal inside him. How was it possible?

He caressed higher, until the heat of her core quivered on his fingertips. She was wet, blessedly so. Blane stroked a finger between her folds, finding the nub of her pleasure. Aliah cried out, her head hitting the door.

He chuckled against her breasts, then came up to gaze into her eyes.

"Ye want me," he stated.

She swallowed and he watched the pulse in her neck jump.

"Say it, lass."

"I do…"

As she said the words he thrust a finger inside her. Her channel was tight, squeezing against him.

"Oh, God," she gasped, her head falling back again.

Blane felt his control was going to snap and soon. Lifting her into the air once again, he stormed to the bed. He had one mission now—to pleasure them both until the bed shook and the walls echoed from their cries.

He laid her on the bed, taking a moment to let his gaze rove from her ruby kissed lips, to her breasts which spilled from the soft gown she wore, down to her slipper covered toes. There was only one way to undress her, to reveal to himself the beauty of her lush body—slowly. He would take his time, kissing each and every inch of her creamy curves, nibbling, teasing until she writhed with a powerful need.

Eventually his gaze moved back up to her face, framed by her golden hair on the white linen pillow. Her eyes stopped him. They were wide, hazy with desire and something else. Something disturbing. She was scared. There was fear in her eyes. That was a slap in the face. A dunk of cold water on his ale-soaked brain.

What was he doing?

Disgusted with himself he slowly backed away from her, shaking his head. Willing his cock to behave. "Apologies, my lady," he mumbled. *Ballocks!*

The fear he'd seen before was quickly wiped from her face, but he couldn't grasp the emotion that replaced it. She rolled over to face the opposite wall, her back to him.

"Shut the door on the way out, Sir Blane." Her voice was cold and he longed to say something to comfort her, to place his hand on her back and offer her…

There was nothing to offer her. He'd already taken too much and he had nothing to give in return save heartbreak. Which it seemed he'd already accomplished.

The wall blurred before Aliah as tears clouded her eyes, stinging them. She tried not to blink, as if doing so would give permission for the tears to fall, for her feelings to be hurt by what had transpired.

Instead, she closed her eyes, ignoring the trickle of wetness that slid over her nose to join its sister tear on the pillow.

She couldn't decide if she was more embarrassed or heartbroken. When she'd left the hall, she'd been determined to put Blane behind her. To move on, and then he'd found her on the stairwell. Said things that made her heart swell, her head spin. *I want much more than that...* His words still echoed in her mind. As if to further push away her reserve, his lips had touched hers and all had been lost.

Whenever they kissed the world melted away. She became boneless in his arms and desired nothing more than the pleasure of surrounding herself with his scent, to run her fingers through his thick hair or along the corded muscles of his arms. Her body still pulsed with the passion he'd ignited.

Blane made her feel beautiful, desirable. He made her feel she was more than what she was. Made her forget the pain of what brought her into this world—the guilt of having caused her mother's death. Prompted her to think there was more to life than what she'd sentenced herself.

But as they grew closer, the turmoil only seemed to get worse. He literally was shoving her away. She didn't know what to make of it, and she was certain she couldn't take much more. They'd both had too much to drink. They'd both let the heat of the moment take over.

Swiping away a tear, she rolled onto her back, sinking into the soft mattress and flopped her arm over her eyes. He'd done the right thing by leaving and once more she found herself feeling more stupid than anything else. How she wished for Arbella's company. She needed someone to confide in. To talk to about her feelings and how insane she felt whenever she tried to make sense of what was happening.

Not that her sister was worldly in the ways of men, but Arbella had always paid attention to relationships and the interactions between people. If anyone could help her to decipher her feelings, it was her sister.

A deep sigh escaped her. Arbella was not here. And she wouldn't see her sister for several days—in which time she'd have to see Blane again.

A soft tap sounded at the door. Aliah tried to ignore whoever it was, praying it was not the man himself returning.

"Aliah?"

A wave of relief filled her, 'twas Lorna.

Pulling herself up, she realized when the cold air hit her bare breasts she'd not fixed her gown. She hastened to do so, then climbed from the bed, pulling the door open a crack.

Lorna stood alone in the corridor, a tray in her hand filled with small bowl of sugared almonds, a jug and two cups. "May I come in?"

Aliah nodded, not trusting her voice. Her throat felt swollen, achy. She was sure to start sobbing as soon as she spoke.

Lorna glided in, softness embodied, and offered Aliah a warm smile as she shut the door behind her and set the tray on the table by the hearth.

"I see the maid has yet to light your fire." She clucked her tongue then went about setting up the logs and lighting them with a flint. "I have called for your bath. They will be here soon."

"Thank you."

"None required." She smiled, but it wasn't the exuberant smiles she'd displayed in the great hall, this time the turn of her lips showed concern. Rubbing a hand over her belly she sat in one of the chairs before the hearth. "Will ye join me?"

Aliah nodded and took the seat opposite. Lorna took a few minutes to pour out two cups of almond milk and offered Aliah some of the sweet nuts. She took a few, enjoying the crunchy sugared treat.

"Judging from the way ye look and the way my brother is storming about the castle, I'd say something's happened between the two of ye."

Aliah sucked her lower lip into her mouth, not wanting to say anything, but at the same time, wishing to explain everything.

"I remember when I first met Jamie. My heart beat so rapidly in my chest whenever he passed I thought I'd burst. I found myself making up reasons to be near wherever he was. And then he kissed me and I felt as if the whole world was crashing down around me, and that I was being lifted into the heavens."

Aliah's eyes widened. She'd never heard someone talk about kissing before — and to hear it told exactly as she felt...

"'Twas over for me then. I was changed. I was enraptured. I was in love." Lorna gave her a pointed look. "Do ye know what I'm saying?"

Aliah shook her head, kicked off her slippers and tucked her feet beneath her, grabbing another handful of nuts.

"I think ye do. I can see the way ye look at each other."

Blane looked at her a certain way? Aliah nearly bit her tongue instead of a nut at that realization.

Lorna nodded. "I wasna particularly aware of my feelings either until telling my younger sister a romantic tale. Seems we dinna quite realize such ourselves until it's pointed out to us."

"Aye," Aliah said softly in agreement.

Another soft knock came at the door and Aliah stiffened. He'd come back.

"That must be your bath." Lorna answered the door, allowed several servants to carry in a large wood tub and a few steaming buckets of water. They left, only to come back with more and more buckets of water until the tub was filled halfway. Steam swirled into the air, quickly squelched when they added a couple buckets of colder water to cool it down. Lorna dug around in the wardrobe against the wall near the door, pulling out some linen towels and soap. She pushed one linen towel into the tub, lining it and set the other on the bed. "Come on now, in ye go."

"My lady, you don't have to help me, surely a maid would be more than willing..."

Lorna waved away her words. "Och, I told ye to call me Lorna. 'Sides, what kind of mistress would I be were I not to offer up a good hair washing to a lady? Come now, I dinna mind."

Aliah stood and walked over to the tub, watching several bits of something floating in the water. "What's in it?"

"Dried heather and lavender. Makes the water smell sweet—and your skin when ye're done. 'Haps next time ye come for a visit, I could show ye how to have a milk bath." She ran her fingers up her arm. "Makes my skin as silky as...well silk." She giggled.

Aliah had never had a sweetened bath—nor a milk bath. She quickly stripped off her clothing and climbed into the tub, letting the warmth of the water seep into her muscles and bones. The scents of the heated flowers encompassed her, relaxing her. Aches seemed to melt away. She'd not realized how sore she was until that moment. Leaning her head back on the rim, she stretched her legs to the end of the tub, rubbing her toes on the wood.

"This is heavenly, Lorna."

"Oh, aye. Jamie gets so irritated, but I have a bath nearly every day."

"Truly?"

"Aye. I love to sit and reflect on the goings on of the day. Do some of my best thinking in a tub. And then of course, there's always the fun of it."

"Fun?"

Lorna's cheeks flushed a rosy red. "When ye're married, ye'll know the meaning of it."

Aliah's own face heated as she took the woman's meaning and visions of Blane climbing into the tub with her came to mind. Instantly her nipples hardened. She sank into the water to hide her reaction, thankful that Lorna had turned from her to gather a linen square.

Turning back, she handed the square to Aliah with a ball of lemon scented soap.

"Mmm, that smells wonderful."

"Aye. I love lemon, 'twill help to clear your head. Dip your head a bit."

Aliah did as she was instructed and when she came back up, Lorna started to wash her hair, massaging her scalp. She allowed herself a few moments to luxuriate in having her hair washed and then rubbed the ball of soap on the square, washing her arms and legs.

"Dunk for a rinse," Lorna said.

Aliah sank beneath the water, rubbing the soap from her hair. When she rose, Lorna pulled her hair over the back of the tub and started to brush it.

"I've heard that your sister is verra happily married," Lorna said.

"Arbella?"

"Aye."

"Have you seen her?"

"Not yet. We had planned a visit after the bairn is born. Magnus and Arbella will come here to Glasgow, then when the bairn is old enough to travel, Jamie has promised we will visit Dunrobin."

"Dunrobin?" The name sounded mystical.

"'Tis my clan's castle in the Highlands."

"Oh. Blane never mentioned the name. He told me of Sutherland."

"'Tis the name of our holding."

"I see. What is the castle like? What is Magnus like? How do you know they are happy?" Aliah's questions came out one after the other and instantly she laughed. "I'm sorry."

Lorna chuckled. "Dinna be sorry. I shall answer each of your questions. The castle is imposing, but beautiful. Full of life. The clansmen and women are a close-knit group and do so much for each other. I miss it. 'Tis not as overlarge as it is here, but is still impressive. Magnus is much like Blane. They are both large, Magnus is lighter in coloring. Both have a stubborn streak that is…frustrating. But they both have hearts of gold." She paused a moment, working out a snag in Aliah's hair. "I know they are happy because I received a letter from your sister stating as much and inquiring about a visit."

"Truly?" Aliah was hurt that her sister had written to Lorna and not to herself.

"Aye. Dinna let your heart be saddened, Aliah. Your sister mentioned ye in the letter and that she missed ye and hoped ye'd be able to visit her."

That only made Aliah feel worse. If she'd entered the church, she would probably never see her sister again. Her heart ached with that thought. It'd never truly bothered her before now.

Aliah nodded, accepting Lorna's words.

"Ye know, one can always choose one's own path."

"For a man mayhap," Aliah countered.

"Nay, not so." Lorna stood and grabbed a linen towel, offering it to Aliah. "There are ways to get what we want too,

Aliah. Ye just have to figure out what your path is and follow it."

Lorna's words did not make any sense at all. If her father forced her to marry, she would have to marry. If she ran away and joined the church, Mother Superior would decide her future. Aliah didn't see how she was in charge of it at all.

Blane's sister only smiled. "Ye'll understand soon. That I know. I shall see ye in the morn."

Aliah stared at the closed door until her skin was covered in gooseflesh and her teeth chattered.

"Ye know naught of what ye speak." Blane paced the small square of space available to do so inside Montgomery's library.

The laird sat in a large oak chair, booted feet crossed at the ankle atop his old worn desk. Candlelight flickered shadows on his face and illuminated the stark walls. The laird's arms were folded over his chest and that idiotic smile still graced his face.

"And why do ye keep smiling at me like that? Ye look like a madman!"

Montgomery's grin only widened.

Although his sister's husband was an enormous annoyance, Blane was mostly angry with himself. He could not believe the way he'd treated Aliah—and that his cock was still engorged with the need to fill her. Luckily his pleated plaid and sporran did their job of hiding the evidence. But it didn't still the pulse, or the heat rushing through his body. Angry. Lusty. Angry...

"Look, Blane, stop your fashing like a virgin lass. 'Twill do naught but drive ye mad."

He was already there. Blane stopped pacing, dropped into a chair, crossed his arms and glared at his brother-by-marriage. "What do ye suggest?"

Montgomery shrugged. "Marriage?"

"Nay." He wasn't about to explain to Montgomery why he couldn't offer.

"I canna imagine what your reasons are for denying her." The man raised a challenging brow.

"I didna ask ye to."

Montgomery shrugged. "Ye're right 'tis none of my business, save I wasna the only one that watched ye chase her from the hall and ye were both gone an ample amount of time."

"Ye'll not compromise her reputation," Blane demanded.

Montgomery shook his head. "I would never. What of ye?"

That hit like a punch to the gut. He *had* compromised her. Making threats to his brother-by-marriage was ridiculous when Blane had accomplished that feat with heady flourish.

"She deserves better," Blane muttered half to himself.

"Any woman of value does."

"Bastard." He gritted his teeth against the urge to grab the man by his collar.

"Ye take my meaning the wrong way, man!" Montgomery laughed. "'Twas the same for me with Lorna. Now afore ye go and rant at me about the way it went, let me finish."

Blane closed his mouth, letting the insulting words die on his tongue.

"When a man falls for a woman, he always thinks she deserves better. He canna imagine that she would desire him, for he holds her so high above himself. I'm not sure it's a feeling that ever leaves a man."

Blane pursed his lips, his jaw tightening. He wondered if Montgomery was aware of how profound his words were. They were all well and good for *him*. The man was here with his wife.

"My situation is different than yours. 'Tis different than Magnus'. I am a traveling merchant. Ye're a laird."

Montgomery shook his head, disappointment showing on his face. "Ye're more than a traveling merchant, Blane. Dinna be an arse. Ye're a knight, a warrior. Ye're in line for one of the most powerful clans in the Highlands. Ye feed your clan. Ye're an important man. Dinna insult the rest of your family by naysaying your worth."

Blane blew out a breath of disgust. No one had ever said anything to him like that before. Shown him his own worth. Shown what an arse he was. And yet, Montgomery didn't even know the half of it. Even if Blane believed the man, ultimately, Blane was a coward and responsible for his parents' death. That was a demon he'd fight until his last breath. He didn't deserve happiness or the warmth of Aliah's embrace.

Shoving from his chair, he stormed from the library.

Chapter Seventeen

The following morning, the castle woke at dawn and with it Aliah pulled herself from the comfort of her soft bed and headed down to the great hall. She was hoping to avoid Blane, but when she arrived, it appeared that everybody had decided on an early meal.

She took her seat between Lorna and Blane, mumbling greetings. A servant presented her with a steaming bowl of porridge, dribbled with honey, sliced apples and chunks of walnuts. Just a hint of cinnamon reached her nose and had her mouth watering. Eagerly she dipped her wooden spoon into the bowl. The porridge reminded her of home. Arbella had often ordered them an intricate breakfast of soaked grains.

As she ate, Blane leaned into the table, looking over her toward Lorna. "We've appreciated your hospitality, but must make haste after the meal. Winter is coming and I'd rather not get caught in a storm."

"Oh, aye, that would make your travel quite heinous," Lorna agreed.

"We shall see ye in the spring then," Montgomery said. "'Twas our pleasure to have ye, even if 'twas so short a visit. We *value* your company."

The way he put an emphasis on the word *value* puzzled Aliah. She shook her head, dismissing it and continued to eat her porridge. Men were like a foreign species and she wasn't sure she had the energy to figure them out quite yet. She was still trying to decipher her own line of thinking and just exactly how she was supposed to take control of her own future. Sitting beside Blane, she was a mess of confusion. Her body wanted to lean close and her mind tried to get as far away as possible.

The meal was over all too soon, and their things were packed and horses readied. Even Frosty appeared eager to leave, as if he knew he'd soon be reunited with Arbella. Aliah hugged Lorna tight, thanking her for her company and guidance. Lorna wished her well and hoped that she'd be seeing her come the spring. Aliah couldn't make any promises and simply nodded. Truth be told, it looked more like she'd be safely ensconced in an abbey by then.

Aliah pulled her cloak tight around her after Blane assisted her in mounting her horse. The sky was still cloudy and threatened rain. The sun tried to shine somewhere above, making the clouds glow silver.

She heard Blane address his men as they exited the gates of Glasgow Castle, "If we ride hard, we'll make it to Stirling before nightfall. 'Tis better we camp beyond the bridge if we can make it."

Liam glanced at Aliah with a raised brow and she quelled the need to hit him. She lifted her chin, deciding that she would show them all she could muster the strength just as well as the rest of them. As soon as they were on the road, the men urged their horses into a gallop and Aliah did the same. She rode in the middle of the warriors, and if for any reason her horse started to slow, one of the horses behind nudged it along. She was at a disadvantage given that their mounts were used to riding this hard—well trained warrior horses. Hers was simply a borrowed mount from the Kerrs. Well cared for, aye, but it was not as well trained. Aliah did manage to keep up however, and even when her bladder screamed for them to stop, she held it.

The importance of proving she could be as strong as the rest of them outweighed the need for relief. However, when they did stop to water the horses, she was all too glad to jump off and run to the nearest bush. Blane chuckled as she passed and when she returned he eyed her with what she thought was a new-found respect.

When she went to remount, he stilled her with a brush against her arm that sent tingles racing along her flesh. Flashes of the night before threatened to fill her mind and make her weak in the knees but she refused to pay them heed, for she too remembered his rejection.

"We will rest for a few moments and eat. Dinna want to work the horses to the point of exhaustion."

Aliah nodded, glad for the reprieve and a chance to stretch her legs. Blane handed her a cold leg of fowl, which she quickly devoured, tossing the remains to Frosty. Her hound growled with delight and nearly swallowed the bone whole. All too soon they were on the road again, weaving in and out of the trees and lucky to remain undeterred by anyone.

The land grew hillier as they climbed and descended ridges, crossed moors and burns, then climbed over another vast rise. The wind was brisk upon the inclines and calmed somewhat on the planes. They passed quiet villages, shepherds and their flocks, merchants traveling with their wares, and those who harvested the last of the fields. No one seemed to have any interest in them beyond an initial weary glance. Finally, they came to Stirling, remaining hidden in the forest to the south. Aliah stared at the impressive castle, perched atop a hill in all its magnificence. 'Twas an amazing feat that the Scots had been able to wrestle it from English hands. Then again, she eyed Blane, if they were all as brawny and determined as he was, it wouldn't have been so hard.

Blane had told her of the great warriors who led the Scottish War of Independence—William Wallace at their head. Aliah was uncertain what he looked like, but assumed he must be a brutish sort of man to lead a whole country to rebellion. She respected and feared him—and those feelings, she would never admit to. Her thoughts would be treasonous to her own country and allow the Scots to laugh at her.

Blane nodded to a few of his men who quietly dropped from their horses and fanned out in opposite directions. By now she knew the routine. His men would check that it was safe to exit the cover of the trees and make their way over the wide meadow. They'd not be covered and an ambush was likely should any of the enemy lie in wait. He'd been right about arriving before nightfall, but not by much. The sky already had a pinkish glow, causing Sterling to look ethereal. A golden glow surrounded the towers and walls. Being quite the homebody, and only traveling to court on a couple occasions, she'd not seen a castle so glorious as this one. The hill was covered in purple thistles and other fall flowers. Fields were barren of people with the sun beginning to set, and only a few sheep and cattle dotted the expanse. From the village surrounding the castle, smoke swirls curled from chimneys. So beautiful. Serene.

Judging from what she heard in the air now—silence broken only by an occasional bird chirping—the place did not seem threatening. There were no shouts or cries of pain. Simply peaceful, as if she gazed upon a fantasy town and its castle.

Soon Blane's men returned, nodded and remounted their horses. As one, they moved from the trees, trotting along the dirt-packed road toward the castle.

"The bridge is beyond, across the River Forth. Just rebuilt after Cressingham and Surrey saw it destroyed."

Aliah nodded, feeling the power of what that bridge meant. Her sister had fought for her life on that bridge. Found love there. While Aliah wasn't afraid of love, she could do without fighting for her life—and she could do without what love brought. Marriage, children, pain, loss. Aliah didn't want to leave a child behind the way her mother had left her—even if it was God's will. A shudder passed through her and she sent a prayer up to the Lord that they made it over the bridge unscathed.

Luck was seemingly on their side. With Stirling teaming with Scots, not a one minded their passing. But there was no telling what eyes watched them from beyond the trees. The hooves of their horses clopped over the newly built wooden bridge in an ominous echo. No one said a word as the water churned and swirled beneath them. The current, quick and vicious, waited for someone to fall so it could carry them away. A swift wind blew, whipping Aliah's hair, with a sting, into her face. For a moment, she thought that victim would be herself. The water would be frigid, soaking quickly into her cloak and gown, dragging her to the bottom. She clutched her cloak tighter, sinking into the fabric, wishing it was thicker. Clenched her knees tauter on the horse and gripped the reins until her fingers hurt.

By the time they made it over the bridge and the trees leading up into the mountains came into view, the sky had darkened to pink with splashes of purple.

"Night comes. We must find shelter," Blane ordered. They picked up their pace, galloping toward the forest beyond.

She prayed he knew of a place to make camp, for after a day of hard travel, her legs were starting to go numb and she worried whether or not she'd be able to stay on the horse. There were benefits to riding with Blane, and that was the ability to rest. Having her own mount left no room for rest. She'd chosen to ride astride to keep pace and now her inner thighs burned with the need to stretch. Even her fingers cramped from having held tight to the reins.

Thank goodness for small miracles. As soon as they reached the trees, Blane slowed their pace and seemed to follow some known trail. 'Twas darker in the forest. Despite autumn having caused many tree's leaves to fall, this forest was filled with firs and pines, which blocked much of the lingering light.

They came to a gurgling stream, over which what little light was left colored the water in pink hues.

"We camp here," Blane said.

The men dismounted and went about the various jobs they each seemed to be assigned to whenever they stopped for a long period of time. Liam erected the makeshift tent for her while several others went about forming a fire. Another of the warriors began frying griddle cakes.

"Would ye like to hunt with me, Aliah?" Blane asked softly by her side. "I've a hunger for a little more than fried griddle cakes and jerky. The food Lorna sent us away with didn't last long with these hungry men." His eyes sparkled with teasing, she assumed because his own appetite was that of several men put together.

Aliah gave a short laugh of agreement, nodding. Tension still filled her and she was wary, but he offered her what seemed like peace and, given they were stuck with one another for a few more days, she chose harmony.

"Mind if we hunt as well?" Liam asked.

Blane shook his head. "We'll take the other side of the stream, ye take this side."

Liam nodded and took two others with him. The rest stayed at the camp to keep watch. With purposeful strides, Blane grasped his bow and quiver from his mount. Aliah wore hers as a permanent part of her wardrobe, feeling safer with it strapped to her back. She'd felt naked when Blane ordered Liam to take it after she'd shot him—and grateful when he'd given it back to her. She issued a command to Frosty to stay at the camp. Best not to have his eagerness to catch his own prey undermine their hunt.

"How will we cross the stream?" she asked.

"Come, I will show ye." He took hold of her hand, engulfing her palm in his larger calloused one. Instinct bade her to yank away, but she kept a tight hold, trusting her heart. Blane's feet crossed silently over the ground whereas hers crunched on every leaf and snapped every twig. She looked down at his feet as they walked, trying to figure out how he walked so silently. Each of his steps was measured, rolling from his heel to the ball of his foot with precision. The muscles of his legs worked in fluid motion. She was amazed to realize that his stealthy walking must have been thoroughly practiced.

Giving it a try, Aliah measured her steps, rolling on her feet, moving her legs with calculated motion. It worked! She had to stop herself from letting out a whoop of glee. Blane turned around and smiled at her, as if he knew what she'd been doing.

There was comfort in his hold on her, his easy smile, while he guided her through the trees. Aliah was both disturbed by it and at the same time felt her heart lighten.

Perhaps what Lorna had meant by taking fate into her own hands had to do with Blane after all. Before she could think further on it, they came to a large fallen tree across the stream. Its roots upended from across the way.

"'Tis not deep, but I'd rather have dry feet."

"Me too," she answered. "How did you know this was here?"

"We camped here afore. I try to remember our route. 'Tis much easier for travel if ye know the land and what it has to offer."

There was so much more to this man than she'd originally thought. Not only was he beautiful and brawny man, he was intelligent, cunning and even if he was loathe to admit it, she saw a sensitive side in him. 'Twas evident in the way he treated her and she'd witnessed him behave toward his sister much the same. He pushed her away because he thought she deserved better, not because he was cruel. As much as it pained her, she knew his intentions were good.

Sensuality was the one part of his being she refused to acknowledge—doing so would only cause her to remember how very close she'd come to giving him her innocence.

"I'll go first. Ye walk behind me, and hold on to me." Blane stepped up on the log, bouncing up and down, getting a feel for it. "Come on," he encouraged.

Her heart leapt. She'd never walked on a log before. Seemed like an easy enough task, and one that many would have tried, but Aliah had never found cause to do so. She tentatively stepped up, feeling the log shift under her added weight, and she lost her balance, grappling with Blane's back for purchase. He chuckled, grabbing hold of her hands behind him and placing them on his hips.

Instantly she felt as though her fingertips were burned. Sinew and bone were carved beneath her touch, and as he walked forward one step, she could feel the motions of his body working beneath her fingers. 'Twas mesmerizing. He walked a few more steps and she found she barely paid attention to the log, so distracted was she by holding onto him.

"How are ye doing?" he asked.

"Wonderful," she sighed.

Blane laughed. "Ye're a natural."

He wouldn't say that on a normal day when she felt clumsier, but holding onto him kept her steady. "Only with your help," she said.

"Ye must have more confidence in yourself, Aliah. Ye're a remarkable woman."

"Thank you." She was touched by his words and found herself smiling. That he would think so highly of her, and even tell her as much, spoke of something deeper between them. Even though they tried to push each other away, they couldn't. Her heart leapt into her throat.

When they reached the other side, Blane turned around, stepped off backward and lifted her by the waist to the ground. They stayed unmoving for the span of several heartbeats, each studying the other, the tips of their boots touching.

"We'd best catch our dinner before the rest of the light fades," she said, interrupting the spell.

"Aye, we will most likely have to find our way back in the dark as it is."

Hand in hand, they crept through the forest, finding a spot to hide just behind some brambles. Once again luck was on their side—a wild pig ventured out into the open, nosing in the dirt. As one, they each took a shot, landing their mark.

"That was timely," Aliah said.

Blane chuckled. "Seems the mountains would like to feed us tonight."

"Aye, and a hearty roast it will be."

Blane lifted the pig over his shoulder and they ventured back toward the log following the light of the moon, crossing it much the same way they had the first time. The men cheered when they returned with meat, especially Liam and his crew who'd come back empty handed.

While the men prepared to roast the pig, Aliah took a few moments to cuddle with Frosty on top of a plaid blanket that had been laid before the fire. There was no denying it felt good to be off the horse and lying about. Aliah also found a certain comfort in being outside. She couldn't help but think how much she'd missed by remaining indoors as a child. There were plenty of times when Arbella and Samuel remained out of doors until the sun had sunk and the moon shone bright. They'd oft had their ears boxed for it, but it didn't seem to stop them. Lying back all the way, Aliah stared up into the dark night sky, dotted with a million diamonds. They'd found the perfect spot to stop, since the stream left the sky open and she could really admire the view.

Never before had she appreciated nature so much. How fortunate Blane was that he traveled so often, that he could breathe in the fresh air, and not have to deal with the strict rigors of a household. Her view was momentarily blocked when Blane stood over her, smiling.

"Admiring the stars?" he asked.

"Aye. 'Tis fascinating." She sat up when he tendered her a wineskin.

"Guess?" he asked.

"Drink of the gods?" she offered with a smile.

"Ye know me too well," he answered. Their fingers brushed as he passed her the wineskin and dropped onto the blanket beside her.

Immediately a part of the evening chill receded as his heat invaded her space. She tried not to laugh as Frosty moved to stretch out his large body between the two of them.

"That or I hoped you weren't going to give me any more whisky," she said with a laugh.

His lips curved up in a lopsided smile as he gazed at her. "Och, lass, I learned my lesson the hard way already."

Aliah dared not mention wine...or how he'd decided to name it Temptation after her. Water was just fine.

He lay down beside her and crossed his arms beneath his head, lifting it. 'Twas almost as if nothing wayward had happened between them. Part of her was content to leave it that way, to sink into this easy comfort they'd developed. The other part of her insisted on speaking to him about it.

The latter won out.

"Blane," she said tentatively. "We need to talk."

He rolled his head toward her, his eyes darkening in the meager fire light. "Do we?"

Blane was offering her a way out of the conversation, to nip her words before they crossed her tongue. How much she wanted to reach out and grasp his offer, but she couldn't. There was too much left unsaid between them. For all the saints, he'd nearly taken her innocence.

"Last night..." she trailed off, unsure of how to begin or even what to say.

He let the silence linger, and she allowed the time of his reprieve to let her mind wander. Lorna had said that she should take fate into her own hands. What did she truly want? Convent? Blane? Piousness? Passion? Routine? Adventure?

Aliah glanced over at him. He still gazed at her, his eyes sparkling, his lips turned into a half smile. There was no judgment there. He patiently waited for her. She could imagine falling asleep to his gaze each night and waking to it each morning. 'Twas a markedly better fate than waking within a cold and lonely bed with only prayer and her fellow sisters in Christ for comfort.

While at one point, the church had seemed best for her, now she knew it wasn't. Perhaps she'd punished herself long enough. Perhaps *this* was God's will.

She wanted Blane. With all her heart. The answer was clear. Aliah wanted a life of passion, adventure. A life she could live with the one man who presented a future shown with promise.

And without a doubt... She knew. Every fiber in her being was aware of it, sparking, tingling, sending shivers of excitement and anticipation along her spine.

She was in love.

Chapter Eighteen

Blane gazed into Aliah's lovely eyes, watching the inflection of emotion as it raced along her face. Lord, he wanted to take her into his arms, to kiss her. His chest tightened with some foreign feeling.

He watched her throat bob, and then her lips parted, silent. She licked her lips nervously, and he waited on baited breath to hear what she had to say. His heartbeat quickened, as though whatever words would roll from her precious lips were the very essence of his survival.

"Blane, I—"

A shrill bird call whistled in the air, cutting off her words. Immediately he was on alert, jumping to his feet and drawing his sword. Aliah glanced around rapidly, fear creasing her features.

"Go!" Liam shouted to Blane, his own sword drawn.

Each of his men took up a battle stance, weapons ready. Without thinking, Blane sheathed his sword, grabbed Aliah's arms, lifted her up and swung her over his shoulder.

Tossing her onto Gunnar, he leapt up behind her and kicked the horse into a gallop, issuing a whistle for Frosty to come and a curse when his injured leg cried out with pain. He didn't look behind him to see who followed. Didn't look behind him to see which enemy had found them — be they Sassenach, outlaw or enemy Scot. That didn't matter. What did matter was getting Aliah to safety.

They crashed through the trees, Blane using his targe to knock low-lying limbs out of the way. They rode fast, at neck-breaking speed. Distance was needed between their enemy and themselves. His men would follow once they'd had a chance to dispatch whoever encroached on their camp. Of that he was certain. His men were the best and he trusted their strength, their abilities, beyond measure.

That shrill whistle had made his heart stop. A cold sweat had started on his spine.

Only that whistle meant the enemy was on top of them. If a minute or two more had passed, Aliah would have been right in the middle of a skirmish.

Whoever it was had been stealthy. 'Haps even followed them from Stirling. One never knew. These were perilous times, with many desperate, treacherous men willing to take risks and many overestimating their own capabilities. That made them even more dangerous.

Blane was grateful that Aliah didn't resist him, understanding the danger they were in. She sat in front of him on the horse, and he could feel her trembling. With one arm wrapped around her waist, he hauled her close, attempting to comfort her. But it appeared his hold did little but keep her atop the horse. She still trembled.

Frosty loped behind them. He was glad for the dog keeping silent, else their enemy would hear his howls and give chase.

To the left the land sharply inclined up a mountain pass. That was the best way for them to go. The enemy wouldn't think he'd take such a dangerous route in the dark, and indeed he might not, save for that reason. Slowing Gunnar, he urged his mount to start his climb. At least a half hour passed, Gunnar slipping twice, before Blane felt they were safely away and they made it to a level part in the rise. The sounds of a waterfall echoed ahead. They broke through the trees beside a pool of water, and he was glad for the light of the moon—it shone on the waterfall, spilling from atop a wall of rock into the pool, and then slowly making its way down the mountain. A sense of recognition hit as he thought he may have stopped here once before.

"I believe there's a cavern beyond the falls, lass," he said into her ear.

She nodded, her head bumping against his chin.

"I'll have to hide Gunnar, he willna fit inside."

Aliah nodded again.

Blane would make sure she was safely put inside the cave first, her dog to guard her while he found a place to tie up Gunnar. He hated to do it. Leaving the horse out in the open like that, without protection. Anyone who came across the destrier would realize a lone warrior was not far behind. Might attempt to find them, or simply steal his horse. 'Twas a chance he'd have to take.

Dismounting, he walked to the edge of the pool until he reached the wall of rock. "We'll have to get a little wet, but I have extra plaids in my bag to keep us warm." And whisky. They would need it. He'd have to feed it to her slowly, with plenty of warning so he didn't end up with the liquid fire spewed all over him.

"All right," Aliah said.

Lifting her into his arms, he stepped into the cold water, trying to keep her as dry as possible. Aliah put her arms around his neck and held tight. He slid his feet along the slick bottom, feeling his way through the water. Frosty splashed behind them, not seeming at all bothered by a little swim. The water steadily grew deeper, covering Blane to his waist, and just barely touching the hem and rear of Aliah's gown. He did his best to lift her higher, but the water only got deeper. By the time they reached the falls, he was chest deep in it and she was only dry from her chest up and knees down.

A break in the falls between the falling water and the stone wall allowed Blane to peer behind. He had a momentary fear that he'd remembered the wrong place, but sure enough there was a shallow cave within the rocks—not going back more than ten feet. The moon shone through the water, bathing the cave in silvery light. He let out a breath when he discovered it unoccupied by bear or wildcat. They would be able to keep safe here. Setting Aliah on the ledge, she scooted inside as he lifted himself and then the dog from the water.

Aliah shivered, pulling her knees up to her chest.

"I will go and get my pack and hide Gunnar. Why dinna ye wring the water out of your clothes while ye wait, so ye dinna catch a chill. When I return, I'll have a warm plaid for ye to wrap yourself in."

She eyed him guardedly, but nodded.

Blane offered her a comforting smile. "Dinna fash, I will return. Frosty here will keep ye safe until I do." He rubbed the dog on his head, who then shook himself dry, droplets flinging everywhere.

"If only I could simply shake myself dry," she pondered with an amused curl to her lips.

"Aye, we'd both be a lot warmer then."

"Blane…" She glanced up at him, catching his gaze with her moonlit, wide, blue eyes.

"Aye?"

"Come back, all right?"

Blane knelt before her, stroked her cheek. "I swear it, lass."

Aliah nodded, leaning into his hand, her eyes dipping closed for a moment. His lips burned to caress hers, but he pulled back, not wishing to complicate this night further. They'd seemed to find a calm peace together that would only shatter once more if he were to press his desire on her.

Standing abruptly, he quit the cave, intent on returning with the dry plaids once his horse was safely hidden.

Although she was shivering from being cold and wet, Aliah's insides warmed as she watched Blane retreat from the cave. She couldn't help but notice the way his linen shirt became transparent as it stuck to his broad back, outlining his shoulders and every other muscle. His plaid too was stuck to his solid form, showcasing the line of his legs, the sculpt of his rear...

Ashamed, she averted her eyes. A woman of virtue wouldn't dare look at a man in such a state. Aliah's eyes glanced back. Well, obviously she was no woman of virtue, for not only was she looking, she was enjoying the sight. She gave up trying for purity and instead greedily watched his every move, even craned her neck to observe him glide into the water and walk the several feet to the shore. She sighed with disappointment when he was lost from her view.

Sitting directly in front of her, Frosty stared at her, snorting with what seemed to be disgust.

"Well, if you were a lady dog, you'd be looking too," she retorted.

Frosty cocked his head to the side, staring into her eyes.

"You would," she said, rolling her eyes.

The dog let out a long huff of breath as if annoyed with the line of conversation and instead laid down, staring out the space between the cave wall and toward the water where Blane had disappeared.

Aliah took the time that Blane was away to peel the layers of wet clothes from her body, wringing them out one by one — making sure she did so on the farthest side so as not to get the back of the cave wet where miraculously the floor seemed to be dry.

Once she'd wrung out her chemise, gown and hose, and laid them on the ground, Aliah stood naked, shivering, rubbing her arms and thighs for warmth. She didn't particularly want to put anything back on, for it would only make her colder. Blane would be bringing her a dry plaid to wrap herself up in…but until then she was standing stark naked. She glanced at the dog. Frosty was big, but not big enough to hide her entire naked form, and besides the animal was so enraptured with Blane he was sure to run toward him when he approached, uncovering her nakedness.

Still… Blane could come back at any time, finding her like this, shivering, nude. Her nipples were tight from the cold, but tingled with her thoughts of Blane.

Aliah stared down at the taut peaks. Why did her body make it so much harder for her to pretend she didn't have feelings for him?

Love… Her heart leapt, feeling as though it soared with just that one thought.

A splash in the water, made her jump. "Oh no," she muttered. Taking quick steps, she picked up the first piece she could grab, throwing her chemise over her head, and hurriedly shoving her arms into place. As Blane hoisted himself onto the ledge, she finished tying the ribbon tight and yanking it down over her knees, though the wet fabric clung to her flesh.

Standing tall in the moonlight, Blane stopped dead in his tracks, his eyes pinned to her, raking over her form. His lips pressed together, jaw tightened, and even in the darkened light she could sense his gaze changing, filling with passion. He let out a slow breath. Immediately she understood her mistake.

If she could see through his shirt… Glancing down, she took in what Blane did—shadowed, rigid nipples pressed to the thin, transparent fabric. Being wet, the chemise clung to her form like a second skin. Outlining *everything*…

Blane cleared his throat and whirled around. "I, uh…" He started to rummage in his pack, then thrust a plaid behind him. "Here."

Face hotter than a blaze, Aliah grappled for the plaid, her fingers trembled making it harder. Finally, she took hold of it, wrapping the fabric around her shoulders and clutching it in front of her. Within seconds she was cloaked in warmth.

"Are ye…covered?" he asked.

"Aye," she squeaked, mortified.

Then Blane turned back around, his face still filled with want, and tremors passed through her—not the ones she'd experienced from being cold. Nay, these tremors were warm…hot even.

"I'm sorry… You said to wring out my clothes."

"Aye."

"You came back quicker than I thought." She found her eyes wondering over his shadowy form, still soaked with fabric clinging to him. Her breaths quickened and she pulled the blanket up to her mouth, trying to hide the way she licked her lips, yearning for what she couldn't have. Then she said something she'd never in her wildest dreams imagined saying to a man, but what was worse was the images that flashed in her mind. "You'd best take off your clothes."

Without taking his eyes off her, Blane tossed his pack somewhere into the back of the cave. She heard it bounce with a soft thud. Eyes wide, frozen in place, she watched as he unlatched the pin from the plaid at his shoulder, letting the fabric drop. Her gaze locked on the fabric of his shirt, clinging indecently to his broad chest. Blane's nipples, tiny dark dots, were taut. She couldn't recall a man's nipples ever having the effect on her that his were. Then again, had she really witnessed many naked chests? Her breath caught, insides quivered. The wet shirt followed the dips and ridges of his muscles and her hands itched to reach out and stroke each one. With deliberate slowness, Blane reached up and untied the strings at his neck, allowing her to see actual smooth, muscled skin. Her mouth went dry.

Aliah's feet remained rooted in place. She felt ethereal in this magical place. The sound of the waterfall, the silvery light of the moon, this man, so unbelievably handsome and with a look of sensuality upon his face geared just for her…

Part of her knew this was wrong. That to feel the way she did, both physically and emotionally, was bound to get her into trouble. But she didn't care. She wanted to watch him undress. Wanted to touch him. Wanted to tell him how much she loved him. To show him how much *they* made sense. Blane would only fight her on it. Some part of him wouldn't allow her in. The damaged part that he'd hinted of. Consciously he would push her away, she knew that. 'Haps though, she could show him the right of it. Show him how much being together would only make their two worlds perfect.

Aliah took a step forward, faltered as he reached for the edges of his shirt and pulled it up over his head. That too he tossed. Her eyes were riveted on his flesh—smooth, muscled flesh. A long scar curved wickedly over his ribs, intimating at some deeper struggle. A male had never entranced her more.

Blane's eyes were still connected with hers, as if he challenged her to continue watching. She was up for the task, her lip curling slightly in invitation. A shudder of pleasure passed over her at the boldness of her actions. She was tempting this man. Blane had already called her temptation itself once... Now she toyed with him, wanting to see just how far he'd go.

His fingers fiddled with his sporran, undoing the leather strap, he tossed it somewhere. The corded belt came next and with it...his plaid pooled at his feet. Aliah's eyes widened, stretching so far open she swore they'd pop from her head.

Blane was naked. Gloriously, frighteningly, naked.

Nude, muscled flesh.

Aliah's breath caught. Her heart stopped.

Blane stood tall, proud. The breadth of his chest rose and fell evenly, as though this were a normal occasion, but the way he clenched and unclenched his jaw showed her the opposite. Hungrily, she looked him over, her eyes riveted on the middle part—the part that she'd felt pressed against her more than once.

'Twas long, thick. Silky looking and hard at the same time. Looked like an arrow, pointing straight toward her. 'Twas a little frightening and she supposed if she were to see a man naked for the first time, bathed in the shadows of night and the silver moon was the best way.

Between her thighs, she felt a quiver. The mark for his arrow seemed to wait for him to hit home. Aliah swallowed, and slowly pulled her gaze from the impossible, for he would never fit inside her. She should end this game now. 'Twould cut down on some of the embarrassment of... Of what? She had no idea what happened between a man and woman, other than what Blane had already showed her and what Glenda had whispered of—the latter she'd not believed.

Instinctively, she knew he would place his shaft against the core of her, the place that was now damp and clenching. Shivers snaked up her spine, despite the warmth of the plaid now surrounding her.

"Will ye share your warmth with me?" Blane gave her a half smile. "I'm afraid, 'tis the only dry plaid I have."

Aliah glanced down absently at the plaid draped over her. His words seemed to sink in and register slowly. The only plaid he had… And he was completely nude…

Her throat felt like it was swollen shut and her belly did one flip after another. She found herself nodding without realizing it. Still he beckoned her forward, one hand outstretched toward her. Aliah stepped forward, the cave floor cold beneath her already frozen feet. His hand captured hers, and she found herself swiftly tucked against him. She clutched tight to the plaid, keeping that singular barrier between them.

"'Tis a little better, but I was hoping to share the inside of the plaid too," he teased.

Aliah nodded, but didn't let go.

Blane chuckled. "Should I put my soaking wet one back on again?"

She nodded, then shook her head.

"Ye confuse me, lass," he said softly. "I return to find ye painted like a goddess against nature's backdrop." He nuzzled against her neck, sending shudders through her limbs. "Ye are so beautiful, so perfect…even if ye are stubborn." He said the last part with a little nip of her ear. "But I willna compromise ye…unless ye want me to. And I willna do it without ye saying so. Even if every muscle in my body strains to feel ye against me."

Every muscle in her body strained too. Every inch of her flesh yearned to be touched by him. Her lips burned for him to nuzzle his way upward to capture them in a kiss. He wanted her, he admitted it. Was it enough?

Aye. For now. This was how she would show him. And if it wasn't meant to be, then at least she'd tried and hadn't condemned herself to a life of 'what if?'

Aliah opened the plaid, pressed her chest to his. "I want ye to."

Chapter Nineteen

"This canna be undone," Blane whispered, his eyes locking on Aliah's.

"I know it." Her lips quivered, partly from excitement and partly from fear.

"*Mo creach*," he said through gritted teeth. His brow furrowed into a frown.

For a moment, Aliah was afraid that he'd changed his mind. That he didn't want her as he'd said and she'd only made a fool of herself. Then his mouth crushed to hers. His arms snaked around her waist, hoisting her nearly off her feet. The warmth of his nakedness flush against her unsettled her senses.

Blane's tongue slipped into her mouth, dueling with hers, tasting, caressing, teasing. As always when he kissed her, her body went wild—frissons of pleasure firing throughout. Aliah was soaring, an ethereal being floating on clouds. Her mind was numb to everything but Blane. She rubbed wantonly against him, gasping at the feel of his shaft nearly touching her bare mound. The thin-as-air chemise was no barrier, it was just in the way.

Aliah moaned into his kiss, threading her fingers through his hair, then down his neck, feeling the pulse in the side. His neck was not the only thing that pulsed. He rocked his hips back and forth, tantalizing her with every slide of his rigid member. His movements only made her own body throb more. She was coming undone. Control was slipping away and there was nothing she could do about it. Nothing she *wanted* to do about it. She was going to let herself go, give permission for this one night of passion and see if it led to a lifetime of bliss or only a precious memory.

Sharing her love with Blane, sharing her body... Seemed like the most glorious thing she could do. The one selfish act she could indulge in. The deciding factor in her life. Beyond all those things, she loved this man, and she wanted to love him in a way that would leave them both with an impression on their hearts. Gently, Blane disentangled his mouth from hers. Even when the cool air hit her overheated lips, she left her eyes closed for a moment longer, trying to catch her breath. When she opened them, Blane smiled down at her, his eyes showing a mixture of desire and...she dared not name it, but the emotion he showed was very close to what was in her heart.

"Ye're so warm," he said, his fingers sliding over her hips. "But I think ye'd be warmer without this on." Blane tugged at the chemise.

Aliah stepped back a foot, dropped the warm plaid to the ground and slowly tugged at the ribbons at her throat. The chemise fell open to reveal the tops of her breasts. Blane's gaze remained fixed on the flesh she revealed. He stepped nearer, closing the distance between them and reached out, trailing a soft caress from her collarbone down to the valley between her breasts. Her breath hitched, came erratically, making her chest rise and fall rapidly. Euphoria set in.

"I've never seen anything so exquisite."

She wanted to disagree, to say that surely a man of his prowess had seen plenty, but she didn't. He had eyes only for her, and she'd not let anything spoil this moment.

"Are ye certain ye want this?" he asked, his gaze traveling back up to hers.

"Aye." She bit down on her lip when she'd nearly confessed her feelings for him.

"Me too," he said. He cupped her breasts through her chemise, thumbing over her nipples, sending fresh tremors through her.

This was really happening. Nothing would stop them this time. No interruptions. Neither of them backing out.

Blane bent down, kissing her collarbone and lightly pushing the chemise from her shoulder, following its trail with his lips. His mouth was so warm on her flesh. She never felt more decadent. He repeated the movement on the other side, and she rolled her head in the opposite direction, sinking against him. Her knees felt weak, her entire body boneless.

A waft of cool air hit as the fabric of her chemise pooled at her feet. She attempted to kick it away, but her toe caught on the fabric. She groaned inside, wanting this moment to be perfect, but her nerves foiled it. Aliah shook her leg, trying as hard as she could to get the gown away, but it didn't work. Blane pulled back, laughing.

"What are ye doing?" he asked.

She looked down, embarrassed to see that she'd kicked her toe right into one of the ribbon loops. The humor of it hit her. "Trying to get rid of my chemise," she said with a laugh of her own.

"Let me." Blane knelt down on one knee before her, but instead of rescuing her toe, he kissed her right on the navel.

Aliah sucked in a breath, her hands clasping his shoulders with a slapping sound. She steadied herself from falling completely. Amazing that he was able to turn her clumsiness into something sensual.

"Mmm…" Blane murmured across her flesh as he kissed circles around her navel, then over to her hip.

Aliah could barely breathe. How was it possible that by him simply kissing her belly, he could elicit such a reaction from her? Her heart skipped a beat, her thighs quivered. She clenched her thighs tightly, but that only made her balance more precarious, and made her core convulse with the need for… She didn't know.

Blane kissed his way down her thigh, all the way to her knee. He took her foot, and placed it up on his bent knee, freeing her toe. But he didn't stop, didn't let her go, he tickled her foot with his fingers as he kissed the inside of her knee.

"Your skin tastes like the purest of honeys."

His teasing about honey pies came to mind, but she thrust it away, focusing on the way his tongue swirled up her inner thigh.

"I must have more of your honey…" he murmured.

What was he talking about? She couldn't fathom. Couldn't follow, not when his hot breath touched against the dampened curls at the apex of her thighs. Aliah raked her nails up the back of his head, gripping his hair tightly.

Then his mouth was on her… Kissing the very heat of her. She cried out, her hips jerking forward.

"Blane, what… What are…you doing?"

"Loving ye." His words were simple, but the impact was strong, made even more so when his tongue swirled between the folds of her sex and she felt as though she were floating in a cloud of pleasure.

He held her steady with one arm wrapped around her buttocks, his hand splayed hotly on the small of her back. Blane's mouth worked magic. He kissed, suckled, licked. He pushed her thighs wider apart, gaining more access to the slick, quivering folds and the nub firing pleasure with every breath she took. Blane was a master at the craft of pleasuring, she was sure of it. Aliah's head fell back, moans cut from her throat sounding feral, animalistic. Never before had she thought... Everything she knew, believed in, 'twas all flipped this way and that the moment she laid eyes on this man. The moment he knocked at her door.

"Och, lass, ye taste so good."

Every word he spoke vibrated off her sensitive flesh, played with her thoughts. Made her feel alive. More alive than she'd ever felt before. Then he took her nub in his mouth, sucking with just the right amount of pressure. She felt herself coming undone. Felt the spiral upward, as pleasure radiated throughout her. Her sex quivered, spasmed, and a cry tore from her throat that she swore echoed off the walls of the cave. Aliah dug her fingers into Blane's shoulders, seeking an anchor so she wouldn't fall over. He held tight to her, his hands at her hips, keeping her upright when she was sure her knees could no longer hold her.

He continued to kiss, lick and nuzzle her until the spasms subsided, until her breaths were no longer ragged indrawn gasps and the pressure that had steadily climbed and peaked began anew. Still she trembled, felt as though her skin were on fire. Opening her eyes, which she'd just realized were clenched tightly closed, she gazed down at Blane. Pleasure and pride shown in his eyes.

"Ye're one tasty treat for a man."

Aliah cocked her head to the side, a smile touching her lips. "Is that what you meant by honey pie?" Her face flamed from asking such a question, but she was pretty sure she was correct.

Blane laughed hard, his head falling back. "Och, lass, ye will have me undone. I canna believe I said something so scandalous to ye." He spread the plaid out on the floor and then swept her off her feet, laying her on top before quickly coming over her. His nose touched hers, one thigh rested on top of hers, his shaft pressed hard and pulsing against her hip. Unaware of how it was possible, tremors of need ran through her once more. She truly was a wanton, for even when he'd dined on her moments before, it appeared it wasn't enough for her insatiable body. He braced himself on his elbows. "'Twas the best pie I've ever had."

He nudged her thighs apart, settling himself between them, his member resting against her core. Aliah pressed upward, wanting to be closer, enjoying the sparks of pleasure that jolted with each rub against his thickness. Wanting to join with him completely, to feel for these precious moments that she was his and his alone.

"I..." How did she say what she wanted to? Honestly, she supposed. "I enjoyed it very much."

Blane smiled with raw male sensuality. "I noticed. Ye found your release, 'twas powerful."

"My release..." she trailed off.

"Aye, that powerful firing of sensation that" —he kissed her neck, his teeth scraping over her flesh as his body molded hotly against her core— "made your body quiver, your breath catch and your heart stop."

Aliah closed her eyes, lifted her knees up around his hips to be closer to him and stroked her hands over his rippling back. "Aye, that is how it felt."

Blane caressed one of her thighs, scraping his calloused palm down until he gripped her derriere. "I've never met a woman with as much passion and fire as ye." His eyes locked on hers, intense, and she could see he told the truth.

Aliah smiled, traced her fingers over his stubbled cheek. "You've changed my opinion on a lot of things," she whispered.

"Like what?" he asked softly.

"Life. Everything." Her hand moved out as if indicating the world. "I was so sheltered before now. I feel as though I've grown in many ways since I met you."

Shadows crossed over his features, and Aliah realized she might have said too much. She didn't want this moment to be ruined, didn't want it to end. Not until they'd both found release as one. Reaching up she pressed her lips to his, sliding her tongue along his lower lip. Blane growled deep in his throat, his hand pressing to the back of her head. He kissed her deeply, saying so much more with that kiss than what he was willing to with speech. Aliah understood it, accepted it, drank it in.

Her plan would work, she was sure of it. Now was not the time for talking, and she knew that too. Now was the time for making love.

Blane caressed her everywhere, stroking, tickling, massaging. His lips pressed hotly to her breasts, his tongue teasing her turgid nipples. She did the same to him, delighting in the feral moan that came from deep in his throat. Aliah grew bold, sliding her hands over his chest, the light crisp hairs tickling her fingertips. Bolder still she was, touching his thighs, running her nails lightly over the muscles. Aliah touched him everywhere as he'd done to her. Hips, chest, back, arms. His body was so different from her own, enticing her to do things, to feel things, she'd not imagined possible. Then she grew boldest of all, stroking down his muscled belly to the thick shaft that jutted from his pelvis. She took hold, wrapping her fingers around his length, marveling at the breadth of him, and the silky feel of his flesh.

"Och, lass…" he trailed off. The veins in his neck pulsed, and his face looked strained. He was losing control.

Aliah stroked upward, brushing over the tip which made him gasp and made her all the more eager to do so again. He crushed his mouth to hers as she stroked him, laying claim to her just as she was doing to him. Then his fingers touched the

214

folds of her sex, slipping between. He slid one inside her, stretching her. It felt so good... Aliah moaned and squeezed his shaft as he pushed another finger inside.

"Do ye like that?" he asked between kisses and nips of her lips.

"Aye," she moaned.

"God, lass... Ye'll have me undone afore my next breath." With those words he swiped her hand from his shaft and settled more fully between her thighs, the tip of his member pressing against her opening.

"I want ye now, Aliah. Tell me ye want me too. If ye want to stop, we can. I promise." His voice was husky, filled with tension and desire.

"Nay, I want you," she whispered, lifting her hips.

"Thank ye..." Blane took her mouth once more in a carnal kiss, making her delirious, making her forget...everything but him.

When she thought she'd drown with passion, he thrust his hips forward, sinking his shaft deep inside her. A pinch of pain vibrated from her core, and she whimpered. Glenda was right about something else after all. Blane stilled his movements. Placing a hand on either side of her face, he brushed stray hairs and a few tears away. He stretched her, filled her. Although she'd feared he wouldn't fit, somehow he'd managed to push inside her.

"Aliah, look at me."

Swallowing, she blinked open, staring into his darkened eyes. His face was calm, showing a shadow of concern.

"Are ye all right?" he asked. "Did it hurt much?"

She nodded, shook her head. Licked her lips. Shifted. Something happened. The pain dissipated and was replaced with a needy, aching throb. "It hurt a little, but I'm starting to feel a better." She moved beneath him and pleasure washed over her. She did it again, disbelieving, and was once more rewarded with the same sort of delicious frissons that shot through her when he'd kissed her *there*. "Oh..." she murmured.

"Feels good?"

"Aye."

Blane shifted too, pulling his hips away, his shaft dislodging from inside her, making her feel empty. That didn't last long though as he slowly, gently pushed back inside and sparks of wondrous sensation lit through her.

"What about now?"

She nodded, biting her lip. "Oh, aye." She was surprised with the sound of her own voice. It didn't sound like her. Sounded like a completely different woman. A sensual woman. A woman who knew what she wanted.

Blane touched his forehead to hers, inhaling deeply. "Och, woman..."

Aliah lifted her knees higher around his hips, feeling compelled to hook her ankles at his hips. He sank deeper inside her and the sensation was even more powerful.

"Ye'll be the death of me," Blane said huskily as he continued his measured movements.

Aliah grew restless, wishing he would... What? She wanted to shout out with pleasure, with frustration. She bucked her hips upward, dug her nails into his shoulders, kissed his neck, his lips, sucked on his tongue.

"Blane, please," she begged, not even sure what exactly it was she was pleading for.

"What, tell me?"

"I don't know, I simply want..." She moaned as he quickened the pace, thrust harder. "Oh!"

"This is what ye desire?"

She nodded, arching her back.

"I want to please ye," he whispered against her ear as he licked the shell and scraped his teeth over the lobe.

"You please me," she answered, her hands brushing hard down his back, sinking into the muscles, pressing him even closer than he already was. "Do I...please you?" she panted, her insides quivering, muscles constricting.

"In so many ways," he answered.

Blane stroked her hair, her cheeks, kissing her tenderly over her face, then moving toward her neck and kissing her at the hollow and side until she shivered and her nipples tingled.

The time for talking came to an end as they both sought to pleasure the other and to hold back as much as they could from release. Restraint made the pleasure all the more intense. Aliah's limbs shook uncontrollably and Blane's muscles trembled under her fingertips. Both of them panted and moaned beneath the moonlit falls. The noises they made were coupled with the splash of the waterfall. Anytime she came across a waterfall in the future, she'd never be able to look at it the same way again. Thoughts of Blane, of this most perfect, sensuous moment would forever cross her mind.

"I dinna think I can hold back much longer," Blane ground out.

"Then don't."

He obeyed her, quickening his pace, gripping her buttocks and lifting her higher. His lips captured hers as he drove repeatedly deep inside her. Aliah rose with each of his thrusts, meeting his hips. She clung to him, traveling with Blane to the heights of passion they created.

"Please...tell me your release is within reach," he said.

Aliah sought to find her voice, nearly choking when she did. If he meant that powerful fire... "Aye!"

If possible, he thrust harder, deeper, taking complete control of her body. Tremors began in her core, radiating outward. Her mind became blank of anything beyond ecstasy, Blane, love. When the eruption occurred, Aliah cried out his name, her entire being quaking with exquisite pleasure.

"Aliah!" Blane called, shuddering above her. His entire body trembled and a guttural groan echoed from his lips making her shiver. He thrust deep once, twice, then a third time before becoming still. Blane collapsed nearly on top of her, save for his elbows bearing the brunt of his weight.

They were silent for several minutes, their heavy breaths mingling with the sounds of the waterfall. Their limbs entwined, fingers laced through one another's, surrounded by the heat they'd created and the beauty of nature.

At some point, Blane climbed up and ripped a cloth from his pack, wetting it in the falls, sprinkles dripping down his thick arm. He brought the chilly watered rag between her thighs. She jumped from the frigid cloth touching the very heat of her, but soon welcomed the coolness as he washed her.

They gazed into each other's eyes as he did it. The significance of what had just happened was not lost on Aliah. She'd made love to a man. But not just any man — Blane. Love gripped her heart, making it clench. She wished more than anything to share with him how she felt, but knew that it was not the right time.

Blane collapsed beside her, pulled her flush against him and wrapped them up in the plaid. Warmth encompassed her.

"Ye are," he paused, "everything a man could ever dream of."

The enormity of his words filled Aliah's heart with happiness. In his own way, he shared her feelings.

Smiling to herself, after several minutes Aliah whispered, "I would not have given myself to another."

Blane snored softly. He'd not heard her admission. She didn't let disappointment shadow the beauty of what they'd done together. Instead, she curled up in his warmth and vowed to make him see the right of things.

Chapter Twenty

Blane woke refreshed. Stretched his arms over his head. He hadn't slept so well in months. A movement of warm, naked flesh against his jolted him.

Aliah.

The enormity of what happened the night before came ricocheting to the front of his mind.

He'd taken her virginity.

Bastard. He was a complete and utter fool. In what world had he thought such an act would be acceptable? Did he think he could bed her and just toss her aside? While the prospect of having her at his side for a lifetime filled him with joy, it also caused him a wagon load of anxiety.

Guilt over his past ate at him. He couldn't bring her into his damaged world. Couldn't expect her to nod and smile as he left time and again on the many journeys he took throughout the year — bent on revenge and nothing more.

Aliah deserved better than that.

And now he'd taken the most precious thing she had. The bargaining chip she had for a good marriage. The virtue she needed to join the church. He'd forever ruined her. Not to mention a child could be begotten from this joining. Blane wished he could blame drink for his lack of thought, but that was not the case. He'd had only a few sips while they lay on the blanket at camp waiting for the wild pig to roast. Nay, he'd been clear-headed as he made love to her. And enjoyed every damn minute of it.

Tossing his arm over his head, he tried not to groan aloud as he thought of every possible repercussion from his selfish act. Aliah was sure to hate him the moment she woke. She was sure to curse him to Purgatory. Her father — once he was located, since he'd not yet been found when Blane left Dunrobin — would seek retribution. That was another thing. When Aliah realized he'd lied about her father, she'd never trust him again. Magnus and Arbella would surely take him to task.

Damn.

Aliah shifted again beside him, her silky arse rubbing against his hip. She moaned a little in her sleep, reminding him of the way she'd responded to him the night before. The woman was a hellcat. A fiery, passionate lover. Admittedly, a large part of him was proud to have been her first lover. An even larger part never wanted her to love another again.

Mayhap it was possible for them to be together. A war started inside him between his desire for a life with Aliah in it, and the revenge he sought against his parents' murderers. Blane had always thought to condemn himself to a life of work. Never thought to allow himself the indulgence of a family, people to love and who loved him in return.

From the moment he'd met Aliah, that desire, that need for his own family had begun to niggle its way inside his thoughts, his heart. What had she done to him? Turned him from a hard, vengeance-seeking warrior, to a lovesick pup. He had to harden his heart. He couldn't allow that to be the way of it. He had to be strong. Finding his parents' killers was his number two priority—number one having always been to take care of the clan the best way he could.

Where would Aliah fit into his plans?

She wasn't likely to want to travel with him to market—and he wasn't likely to let her. Too dangerous. He didn't want her in the middle of any skirmishes, didn't want her exposed to so much danger in the wild. Besides that, with each trip to market he made, he tracked clues to his parents' killers. That was not something he ever wanted to expose her to. Not while the bastards still lived.

There was no room for her in his life. Not yet anyway. If he ever came to find and slayed the murderers, it was possible... But who knew when that was going to be, and Blane couldn't ask her to wait for him until then. He wouldn't be able to explain to her why he asked her to wait, and she wouldn't understand his request. Women wanted answers and Aliah in particular didn't like not being informed. Such a bid wouldn't sit well with her, would only make her angry, and then she'd most likely resent him.

Truth be told, as much as he wanted to try and make it work, he had some serious doubts.

"Good morning," Aliah murmured, rolling over and tossing a long, lithe leg over his thigh.

She had the body of a goddess and he couldn't help sliding his hand up the proffered leg. He glanced down to see her bright blue eyes gazing into his, filled with tenderness. There had to be a way... Or else he had to put her aside now. And he couldn't do that. Not yet.

"Good morning, lass." Blane kissed her forehead, breathing in her lemon-scented hair, enjoying the softness of her skin.

"How did you learn to speak with an English accent?" she asked, her voice still sleepy. "You speak it so well, I'd not be able to tell that your true voice is so filled with a brogue."

Blane chuckled. "'Twas actually a game when I was a child. The English have long been a thorn in a Scotsman's life. My father brought many Sassenach prisoners home. Mimicking them, I used to walk around the bailey and keep pretending to be a Sassenach coward. The other children gained a lot of laughs from it and even my parents—" He paused a moment, his smile faltering, not having spoken of his parents in some time. "Even they thought it was good entertainment. So, I suppose, practicing so much at a young age helped me to hone it well."

Aliah smiled. "Sounds like you were quite a jester as a child."

"Aye." Until that fated day... He still play-acted for the others, but it was never the same. From that moment he practiced so he might one day find the vile lechers who'd taken his parents from him. "What of ye? Were ye a jester? Somehow I dinna think so."

With a brow raised, she imitated his brogue, "Oh? What makes ye think I wasna funny?"

Blane chuckled, "Ye're terrible!"

Aliah smacked his shoulder, bit him gently. Blane rolled over, pinning her beneath him.

"Ye were the serious type, I gather. Your head in a book. Praying for every childhood mishap that befell ye and mayhap even taking penance for the sins of others."

Aliah gasped in mock exasperation, then sighed deeply. "You're right. Last night was the first time I've ever done anything for myself."

Mentioning what had happened the night before made Blane's blood run hot, surging toward his cock faster than an arrow to its target. Aliah's eyes widened, feeling his arousal pressed so hotly against her.

"'Twas the same for me," Blane whispered, seriously. "We both took what we wanted."

"And we gave…" She bit her lip.

"Aye." He wanted to give again — which he did with gusto.

Their bodies satiated and slick from lovemaking, Blane rolled to the side.

Several moments of silence passed before Aliah spoke again. "Where will we rendezvous with your men?"

Reality came crashing back. "We shall meet them at the hollow tree."

"Where is that?"

"'Tis a short ride from here."

"Will they be waiting?"

"Aye, most likely they've sent out scouts already." His men would have found the spot he'd shouted to Liam before riding away, after the skirmish with whoever surrounded them. But his men would have also known that Blane would find a safe spot for Aliah before risking darkened woods and their capture to find the hollow tree.

"What is the hollow tree?" Aliah's fingers drew light circles over his chest, driving him wild.

He clapped a hand over hers, flattening it to his chest. "'Tis a tree we've marked as one of the many rendezvous points along our route in case we are separated."

"Have you had to meet them there before?"

"Only once."

"What happened?"

"English." Blane lifted her hand to his lips and gently kissed her fingertips. "We'd best dress and head out."

"Aye. Our clothes are most likely dry by now."

"Hopefully. We willna dress until we reach the other side. Dinna want our clothes to get wet again."

Aliah nodded, her cheeks turning pink.

"Come, let us depart, else they may happen upon us when ye stand so gorgeously nude along the water's edge." His words had Aliah bouncing to her feet, and Blane itching to reach out and touch the lushness of her skin, the curves of her hips and rear. Her rosy nipples were hard as her breasts swayed while she walked to gather their garments. Seeing them standing, Frosty jumped from his spot near the waterfall as if he'd only just noticed their presence.

"Here, I'll put the items in my pack."

Aliah handed him all of their clothes, and he rolled up the plaid they'd slept in, then strapped the pack to his back and secured his weapons. For a moment, he thought about pulling her into his arms, carrying her into the water, then thought better of it. If her silky skin touched his... They'd not be leaving this cave for at least another hour. With that thought, he plunged into the icy water, careful to keep his pack dry.

Frosty followed him, splashing hard and a more timid Aliah slipped into the water with a squeal, her womanly curves quickly concealed by the frothy swirls. A swift rush of desire filled him and along with it a tender, cramping in his heart. He thrust his feelings aside. While he'd originally told himself that she could be his for last night only, he wanted her all the more now. For more than lovemaking. But in all reality, once they reached Dunrobin, she could no longer be a part of his world. How could she? Her father would surely never allow it... And yet...

When they reached the bank, Blane tossed Aliah her clothing as she shivered and rubbed her hands furiously over her limbs. He had to use sheer force of will not to look at her. But dammit, he couldn't help a peek or two as she slid her chemise over her head and all her creamy skin disappeared. Now that the garment was dry, it wasn't as easy to make out her form beneath it. That didn't stop him from imagining though. He'd seen plenty, memorized every detail. Every dip and curve.

"Will you dress or just stand there staring at me out of the corner of your eye?" she asked with smirk on her face.

Blane gritted his teeth at having been caught. So much for subtle.

Aliah stepped forward, her eyes sparkling with mirth. "Not that I mind your state in the least." Her gaze hungrily devoured his form, and Blane felt his face heat. He was blushing — again. With a growl, he yanked his shirt over his head. Once he was dressed he stalked the rest of the way toward her, hauled her up against him and crushed his mouth to hers. Immediately his body was on fire and he was glad to have had the forethought to dress before taking her into his arms, else he'd have her up against a tree... And in reality that was still a possibility.

Frosty let out howl, baring his teeth at something in the woods.

Yanking Aliah behind him, Blane withdrew his claymore, standing at the ready. Keeping a keen ear for any sounds out of the ordinary, he watched the forest closely. It appeared normal, peaceful. The branches swayed in the breeze and the morning sun crept down lazily. A few birds called and from his right a squirrel scurried up a tree.

Yet, the hound's hair was on end and he continued to snarl, staring at the same spot as Blane. He saw nothing.

Then he heard it. Just the faintest sound — a soft, swishing in the air. Someone crept toward them. Blane contemplated running toward where he'd hidden Gunnar, but he had no idea how many surrounded them or where they all stood. He could run straight into a trap.

"Stay close, lass, be ready," he said quietly.

"For what?" she whispered, fear in her voice.

"For a fight."

"I am ready," she said, and he heard her nock her arrow.

"Show yourself!" he shouted into the trees.

Less than a minute passed, feeling like forever, when Liam stepped from behind the trees, arms raised. "'Tis only us."

From behind several other trees men from their entourage stepped forward. Frosty growled at the men, but with a flick of Blane's hand sat on his haunches.

"Dinna sneak up on me like that again," Blane ordered. "Although, I should be grateful the lot of ye did it so well."

"Apologies, sir, we thought it might be ye, as we saw Gunnar tied to the tree, but one can never be too sure."

"How long have ye been here?"

"Just now."

Good. He hoped Liam told the truth, else the man had seen Aliah's lovely, nude form. "I take it ye were concerned when I didna meet ye at the hollow tree?"

"Aye," Liam nodded, looking them both over. "Ye are unharmed."

"Aye. We hid in the falls." Blane sheathed his sword. "What of our group?"

"Seamus took a nasty wound, but we've sewn him up, poured enough whisky down his throat so he's snoring like a bairn. Angus was not so lucky." Liam frowned.

"Angus is dead?" Regret filled Blane. He hated to lose a man.

"Aye."

"Dammit," Blane said through gritted teeth. "Who was it?"

"I didna recognize the men who attacked."

"How many were there?"

"About a dozen or more."

The familiar feeling churned in his gut. "English?"

Liam shook his head. "Well, a few English, but mostly Scots."

"Clan?" Every muscle tensed in Blane's body.

Again Liam shook his head. "I dinna know. They wore old, ragged looking plaids—outlaws it would seem. They were a fierce lot. Not loyal to Scotland, we gathered that much."

Mo creach! Blane swallowed the bile rising in his throat. They sounded like the men he'd been searching well over a decade for.

"And the Sassenachs, did ye get a name?"

"Surrey."

Aliah gasped.

"Damn," Blane muttered. The same men who'd been at the Kerrs. He prayed his dear friends were safe and it was only a coincidence. "They were at the Fir Tree."

Liam looked surprised to hear it. "But the men at the Kerrs were going to bed down for a night or two."

Blane huffed a breath. "Something must have sparked them to follow us."

"You don't think—"

"No, the Kerrs would never intentionally betray me."

That made him wonder how they had come to follow them. Mayhap the scoundrels had left something in the barn and witnessed Blane and his men take off when they went to retrieve it. Or mayhap Master Kerr hadn't been able to come up with a reasonable excuse as to why Gunnar was gone. Maybe he'd even told the English lord the horse had been stolen, which only made Surrey want it more. The possibilities were endless— and the last one that came to mind was even more disturbing, but he thrust it aside. None of his men would betray him. They'd been together too long. He would have ferreted out a traitor long ago.

"What of the enemy? How did ye leave them?"

"We killed at least three of the Scotsmen, but the rest ran."

"Damn," Blane said again, disappointed. "Let us hasten to Dunrobin, so I might reunite Lady Aliah with her family. As soon as we've rested the horses we'll set out and meet Surrey and his band of traitors once more. We'll not let that mob of maggots hurt another."

Liam nodded as did his other men, vengeance lighting in their eyes. The men retrieved their horses and Blane took Aliah by the hand and moved toward where he'd tied Gunnar. After settling the saddle, bit and pack in place, Blane helped Aliah to the top, then took his place behind her.

When they reached the hollow tree, Seamus was cursing fiercely, and the men were trying to get him to calm down enough to swallow a large portion of whisky. Aliah looked on, horrified at the blood-stained bandage thickly wrapped around his middle. Catching Liam's eye, he nodded. He'd let his men attend to Seamus and keep Aliah away until they'd had a chance to calm him. Blane took her to the stream a short distance away, and hidden by trees.

"Will he live?" she asked, dipping her hand into the water and bringing a sip to her mouth.

"I dinna know."

She nodded. "He is bleeding much."

"'Tis more a fever I worry over."

"Will we stay here until he's able to travel?"

Blane shook his head. "Nay. He must travel with us."

"How?"

"He will be tied to one of the other men. With an enemy upon us, staying in one place too long is impossible and dangerous."

Again she nodded, looking into the distance, deep in thought. Her brow was wrinkled and her mouth thinned in concern.

Blane knelt beside her, lifted her chin. "Tell me."

She shrugged. "I was just thinking about my brother Samuel. He is fighting for King Edward in France. I hope that he has men surrounding him as honorable as you."

Honestly, if they were English, Blane doubted it, but Aliah and her sister Arbella had proven that not all the English were as he thought. "If he's as good as ye, then I'm sure he's endeared himself to his men."

Her eyes lit a little at that. "He is a good man. The best of men."

"Surely, not *the* best," he teased.

Aliah laughed. "Are you wanting to be the best?"

"Only for ye."

Her gaze turned serious, eyes flaring with emotion, desire. "For me, you have been."

Blane's chest tightened uncomfortably and his stomach did a little flip. Aliah was so beautiful, courageous, intelligent, fun… He didn't deserve her.

Montgomery's words came back to haunt him. *When a man falls for a woman, he always thinks she deserves better. He canna imagine that she would desire him, for he holds her so high above him. I'm not sure it's a feeling that ever leaves a man.*

Was that what was happening? He'd refused to believe it before. Didn't want to acknowledge the possibilities, but now… Blane shook his head, took Aliah by the hands and stood. He would banish such thoughts from his mind the only way he knew how. Placing his hands on either side of her face, he bent low and kissed her. At first, he meant it to be a sweet kiss. To calm her, comfort her. However, as soon as her warm lips touched his and he felt the velvet of her tongue, he lost the ability to kiss her sweetly. Judging by the whimpers coming from the back of her throat, and the way she molded her body to his, rubbing wantonly, Aliah didn't want to be kissed sweetly.

Blane threaded his fingers into her hair, unwinding the tight plait she'd formed at the cave. He loved the feel of her silky hair, loved how it tickled his palms. He moaned against her soft lips as she wrapped her arms around his waist, massaging the sides of his spine.

He was surprised by how right she felt against him. How perfectly she fit against his frame. Kissing her was like a dream he never wanted to wake from. Heaven on earth.

"I feel so hot," Aliah whispered against his lips.

Holy Mary…

"'Tis the heat we create whenever we kiss," he murmured. "Whenever I look at ye." He nuzzled down her neck, taking in the soft moans she made and becoming all the more entranced by her.

Oh, how he wanted to make love to her again… To sweep her up in his arms and —

Aliah's leg came up, hooking around his hip and she pushed her pelvis into his. Blane groaned, his cock straining to reach for what she offered.

"Aliah… If we dinna stop, I willna be able to."

"Then don't."

Who was this bold temptress that lured a man into the warmth and sensuality of her embrace? She was the perfect match for him… A woman who could take him away from his worries, make him believe he was better than the fate he'd given himself.

"Are you worried about your men hearing? Do you think they will come to find us?" she asked, starting to pull away.

He couldn't have that, not when he'd just admitted to himself how he truly felt about her. Blane loved her. If she was offering him another chance to feel that love, to express it in the best way he knew how, he would, for in a few days he may end up breaking her heart and he hoped she'd at least remember these tender moments.

"Nay, they willna. They're busy with Seamus."

Blane stroked down her back, gripped her bottom in both hands and lifted her off the ground. The sun hit them at the perfect angle, warming the air unusually for late fall. Aliah wrapped her legs around his hips, her arms around his shoulders. Glancing around, Blane found a tree with a nice patch of grass beneath it. Whipping off his plaid and shirt, he laid them on top of the grass and sat down, leaning against the tree. Aliah stared at him, her eyes riveted to his swollen cock. Blane curled his lip in a wicked smile. He beckoned her forward.

Blane could almost see her breath catch. Aliah stepped forward, then stepped back.

"Come here," he said, his voice coming out husky.

Aliah shook her head, then pulled off her gown, her chemise next, until she stood naked before him, shivering slightly.

"Ye didna have to take it off, 'tis cold," he said softly.

"I wanted to," she answered. "'Tis not so cold."

In the full light of the mid-morning sun, she was even more glorious than by the light of the moon. Her shoulders sloped onto slender, shapely arms. Breasts, rosy tipped and the perfect size to fit in his hands. Her belly was flat, smooth. Hips round, full and legs that went on forever. Between her thighs, a light thatch of golden curls. Now it was Blane's turn for his breath to catch.

She sauntered toward him like some fairy nymph, bent on seducing him and making away with his belongings. Well, she could have whatever she wanted as long as she stayed naked just like that.

Blane beckoned her further. This time Aliah didn't hesitate until she reached him, placing her toes on the bottom of his foot and stroking lightly.

"Shall I lie beside you?"

Blane shook his head, held out his hands. "I want ye to ride me, *mo chridhe*."

Aliah's eyes widened, but still she came forward, planting a foot on either side of his thighs. His cock twitched as he stared up at her, so boldly placed before him. He wondered if she had any idea how much she affected him. Blane ran his hands up and down her silky calves, tickling the backs of her knees.

"Now kneel down."

She did as he instructed, the heat of her channel settling on top of him. Blane let out a short groan.

"Like this?" she asked, scooting even closer to him. She placed her hands on his shoulders, positioning her opening on the tip of his shaft.

Swallowing hard, he tried not to thrust upward and take her completely. "Aye, like that."

"I didn't realize it was possible like this," Aliah said breathlessly.

He nodded, unable to speak. For certain, never in his life had he felt so heavenly than he did with Aliah.

"I'm not hurting your leg?"

"Nay, lass. When I'm with ye, the pain is naught." He spoke the truth, his wound forgotten until she'd mentioned it. Blane reached up to trace over her cheek and jaw, bringing her face closer so he could kiss her.

She trembled a little and he realized she could be cold, even if she'd professed her warmth. He grabbed the length of his plaid and wrapped it around her shoulders.

"I dinna want ye to catch a chill," he whispered as his mouth traveled from hers down her neck and over her shoulders. "'Tis unseasonably warm, but then again, I'm used to the cold."

Shivers wracked her body. "I am not cold at all," she murmured between sighs. "You make me feel very warm."

Blane cupped her breasts in his hands, marveling at the silkiness, the warmth of her skin. Her breasts fit perfectly in his palms and her nipples pebbled, beckoning him to taste them.

He wasted no time, teasing her slowly by breathing hotly on the rosy tips, flicking his tongue out to tease her sensitive flesh and then drawing her nipples into his mouth.

Aliah whimpered, rocking her hips against him, her fingers scraping up and down his chest, massaging his arms and shoulders. Blane wanted them to linger like this for hours, touching, exploring, sighing, but he was aware that if they were gone too long, Liam would come looking for them. To be caught like this was not in either of their best interests.

With that thought in mind, Blane took his cock in hand and guided it through the slickness of her folds, finding the entrance to her channel. "Ye're ready for me."

"Aye." Her voice was sensuality embodied. "I want you inside me."

There was something in her tone, in the glaze of her eyes, that had his heart speeding up and a shudder racing down his spine. Or maybe it was simply that *she'd* said it. The only woman he'd ever truly cared for…

His thoughts were taking a turn toward forbidden ground again. Blane had to banish them quickly. Gripping her hip with his free hand, he thrust upward, burying himself deep inside her. Before Aliah could cry out, he claimed her mouth with his, absorbing her moan of pleasure.

"Shh…" he whispered. "We dinna want any warriors coming to your aid."

"Oh no." She shook her head. "You're all the warrior I need — and I don't need saving from you."

Again her words played with his mind making him feel things that he shouldn't, making him wish for things that weren't meant to be. He was glad when her forehead fell to his shoulder and she kissed the side of his neck. His thoughts were soon consumed with pleasure. Aliah was a natural at lovemaking, her hips swaying in rhythm with his thrusts. They moved slowly at first, just enjoying the sensations of being joined, but soon, Aliah was whimpering, seeking his mouth for deep, carnal kisses to cover the sounds of her moans. Truth be told, he needed to kiss her as much as she wanted to be kissed. Blane's throat burned with the need to shout out his pleasure. Bracing his hands on her hips, he increased his thrusts, his hips pumping at a rapid pace.

He was almost there... Ready to reach that pinnacle of pleasure. But not until he was sure she too found an earth-shattering release. Reaching one hand between their bodies, Blane sought out the tiny nub of pleasure between the folds of her sex. He found it, throbbing and slick. With a few strokes of his fingers, her legs started to tremble against his thighs. Her breath hitched, and she sucked hard at his tongue. She was close, he could feel it. Her channel tightened, squeezing him hard. Then with a muffled cry, her entire body shuddered, her insides clamping tight and releasing in minute vibrations against his cock.

That was too much for Blane. He couldn't hold back if he wanted to. Her release brought on his own uncontrollable one. Intense pleasure shot up and down his spine, surrounding him, embracing him, and bursting outward. His seed rushed in a hot torrent into her body, leaving him spent completely. Ready for a lazy nap.

They stayed connected for a few moments until their breaths returned to somewhat normal.

"'Twas still amazing," Aliah mused.

"Still?"

"Aye, I had thought that it could be no better than it was in the cave."

Blane smiled crookedly. "Gets better every time."

Aliah's eyes widened, her hands resting gently on his shoulders. "Truly?"

"Aye."

She shifted, making his cock, which was still inside her, begin to grow hard. Damn. He'd never bedded a woman and been so ready to make love to her again. If they weren't where they were, in the situation they found themselves, he'd roll her over and ravage her once more.

As it was, he could almost count on Liam arriving any minute to make sure they had not been set upon by outlaws.

Blane gently lifted Aliah from him, and taking her hand led her to the stream where they both regrettably washed away their lovemaking in the frigid water. An awkward silence fell over them as they dressed, both staring at the other, and for Blane, he wasn't quite sure what to say.

He was overcome with guilt. With the need to apologize. Every time he glanced her way, Aliah looked as though she wanted to tell him something, but then she'd turn away. He didn't know where to go from here. If he should confess his love or keep it to himself. If her father was going to marry her off to another man, or she chose to go into the church, then it seemed better to keep his feelings to himself. Yet, if he could somehow change her mind… Blane shook his head. He wasn't ready to put his heart out there. Not when her future wasn't her own.

Regret chewed at his belly. Not for having made love to her. If he had his life to repeat, he would do so again. He regretted that which had yet to happen—and which he prayed did not. He never wanted to hurt her.

Taking a deep breath, Blane stepped toward her, gripped her hand in his and gazed into her eyes. "Aliah, I must apologize now."

"Why?" Her eyes searched his, confused.

"For taking what wasn't mine. For compromising ye."

Aliah stared into his eyes for the span of several heartbeats and then quietly said, "'Twas mine to give. You should not apologize for showing me what pleasure is. For offering me a few moments of bliss."

"But—"

She shook her head, held up her hand for him to stop speaking. "Do not sully what we've shared, Blane. 'Twas beautiful and something we both wanted and enjoyed. I don't regret it and you shouldn't either."

He nodded, unable to speak because his throat had grown strangely tight.

Chapter Twenty-One

They returned to camp in silence. The men were nearly packed up, Seamus already tied to another knight upon his mount.

"If we hurry, we might make it to the Sutherland border within the next few days," Blane told Liam.

Once they were on Sutherland ground, he would feel a lot safer. At any time during the day, the borders were patrolled by a group of Sutherland warriors. Most likely they would be near as well—Magnus would be expecting him soon. The Sutherlands were a strong and powerful clan and not many were willing to pick a fight with them. That didn't mean that those that followed wouldn't try. In fact, Blane was fairly certain they would. The cowards, if they were who he thought they were, wouldn't hesitate to cross over as they'd done over a decade ago.

But this time he'd be ready for them and he wouldn't let them escape with anything but quick passage to Hell.

Aliah's horse was readied, and Blane watched with a bit of disappointment as she mounted on her own. He wished she'd ride with him, but that might be a bigger distraction than he needed. Climbing onto Gunnar, he gave the signal for them to move out.

They rode hard, taking only one break to rest the horses and eat a quick meal before they were off again, climbing over ridges as they made their way north. They traveled hard for several days. The temperature steadily dropped, and by the time the sun started to set on the fourth day, Blane could just make out the puffs of his breath as his hot air mixed with the chilling temperatures.

Aliah shivered on her horse, despite her cloak and an extra plaid that had been provided for her.

"'Tis colder here," she murmured as they left the road, following a path through the trees until they came to a small crofter's hut just over the border where Blane and his men usually made camp.

"Aye, and 'twill only get colder. Once we've a fire lit, ye can warm your fingers and toes by it," he said with a smile.

"Sounds heavenly."

The men went about caring for the horses while Blane gathered firewood to place in the small hearth at the rear of the hut. A hole in the ceiling sufficed as the chimney, but didn't do its job so well, and much of the smoke ended up floating near the ceiling. That didn't seem to matter to Aliah. She found a stool and scooted close to the fire, extending her hands and rubbing them together. Frosty curled up right beside her.

Seamus was placed on a bedroll in the corner, cool compresses to his forehead and whisky poured onto his wound and then dripped into his mouth. He'd become delirious en route, and burned hotter than fire with fever. There was nothing they could do save continue on. Blane prayed he'd make it to Dunrobin soon so a healer could be fetched.

"Better?" Blane asked, pulling up another stool beside Aliah.

"Aye, my fingers are starting to thaw."

"Some of the men were wondering if ye'd be willing to make your stew again?"

Aliah's eyes lit. "Truly?"

"Aye, they are tired of jerky and oatcakes, want something warm. We're not likely to find another wild pig to replace the one we lost. A hot broth might also do some good for Seamus as he's not eaten hardly a bite in days."

Aliah nodded. "I'd be happy to."

"Good. I'll gather a few things. Liam's already set out to catch a rabbit or two. There's a pot over there." He pointed toward a high table that had a few dishes piled on it.

"Do you come here often?" she asked, gazing around at the cozy hut.

"Every few months. We've been lucky no one has taken our supplies."

Aliah nodded. "Is there a well or burn nearby I can get water from for the pot?"

"A burn, just a short walk behind the hut. There's a small garden in the back that despite no one tending to it, seems to still grow a few things. I'll get the water if ye want to see what vegetables ye can rummage up? There's barley and spices on a shelf somewhere."

Aliah agreed, following Blane from the hut. While he went to get some water, she dug around in the dirt finding a few parsnips, carrots and onions. The stew turned out even better than the first time she'd made it, and although they were all on alert for the enemy who never ceased to pursue them, there did seem to be an air of relief now that they'd reached Sutherland ground.

They joked around the small fire, the men crowding into the small hut. Even Seamus in his delirium sipped some of the broth. At last, Blane called an end to the revelry. They had to rest and wake up early enough to clear out just after dawn. The quicker he was able to leave Aliah safely at Dunrobin, the faster he could turn around and reach his enemy on solid ground.

Most of the men bedded down outside, save for Seamus. The rest took first watch. Blane made sure Aliah was safely tucked inside with Frosty while he joined those on watch. Last time they'd been attacked at night, and he didn't put it past the cowards to do so again. Blane was mildly surprised when hours later his watch was up and not a single thing had occurred. He was grateful too.

Creeping into the hut, he saw that Aliah was curled up on the floor beside Frosty. Seamus snored, appearing less agitated. The fire was banked, but the room remained toasty. Not wanting to wake Aliah, he made up his bed by the door and was soon fast asleep.

Shouts came from all around. Blane bolted upright on his pallet. Blinking rapidly, he rubbed at his eyes. He was blind. He couldn't see anything. No not blind, it was just dark. And he couldn't breathe. Sucking in a breath, he gagged, hacked, coughed. Smoke.

The hut was filled with smoke. And heat.

On fire. The hut was on fire! The ceiling was an inferno. Red and orange flames greedily licked the thatch, bits falling in sparks onto the floor. A loud crack thundered in his ears. The back wall was engulfed in flames.

Mo creach!

"Aliah!" he shouted, crawling toward where he last saw her. The room was thick with dark smoke and even the brightness of the blaze didn't show him more than the nightmare about to overtake him. He couldn't see anything. His eyes burned, his throat ached. Where was she? He patted at the ground, but couldn't even see a shadow of her sleeping form.

Unexpectedly, Frosty loomed in front of him, licked his face, nipped at his shoulder, pulling him.

Blane let the dog tug on him, praying the animal would lead him straight to Aliah. He searched with his hands outstretched as he crawled, then finally felt the warm lump of her body on the floor. He shook her, but she didn't respond.

"Aliah! Wake up!" he shouted, panic setting in. Placing a hand on her chest he was mildly relieved to feel it rise and fall, but it did so weakly. She wasn't getting enough air.

Frosty barked feebly. The dog had inhaled much smoked. Blane choked and coughed again. They needed to get out. Now.

He glanced around the room, attempting to find another exit, but there was none. The only way to get out was through the front door, likely where the enemy waited. He had to move fast. The fire was quickly consuming the walls. Cracking and a whoosh sounded above, just before a large clump of burning thatch hit his shoulder. He hissed with pain as the sparks singed through his shirt and stung his bare flesh. Brushing the ashes from his shirt, he again reached out to Aliah, rolling her into his arms.

She needed fresh air and quickly, before the whole roof collapsed. He had to get her out of here, even if he'd end up in the middle of the enemy's circle. Blane would beg mercy for Aliah, they could do whatever they might with him as long as they promised to leave her alone.

Leaning low to the ground, Blane sucked in the deepest breath his lungs could hold, then carefully stood with Aliah in his arms. He ran toward where he thought the door was, holding his breath the whole time. Blankets, roof particles and other debris littered the floor. He prayed for strength. If he tripped…

With a thrust of his shoulder, he forced open the door, and burst into the night air, Frosty at his heels. A few yards away, he dropped to his knees, lungs burning, and placed Aliah on the ground. Metal clanged all around him, deafening screams and shouts vibrated through his ears. His men fought ferociously. A bitter battle to the death. He had to join in, had to help. They'd been ambushed. But he couldn't leave her here, it wasn't safe. Taking note that the majority of the fighting was going on closer to the path leading to the road, Blane picked Aliah up again and rushed behind the hut. Keeping a safe distance from the burning building, he placed her behind some brambles.

"Stay. Protect your mistress," he demanded of Frosty.

The hound sat beside Aliah and barked up at Blane, as if to say he would.

Blane wasted no time running back toward the hut. He burst inside, found Seamus' unconscious body and hoisted him over his shoulder, running him to the spot where he'd hidden Aliah. Frosty still stood vigil, the hairs on the back of his neck on end.

"Good boy," Blane said before charging toward the fray.

With clouds covering the moon and the only light coming from the blaze, he still recognized the band of men who fought his own. He'd never forget them. Evil gleamed in their eyes and demon shadows danced on their faces.

Over a decade later, he'd come face to face with his worst enemies.

Issuing a battle cry, he held his sword above his head and ran headlong into the fight. He swung, cut, sliced, thrust, parried. Not one of the lawless jackanapes would leave here alive. Blane took down one and then another, bent on destruction, not only for the death of his parents but for nearly taking the life of the woman he loved. When he thrust his sword into the last of them, he spat on the ground. Collapsed. He closed his eyes and looked up toward the sky, his chest tight, shoulders heavy. Lungs burned, lips were cracked. Exhaustion took over his entire being and he felt as though he too would die here.

A hard clamp on his shoulder had Blane whipping his sword once more, but he stopped when his eyes landed on Liam.

"They are all dead," Liam said.

"Did any get away?"

Liam shook his head.

"How many?"

"Thirteen."

"Surrey?"

Liam nodded. "He too is among the dead."

"'Twill be a problem for the Sutherlands."

"Not if the Sassenachs never find the bodies." Liam's face was hard and determined. He would protect Blane and all the Sutherlands with his last breath.

Blane glanced over the ground, covered in bodies, all of them enemies. It was over. He'd found his parents' killers. Or rather, they'd found him. Had they come to finish the job they'd started? He'd like to think they had, but the cynical side of him thought that most likely they'd killed so many they wouldn't remember dispatching some miserable youth's parents and leaving him for dead. He was surprised by how lifted he felt. He'd expected to feel retribution, not relief. Aliah crowded his mind. She'd made him see there was something to look forward to. A future filled with promise.

"Where is Lady Aliah? Seamus?" Liam asked.

With a heavy arm, Blane pointed beyond the crofter's hut. "I've hidden them." His lungs burned, making his voice raspy. His shoulder felt afire. He was so overcome with fatigue he was in real danger of falling over.

"I will see to them. Ye'd better tend to your arm." Liam called out to a couple other warriors who followed him toward the brambles.

His arm?

Blane looked down at his shoulder. His shirt was completely burned away, and his skin was singed in places, burned worse in others. Now that he looked at it, a dull ache pulsed from one end to the other. 'Twas worse then he'd thought. At least he hadn't sustained any serious injuries during the battle. Other than a few scrapes and bruises, he was fine. Except for the burns. Hobbling toward the creek, he knelt—nearly falling—onto his knees and scooped water onto his arm. The pain. It was almost too much for him to take. The water trickled down his arm, and agony fogged his senses. He moaned low in this throat, but continued to clean the wound despite how excruciatingly painful it was.

How had the blaze started?

The fire in the hearth had been banked when he fell asleep, had Aliah stoked it? Not likely. That meant the fire came from outside, and none of his men had lit a fire to keep warm. They were Highlanders. They didn't need a fire to keep them warm on a late fall night. That meant only one thing.

Someone else had started the blaze. *Damn!*

The world started to spin. Blane blinked rapidly, trying to keep focus. He stared at a tree. Planted his hands on his knees, steadying himself. He focused his vision on the ridges of bark, the trickle of sap. The sun had started to rise although clouds still covered overhead. A mist rolled over the hilly ground and water. The tree started to move. What the hell?

The damn thing was dancing... Then whipped sideways as though pulled from the ground. It was only when his face smacked into mud that he realized he'd truly collapsed. The world still spun and the mist disoriented him. Blane attempted to push up, but he'd no strength. His throat burned, his lips felt so parched... He could barely breathe.

The world slowly disappeared into a tunnel of black.

Aliah blinked open her eyes. The sun was out, but not shining. It was gray overhead and an eerie mist covered the ground around her.

"I wish we'd arrived sooner. Magnus had an idea ye'd be arriving soon, but we'd no idea ye had an enemy on your trail. Wasna the Ross Clan was it?"

Aliah stared with glazed eyes at a handsome warrior who spoke to another man she couldn't quite see. The warrior was tall, looked sort of like Blane, but not quite. He had the same dark hair, chiseled features, raw strength.

"Nay, not Ross men. These bastards have been following us since we crossed the border from England." Aliah recognized Liam's voice — even if he'd refused to talk to her on the first half of their treacherous journey.

"They've not been much of a threat, from what I've heard, but Magnus is forever on his guard. Where is my cousin?" the warrior said.

"Blane is…" Liam glanced around, his brow furrowed.

There was a long pause, and in that moment, Aliah felt a moment of panic. Blane was missing. Her arms were heavy, like she'd been strapped down, and her mouth was so incredibly dry. Who was this man? What happened? Where was Blane?

"I…dinna know. He was going to take care of his shoulder…"

"He was injured?" the warrior who claimed to be Blane's cousin replied.

Aliah opened her mouth to demand information. Blane was hurt! How had he been hurt?

"The bastards set the hut on fire. His shoulder was burned."

"Where would he have gone?" the cousin asked.

"Probably the creek."

"I'll go check on him."

"I'll come with ye."

Then there was silence. Aliah tried to roll to her side, finding it not entirely unmanageable. Her lungs hurt and burned something fierce, and she found each breath stung, but other than that, she didn't appear to be injured.

A massive pile of burnt embers huddled where the hut had once stood. She gasped, then coughed at the sudden rush of air entering her sensitive lungs.

They'd been inside there asleep. And Seamus! Frosty!

Her dog pounded his tail beside her, panting, as he stood vigil. Another glance behind her showed that Seamus was not far away, but was sweating profusely. That was a good sign that his fever was breaking.

But where was Blane?

Her heart constricted. She didn't remember the fire. Didn't remember escaping. That meant he'd risked his life to save her. He'd carried her from the blaze—and been injured in the process.

Pushing up on her elbows so she could get a better lay of the land, she looked around. There was a pile of bodies near the trees. Half a dozen of Blane's men worked with makeshift shovels, digging. Who were the dead? From the conversation she'd overheard, they'd been attacked. The hut had been set on fire.

Her attention was quickly taken in the direction of the stream as Blane's cousin and Liam appeared. Blane was draped between the two of them, his arms over both of their shoulders as they half-carried, half-dragged him toward her.

One look at his shoulder told her he'd been badly burned. The skin was blackened around the wound and flaming red at the center. Blisters bubbled around the blackened edges. The man had suffered much since meeting her—she'd shot him, now he was burned. What next?

Aliah didn't want to think about that. Using all of her strength, she pushed up to her knees and patted the ground beside her.

"Put him here," she croaked.

The men listened without complaint. She bent over Blane. His eyes were glazed, but open.

"Aliah," he whispered, touching her face with his good hand.

"Let me look," she said softly. "Seems like he's cleaned it well. Have you any bandages or salve?" She glanced up at Liam and Blane's cousin.

"Aye, we have some left from Seamus." Liam jogged off to get the supplies.

"I am Laird Daniel Murray," the cousin said, bowing low. He handed her a skin filled with whisky. "Make him drink."

"Lady Aliah," she said, tipping the skin to Blane's mouth. He drank greedily.

"Ah, I've heard much of ye."

Aliah cocked her head to the side, curious. "You have?"

The man was even more handsome now that her eyes had focused. He must make all the ladies swoon. Funny that she didn't feel like swooning herself. She only had eyes for the fallen man at her side.

"Your sister and your father talk of your arrival nonstop."

"You've seen them?" Hope soared through her. "Is my father well?"

"Perfectly."

She frowned for a moment. "You're a laird."

"Aye."

"Then why are you patrolling for another laird?"

Laird Murray laughed, a deep and rumbling sound. "Good question, but alas I will answer it for ye. Magnus wanted to patrol himself, but his wife was feeling a wee bit under the weather—which worried him much. I was visiting and volunteered to come and see about Blane's return."

"Arbella? She's sick?"

"Aye, but 'tis completely normal, I hear."

"Normal?" Dear Lord... Were Scottish women always sick? Or just English ones who lived in Scotland?

"Aye."

Aliah shook her head. "I don't understand."

Murray shrugged and before she could ask him to clarify, Liam returned with the bandages and a small leather pouch filled with a pungent salve Mistress Kerr had provided for Blane's wounded leg. Aliah worked to cover Blane's new wound. He hissed and moaned as she did so, but other than that, he was a good patient.

"Do you have a healer at Dunrobin?" she asked Liam.

"Aye."

"When we arrive, he must see her immediately."

Liam nodded then walked away to tend to the men, but Murray stayed. He studied her with keen eyes that made her uncomfortable.

"Ye love him?" he asked.

"What?" The man certainly was blunt.

"Blane, do ye love him?"

Aliah glanced away. "What a perfectly odd thing to ask."

"Odd? I dinna think so."

"We've only just met." Her stomach flipped. How had the man seen through her so clearly.

"Aye, but I can see when ye look at him ye feel more than just camaraderie."

Aliah shook her head and folded her arms over her chest. "You're mistaken."

"She loves me," Blane said weakly, a silly smile on his face.

Aliah huffed a breath and then coughed. "Men," she murmured.

Chapter Twenty-Two

Blane remained quite delirious for the next couple of hours, most likely from the amount of whisky his cousin Murray kept pouring into his mouth. Aliah rode her borrowed mount, while Blane rode with his cousin. She wanted to tell Murray to quit with the drink. But he'd only think her a ninny — and then tease her more about her feelings for Blane.

No one was supposed to know how she felt. Least of all Blane. Yet, half-drunk on whisky, he'd uttered those words. Sounded a bit like a braggart too. Irritation sliced through her and her cheeks flamed with embarrassment. She had waited with baited breath for him to tell everyone what they'd done together too. His lips seemed too loose to her. Thank the Saints he'd not uttered a word.

Aliah couldn't exactly blame him. The man was in a lot of pain. Had fought a battle, been badly burned and then nearly drowned with whisky. His face was covered in smears of dirt, ash and other things she didn't want to imagine, as was his linen shirt. The garment needed to be burned as well. One sleeve was completely gone and the rest of it looked as though it'd been trod upon by a dozen boars. His plaid didn't fare much better.

The weather matched her mood — grey and chilly. Earlier that morning she'd felt quite the opposite. Warm, lively. Ready to take on the world. To fight for her future. Fear, though, had sunk in. Aliah had to shake it. Had to realize that there was no place for fear in love. She wasn't so much scared of love, but of everything unknown to her. Especially Blane's opinion on the matter. She knew he felt something for her, she simply wasn't sure what. Aliah bit her lip, pressing away the disturbing feelings churning in her belly.

They crested a steep hill, the dirt road rising over top, surrounded by trees on both sides. The riding party stopped.

"That is Dunrobin," Murray said, pointing down into a valley that led straight to an imposing castle which sat atop an incline overlooking the sea. "They are rebuilding the wooden keep into a stone one."

Aliah gazed over the soaring wooden structure, the various stone towers and thick stone walls. Outbuildings were situated within the walls. The Sutherlands were obviously a very powerful clan. Mowbray Manor could fit inside the walls three times over.

Beyond the castle was the sea. Her lips parted in awe as she sucked in a breath. Aliah had never seen the sea. 'Twas magnificent, mesmerizing. The breadth of blue-black water appeared to stretch forever. Dots of white frothy waves coated its expanse. The grey sky touched down on the water and clouds hovered as if waiting for permission to merge with the impressive body.

"Which sea is it?" she asked.

"North Sea."

Arbella was lucky to wake to such a sight each morning. Aliah had thought she was fortunate waking up to the scents of apples and peaches wafting their way through her windows from the orchard behind their manor. Aliah closed her eyes, breathing in. Her lungs still hurt from the fire, and she couldn't smell the sea—only the scents of nature surrounding her, grass, dry leaves, cool wind. Mayhap as they grew closer she'd be able to catch its scent.

The men kicked their horses forward, riding down the ridge. The incline was steeper than Aliah expected and she held tight to her mount, leaning back a little so she wouldn't tumble right over the top. Thank goodness she didn't have Mad Maiden with her or she'd be going over for sure. The trees opened up on her right showing where the loch fed into the sea below the ridge they now rode on. How she'd love to edge closer and peer over the side, but the party continued forward. Aliah would ask Arbella to show her the sea once she'd had a chance to rest and catch up. Flicking her gaze at Blane, she realized that she'd rather he show her. The way he introduced her to new things was exhilarating and he seemed to take such pleasure in nature, almost like he was seeing it for the first time himself.

She guessed that within an hour or two she would be able to hug her sister, her father. Would they be able to see through her façade as Murray had? Would they know immediately all that had gone on between her and Blane? He looked better than this morning, even managed to sit upright. His eyes were open and he stared toward Dunrobin.

"He is well, my lady. I promise ye that," Murray said.

Aliah frowned, which only made the laird smirk. Blane slid his glance toward her, a smile curving his lips, but she could tell from the redness of his eyes he was not completely sober. To add fuel to the fire, Murray gave Blane the wineskin holding whisky.

"When we arrive at Dunrobin, the healer will take good care of him, and then he can sleep off the half-keg of whisky he's drowned himself in."

Aliah raised a brow. "I think 'tis rather you whose been doing the drowning."

Murray laughed. "I can see why my cousin holds ye in such high regard."

"Aye, high," Blane said, his words sluggish.

What did he mean by that? Aliah refused to acknowledge his statement, because doing so would only be admitting that she cared about his answer. Which she did... But she wasn't willing to admit that much to Murray. After Blane was feeling better, they would have to have a serious conversation. One that discussed the future they'd both been avoiding.

Irritation flickered over her again. Why should she have to discuss it with him? Shouldn't the man know that it was right? He'd nearly said as much... showed her how much he cared. Called her his heart when they'd made love. *Mo chridhe.* Blane didn't realize she knew what it meant, that she'd studied Gaelic. But she was completely aware of his confession.

Nodding with renewed conviction, Aliah made up her mind. As soon as Blane was well, she would demand he admit his feelings to her.

Sooner than she'd expected, they crossed under the gate and into the inner bailey amid shouts of welcome. The sounds of construction stopped as those who worked on what looked like a stone tower ceased what they were doing to stare at the newcomers. Aliah was overwhelmed by the noise and the amount of Highland men and women converging on them. But amid the din of it all, came the shout of her sister and the boom of her father's voice.

"Aliah!" Arbella rushed toward her, not looking the least bit ill.

Aliah jumped from her horse, lifted her skirts and rushed to her sister. They clashed together, hugging so tightly she could barely breathe—which only served to make her sore lungs more so. Frosty bounded toward Arbella, breaking the sisters up, he leapt up, his large paws landing on Arbella's shoulders as he licked her face in a frenzy. Arbella laughed and hugged the hound as she struggled to maintain her balance.

"Frosty, boy! I can't believe you're here." Arbella turned back to her sister. "You made it safely." She held Aliah at arm's length and searched up and down her form. "Thank God."

Aliah smirked. "Did you think otherwise?"

Arbella glanced at the large, imposing, handsome man who greeted Blane. That had to be Magnus. Their facial resemblance was striking. "Possibly. But you are well and that is all that matters. I see Blane is injured though." For a moment she turned from Aliah, her brow crinkled with concern. Arbella ordered someone to fetch the healer and for Blane to be carried into the castle. When she turned back to Aliah, gripping her hand in hers, Aliah couldn't help but stare at her sister with awe.

"You are happy. And comfortable." Aliah's voice sounded every bit as shocked as she felt.

"Aye. Why wouldn't I be?" Arbella beamed, glowed even.

"I can think of many reasons, one being that Laird Murray said you were ill."

A twinkle glimmered in Arbella's eyes. "I was, am. But," she leaned in close to whisper excitedly in Aliah's ear, "I am happy for it! I am to be a mother!"

Aliah gasped, then coughed. "Truly?" She glanced down at Arbella's belly taking note of a slight swell in her abdomen. A part of her feared for her sister. Her own mother had died in childbirth, was it possible such a thing could happen to her sister? To herself?

"Don't look so afraid, Aliah." Her sister spoke softly, pulled her close. "I will be fine. I am happy. And safe."

Aliah swallowed hard, nodded, tried not to let her fears take hold. Arbella's next words were a wakeup call.

"You know, Aliah, 'tis a gift to bring a child into the world. Not all can, and not all survive. But you of all people should know it is God's will. There is no blame here on earth for things that can only be defined by the divine."

Arbella's words had a profound effect on Aliah. They didn't erase her fear, or the blame she clutched to for her part in her mother's passing. Both Mistress Kerr and Arbella appeared to be of the same conviction. And it bore further thought. Acceptance that she was not in control of everything. That she was not to blame for things she had no control over.

Arbella nodded. "But enough chatting, here, let me take you to your chamber and get you a nice bath. You're covered in soot."

"Aye, there was a fire..." Aliah trailed off, imagining what a sight she must be.

"Not before I get a look at her." The booming voice of their father Baron de Mowbray broke through the crowd. He ambled closer, clasping Aliah in his bulky arms. Then he too examined her with scrutiny. "You look well."

"I am." Why was everyone surprised to see she'd arrived in one piece? They underestimated her, that was clear. "And you are not injured..."

"No more than my pride." Her father grunted. Looked as though he wanted to ask her a question, but clamped his mouth closed instead. His gaze followed Blane as he walked on steadier feet than she would have guessed into the keep. Blane's gaze met hers and she thought she would melt from the heat of it. Aliah swallowed hard, bit her lip. His green eyes sizzled, making her want to sink into his embrace.

"What happened to your escort?"

255

She jerked her gaze from Blane's to glance at her father. "His shoulder was burned saving me from a fire last night."

"He saved you?" Her father looked surprised.

"Aye. He's a gentleman." She couldn't help the defensiveness of her tone, and that only made her father wing a skeptical brow.

"Why is he limping?"

At that question, she felt heat flame into her cheeks swifter than a gale force wind. How could she admit to her father, her one flaw that he'd lamented of most—recklessness—had been the reason behind Blane's limp?

"That was an accident." Fingers grasping her skirts, she tried to keep from wringing them together.

"What kind of accident?" Her father's voice had taken on a more severe tone and Aliah was catapulted back in time, feeling like a little girl confessing her latest blunder.

Aliah didn't like feeling like that. She was a grown woman. Lifting her chin, she stared at her father straight in the eye as she said, "I may have...shot him."

"Shot him?"

Arbella laughed. The man Aliah had guessed was Magnus came up and casually put his arm over Arbella's shoulder, laughing too and said dryly, "He probably deserved it."

Aliah nodded, then trying to take the attention away from herself, turned her full attention to Magnus. "We've not been formally introduced. I am Lady Aliah, Arbella's sister."

"'Tis wonderful to finally meet ye," he said. "I am Magnus, Laird Sutherland."

He had nearly the same face as Blane, but where Blane's hair was dark as a raven's this man's hair was more sandy in color. His eyes however, were the same intense green and measured her just as Blane's had when they'd first met. But whereas in Blane's eyes she saw desire, affection, in Magnus, she saw friendly regard. She felt like squirming, but used every tool she'd acquired over the years to stand tall with her shoulders square.

"I should offer you congratulations on your wedding to my sister, Laird Sutherland."

Her words were not lost on her intelligent new brother-by-marriage. "Should?"

Aliah smiled. "Aye. If you would excuse me, it appears I am covered in soot and in desperate need of a bath." Lifting her skirts she swept past everyone when she really felt like running. Explaining why she'd shot Blane was not something she was up for.

Arbella caught up to her, slipping her fingers gently around Aliah's elbow. "You don't know where you're going, sister."

"I just want to get away for a little bit."

"I understand. Come, I will show you to your chamber." Arbella led her up a narrow, circular set of stairs and finally into a chamber. A maid arrived, lighting the fire and several men carried in a tub, followed by more servants with steaming buckets of water.

Within minutes, Aliah found herself immersed in a warm tub. Arbella scooted a stool close and sat, staring, her elbow resting on her knee and chin resting on her fist. Aliah started to feel a little uncomfortable. Arbella always saw through her — save for her inner most desire to join the church. A desire that had since been completely destroyed.

"What happened?" Arbella asked.

"When?"

Arbella rolled her eyes. "Don't play coy now. Tell me."

Aliah wanted to tell her sister everything with all her heart, but she knew she couldn't. Instead, she explained how Blane had come to the manor dressed as an Englishman. How when they'd crossed the border, he'd changed into his Highland garb which scared the blazes out of her. She'd thought she'd been kidnapped so, she shot him. Arbella laughed at that. Aliah told her of waking up in a daze after the fire—left out the part of how they'd been attacked in the woods and she'd shot a man. Left out the lovemaking. Left out the part about how she'd fallen madly, deeply, in love with Blane and that meeting him had changed the entire course of her life.

"I know how you feel, Aliah." Arbella spoke softly.

"You do?" *What exactly…*

"When I met Magnus, I was scared out of my mind. Thought for sure I would die. But things slowly…changed."

"Changed how?"

Arbella shook her head and shrugged. "I don't know when, I don't know how, but he showed me a different world. That I could be myself. That I could lean on him. That being married to someone didn't have to be a duty, it could be… enjoyable. Passionate. Loving."

"You sound like Lorna." Aliah scowled and blew out a breath.

Arbella smiled wistfully. "I'm glad you got to meet her. I am looking forward to visiting her in the spring."

"Will you be able to?" Aliah pointed at her belly.

"Magnus will balk, no doubt, but I've ways of convincing him." A wicked smile covered her sister's normally innocent face. Arbella had changed much since she'd left the manor— and it appeared to be doing wonders for her. "But enough of that, I must know. Tell me."

"Tell you what?" Aliah rolled her eyes and sat back, folding her arms across her chest, water sloshing over the sides of the tub.

"You will play modest with me. I see. Then perhaps I should tell you what I saw, what the rest of the clan saw."

"By all means." Aliah pretended to be busy soaping her arms even though her heart sped up.

"When Blane walked by you, he looked at you—and not just in any way. He looked at you the way Magnus looks at me. Intense. Possessive."

"So? Mayhap he wanted to see if I was all right."

Arbella laughed. "You returned his gaze with equal fervor."

Her sister had a point there... She had indeed, and just thinking about Blane's gaze made her feel flushed all over.

"You love him."

"You and Murray must be drinking from the same wineskin."

"Murray? What's he got to do with this?"

Aliah rinsed off the soap and climbed from the tub, rapidly drying off the water drizzling over her skin with a linen towel. "He said the same thing when I cared for Blane's shoulder."

"Murray is quite astute."

Aliah threw down the towel, yanked a chemise over her head and stomped her foot. Placing her hands on her hips she rounded on her sister. "Fine. If you must know, I have come to care for him."

"A-ha! I knew it." Arbella rubbed her hands together.

"You are gaining entirely too much pleasure out of this," Aliah replied with a roll of her eyes. She turned her gaze on the soft looking bed. "I'm tired."

"What will you do? Does he feel the same for you?"

Aliah wished she could peel back the plaid covered blanket, crawl into bed, lay her head on the plush pillows and fall into a deep, peaceful sleep. Instead she had to brush out her hair. Sitting before the fire lit in a metal brazier, she used not quite so gentle strokes to rid her hair of tangles. The heat of the fire helped to dry her hair and warm her chilled skin.

"I don't know."

"You don't know what you'll do, or you don't know how he feels?"

"Both."

"Father is going to have a fit." Why did Arbella sound excited about that?

"Probably. But at least I am interested in a man and not the church."

Arbella took a seat beside Aliah, taking the brush and pulling it through her hair gently. "The church?"

"Aye. In the spring I was going to join the church in secret."

Arbella laughed heartily at that. "Why am I not surprised? Do you know what is most humorous of all?"

"I can hardly wait to hear..." Aliah said sarcastically.

"Just after Blane left to retrieve you, Father said to Magnus that you'd best arrive a maiden."

Aliah grabbed the brush and met her sister's gaze, all seriousness now. "What makes you think I am not?"

Arbella raised a brow, her lips quirking into a knowing smile. "If Blane is half as lusty as Magnus, you're lucky to have not arrived great with child."

"We only traveled for a couple weeks, 'tis not even possible."

Arbella waved away her comments and started to pace the room. "You'll have to wed."

"I don't even know if Blane wants to marry me. He would have said as much, wouldn't he?" Aliah put the brush down and started to plait her nearly dry hair.

"Doesn't matter. He will be forced to."

Aliah shook her head fiercely, jumped to her feet. "I will not marry a man who is forced to wed me. I'll run to the first abbey and take vows before I say 'I do'."

Arbella glanced at her, cocked her head to the side. "But you love each other."

"Then he must wed me of his own accord. Promise me you'll keep this conversation between the two of us, Arbella. I want to speak with him on my own." Aliah despised the desperate urgency in her voice, but she had to make sure that Arbella kept her secret.

Arbella stared at her, a mixture of concern and respect on her face. "All right. I shall let you have it your way, but you should know if the matter is not settled within a fortnight, I will have to tell Magnus."

Aliah nodded, embraced her sister. "Agreed."

"Get some rest. I will have a tray of food sent up to you for supper."

"Thank you, for everything."

"What are sisters for?" Arbella tucked her into bed while servants entered and cleaned away the mess of the tub.

"Arbella, can I ask you a quick question?"

"Aye."

"Was father injured in the battle?"

Arbella shrugged. "I don't think so. He was lost to me within the crowd. He only just arrived a couple weeks ago."

"So the letter Blane gave me?"

"I forged it… I'm sorry."

Aliah laughed. "You know me well. It worked."

When Aliah fell asleep, her dreams were disturbing visions of Blane, fires, screaming. Then of him shunning her, holding his hands out and shaking his head. Pain filled her chest. Heartbreak. Then her dreams turned more wicked and she woke sweaty, her thighs clenched together, nipples tight and her breathing rapid. Not at all the restfulness she'd hoped for, and they left her more concerned for her future than ever before.

Chapter Twenty-Three

"When will ye ask?" Magnus barged into the chamber and walked with steady confidence toward the bed where Blane lounged after he'd bathed and been visited by the healer.

Blane glanced up at his brother through whisky hazed eyes. "Ask what?"

"You know."

Blane shook his head, feeling pain slice over his brow. Just how much whisky had he drunk? He hated to feel like this. Heavy, tired, out of sorts. "I dinna know of what ye speak." He needed food. That would help to calm the rolling in his belly and to clear his head. "I'm hungry."

"I'll not allow ye to eat until ye answer the damn question." Magnus crossed his arms over his chest, trying to look every bit as powerful as he was.

For an ordinary man, Magnus' stance and the fierceness of his gaze might have had Blane blubbering on bended knee, but this was his brother. He respected him, loved him, looked up to him even, but never did he fear him.

"I'll be happy to answer your question if ye tell me what the hell ye're talking about." Blane struggled to sit up straighter, but the pillows were so plush and soft he just kept sinking back against them.

"When will ye ask Baron de Mowbray for the hand of his daughter?"

"Marriage?" Blane did manage to sit up then.

"Aye."

Blane shook his head. "'Tis impossible."

"Nay, 'tis not."

"I canna marry the lass."

"Ye have already lain with her."

Had Aliah told them all? Anger burned in his chest.

"I see the way your mind works, and 'tis clear from the scowl on your face that I'm right—but the lass is not the one who told me. Ye just did."

"What?"

"Aye. 'Twas a trick question."

Blane glowered up at Magnus. "Bastard."

Magnus smiled with pride and shrugged. "Now answer the question."

"I didna plan to ask her," Blane grumbled. "She willna have me and she deserves much more than what I have to offer."

"Ye have much to offer a wife. Ye're a good man, Blane. Ye have yourself, a good home, love."

Love… Was he so obvious? Magnus would think him weak for loving a woman he couldn't have.

"To love is not a weakness, brother, unless ye let it inhibit ye. For me, loving Arbella has only enhanced my life."

His brother had a knack for reading his thoughts. Damn him. And Magnus had a point. Double damn.

"But I am gone for months at a time, what wife wants that?"

Magnus shrugged. "Many wives manage. Warriors leave, and they try their damnedest to return. I will have to leave soon...although I havena broached the topic with my wife yet. She'll be madder than a snake."

Blane raised a brow. "But ye at least have your own home. I have nothing."

"Why canna ye have your own home? We'll build ye one."

He hadn't thought it would be so simple as that.

A knock sounded at the door and Ronan, the youngest Sutherland brother entered the room with Murray. Ronan smirked at Blane. "See ye got yourself in quite a mess."

Blane felt like punching him.

Ronan took a similar stance beside Magnus, arms crossed over his broad chest. He looked much like Magnus, and it was entirely too irritating for a man with a headache. Murray grinned mischievously and copied his cousins.

"Go away, the lot of ye."

"I merely came to wish ye well, brother," Ronan said. "And to tell ye, Magnus, Wallace has arrived. I will depart with him in the morn."

"I've a mind to join ye," Murray said.

"Dinna ye have a clan to rule?" Blane asked Murray in a surly tone.

"Aye. But they want me to marry soon and I've grown wary of the brides they keep parading. Have to keep the laird-hungry lasses at bay. If I'm warring for Scotland's freedom, there's aught they can do to get me married."

Magnus laughed at Murray and then nodded and clapped Ronan on the shoulder. "Ye will make a great leader, Ronan."

"Thank ye." Ronan came around to the side of the bed and Blane grasped his arm.

"Send 'em to hell, brother." Ronan was a fierce warrior, unmatched on the battlefield—save by his brothers and even his cousins. But they all got their licks in. The Sutherlands fighting together was epic. "'Haps I'll see both of ye on the field."

Ronan grinned. "Aye. I willna let a single Sassenach get past my sword. But ye need to stay here and tend to a certain lass." He walked toward the door, then stopped to turn around. "I want to offer my blessings, your future bride is beautiful, and since she's already shot ye, the marriage promises to be filled with surprises." Ronan breezed out, his heavy laughter echoing through the corridor.

"Aye, she's a bonny lass." Murray winked, then laughed at Blane's snarl as he followed Ronan out.

Had everybody already decided his fate for him?

"I've a need to meet with Wallace, brother. He's brought with him the earls of Lennox, Carrick and Strathearn, as well as Robert the Bruce."

"The Bruce?"

"Aye. Wallace came to collect Ronan to help begin training the men through the winter. Come spring, there promises to be a vicious battle. His companions were a surprise to me. Think ye can sober up and join us?"

Blane nodded. "Aye."

"Good. A messenger arrived this afternoon from Master Kerr. The man wanted news of ye. Apparently, right after ye left, one of the vile Sassenachs saw the tail end of your party and they gave chase. I sent word back that ye were fine."

"Thank ye." Blane was immeasurably relieved to know that his friends were safe. They'd done so much for him, he'd hate if they were to suffer for it.

"Where is Heather? I've not seen her come traipsing in as everyone else has." Blane glowered, but in all seriousness, he'd hoped for the bright cheerful smile of his younger sister.

Magnus shook his head. "The lass was in need of a matronly hand. I sent her to stay the winter with Murray's mother."

"Och, truly?" Murray's mother was strict and proper. Heather was the exact opposite. A free spirit, and a saucy lass to be sure. At fifteen summers, she was a hellion, and in a few years when Magnus would have to find her a marriage match, there were likely to be scores of men lining up because of her reputed beauty—all of whom would run when she opened her mouth.

"Aye."

"I pray the woman doesna whip the spirit from her."

Magnus grinned. "I dinna think anyone could. Heather's a strike of lightning to be sure."

His brother was most likely right. If anything, Heather would come back still just as sharp-tongued and spirited, but with a proper curtsy and coif.

Magnus left the chamber and Blane crawled from the comfort of his bed to splash water on his face and refresh his mouth with mint. A few moments later a servant knocked, entering with a tray of bread and steaming cup of tea.

"The laird says ye're to eat this afore ye come down."

Blane didn't waste time digging into the thick brown bread with honey and the warm herbal tisane, feeling his head clear and the rumblings in his stomach calm. His shoulder hurt like the devil, but at least he'd been cleaned up and cared for. Healing had already begun. And he wasn't going to miss a chance to meet the Bruce or the earls who'd knighted Wallace and named him the Guardian of Scotland.

More importantly, he couldn't wait to see Aliah's beautiful face again.

A clipped knock sounded at Aliah's door, wakening her. "Who is it?" she called from bed, part of her hoping it was Blane.

"'Tis I," her father said.

She climbed from the bed and put on the soft wool wrapper Arbella had left for her. "Come in," she called.

Her father entered, his face a mask of concern.

"What is it?" she asked, alarm filling her.

"We must leave at first light."

"What? Why? I've only just arrived."

"Aye, I know it, but we must leave before winter sets or else we'll be trapped in the Highlands until spring. I, for one, have had enough of Scotland."

Aliah shook her head. "Nay, I cannot."

The baron spread his hands wide, frowning. "Why not?"

"I wish to stay with Arbella and see her through her confinement." She was glad to have come up with an easy excuse.

Shaking his head, the baron put his hands on his hips, as if to scold a child. "Nay. 'Tis too far away. I won't stay here and you will return to England with me. There are already discussions going on with several other barons regarding—"

"Nay!" Aliah shook her head hard but refrained from stomping her foot. She couldn't very well tell her father she wouldn't leave until she'd had a chance to speak with Blane. Couldn't confide that she had hopes of a future in the Highlands. "Arbella needs me."

"She does not. She has a husband now. Lots of people here care about her."

"Do you think that marrying makes her family obsolete?"

"Nay, 'tis only, she has a new family now."

Irritation cut a path through her veins. "And do you think that when mother passed, her family did not mourn her loss as much as you?"

The baron took a step back, shocked at her words. Aliah too was stunned at having said them. Pain shadowed his eyes but he quickly looked away. Aliah took his break in eye contact as a cut to her directly.

"I'm sorry that I took her away from you, Father. And I'm sorry for speaking of it now."

His gaze shot back at her. "Is that what you think? That you took her from me?" The baron shook his head. "You didn't take her from me at all. Your mother was happy to bring you into the world. And 'twas God's will that she rise up to the heavens to be with him, leaving you behind, the best part of her." Her father stepped forward, pulling her into his embrace. "Had I known you blamed yourself I would have corrected you a long time ago," he whispered against her hair.

"Do you see why I must stay?"

He shook his head. "Arbella is safe, healthy, strong. I think she will do just fine in the bearing of her child."

"But what of..." Aliah didn't want to bring up her mother again. She bit her lip and looked away, preparing to tell her father about Blane.

"Your mother, God rest her beautiful soul, was already weakened. When she gave birth to Arbella, it was long, arduous. Her body was tiny and our babies did not exactly have an easy path to travel through. The mid-wife advised against her having another child, but your mother..." He paused, blinked up at the ceiling. It looked as though he tried to rid himself of tears. "Your mother wanted another so badly. That was you, Aliah. Before she left this earth, she whispered your name. Told me it meant noble and to ascend. I think she was trying to tell me..."

This time, Aliah put her arms around her father. She wished he'd shared all of this with her earlier in her life, but was glad to know it now. Despite what others had been telling her all along, she couldn't truly believe she was blameless until now. Knowing that her mother wanted her when warned not to try, and that her mother named her… A weight was lifted from her chest, and with it she felt herself floating.

"You still want to stay?" her father asked, pulling back to hold her at arm's length.

Aliah nodded.

"Why do I get the feeling there is another reason?"

She couldn't lie to her father. "I…"

"Does it have something to do with Laird Sutherland's rogue of a brother?"

Aliah swallowed hard past the lump in her throat and nodded.

"Has he…" The baron shook his head. "Never mind. I shall speak to him."

"Nay! Not yet, please."

Her father studied her for a long time, before speaking. "'Tis a father's duty to take care of his children."

Aliah gripped her father's hand and squeezed, imploring him with her eyes. "And I've no wish to take that duty from you, Father. 'Tis simply, in this matter, I would—" Her speech faltered as she searched for the right words. "I am no longer a child, Father, and I—" She puffed out a breath. "I am in love with a man, but I've no idea if he returns my regard."

The baron's eyes turned soft and he stroked her cheek. "Ah, daughter, he does. But I shall let you find that out for yourself."

"Are we still leaving tomorrow?"

He grinned. "Aye. At least I am. I'll wait until after the noon meal to depart and to see if you'll be joining me."

Aliah threw herself into her father's arms. She had until tomorrow to convince Blane of what everyone else already knew.

The great hall was loud and boisterous as Blane entered. His cousin Murray caroused with Wallace and his men at the long trestle table. At the high table, Magnus sat in the middle with Arbella on one side and a stoic looking man on his other side. He had to be the Bruce. His reddish brown hair hung loose about chin length and his beard was well trimmed. He dressed in regal attire, and looked to be about Magnus' age. Much younger than Blane would have guessed. Three other distinguished Scots also sat at the high table. The earls.

"Brother! Come and join us. I've good news to tell ye." Magnus lifted his mug of ale and a smile spread wide over his face.

"Dinna keep me in suspense," Blane said, walking to the dais as fast as his injuries would allow. He bowed before the Bruce then took his spot beside Arbella. He noted with disappointment that Aliah was not present. Returning his gaze to his brother, he waited expectantly for the good news.

"The Bruce came with Wallace, Lennox, Carrick and Strathearn in order to present the Sutherlands with an earldom."

"Magnus is now an earl, and his wife a countess," the Bruce said.

"Congratulations," Blane said, a smile of pride touching his lips. This was a major step forward for their clan. An earldom meant more power, wealth. And responsibility. Not wanting to spoil his brother's excitement, he chose not to ask what the Bruce and the three backing earls wanted in return. "I am privileged to sit beside a countess," Blane said taking Arbella's hand and kissing it.

His sister-by-marriage laughed as her husband glowered over her head at Blane.

"To the Earl and Countess of Sutherland!" Blane shouted, holding his mug of ale high in the air. "May ye forever be blessed!"

The great hall erupted with shouts and cheers, and the rowdy sounds of slurping and mugs being slammed against the wooden table. Above the din, Blane was distracted by a whisper of something innocent. Aliah stood in the arched doorway, her gaze directed toward him. Throat suddenly parched, Blane couldn't move.

Arbella elbowed him. Blane glanced over to see that his sister-by-marriage was nodding her head in Aliah's direction. Jumping from his chair he rushed to greet her, grasping her hand and pulling her sweet flesh to his lips for a kiss. His heart skipped a beat just being that close to her. He could have been completely healed, for in her presence his pain dissipated. All he needed was her. Just her.

Suddenly, her father came into the room, looming beside them. The baron looked at him hard, the same questioning eyes that everyone else seemed to have. Blane glanced down at her hand still clasped in his. Wanting to never let go.

There was no time like the present. "My lord, if I may have a word with ye in private?"

Baron de Mowbray cocked his head to one side and studied Blane. He'd never felt so stripped bare.

"Aye." The lord whirled on his feet and stomped from the great hall.

Blane kissed Aliah's knuckles and then rushed from the room. Once he'd gained the baron's permission to move forward, he intended to make Aliah his wife.

Chapter Twenty-Four

Aliah stared after Blane and her father as they passed under the stone archway that led from the great hall and outside to the inner bailey.

There was only one reason for them to go off together — Blane was going to ask for her hand. Aliah was not about to let them make a life-changing decision without her. Didn't she climb from her cushy, warm bed to speak with Blane herself? To hear him tell her how much he cared, that he believed, like she did, that they should spend the rest of their lives together? She wanted to tell him how much she loved him.

Shaking her head, she grumbled, "Nay," under her breath. They were not going to take that away from her. She wouldn't allow it!

Lifting her skirts she ran after them, slamming out of the oak doors and glancing around the night-darkened bailey. Aside from the moon and stars, only a few torches lit up the area, making long dark shadows dance in circles. She waited a few moments for her eyes adjust and shivered at the cold air sinking into her bones.

Shadows remained, but a few turned into buildings, barrels, wagons, people. Over by the well her father and Blane faced each other in a heated discussion. But laughter coming from their direction made her pause. Mayhap they weren't discussing marriage, after all.

Frowning, she considered going back inside. But her impulsive nature got the best of her. And this time she'd be damned if she would feel guilty about it. She stormed over the dirt and grass. The two traitors had the nerve to cease talking, and to stare at *her*.

"Daughter, what are you—"

"Aliah, lass, 'tis cold—"

Both men spoke at the same time, then looked at each other with wide grins. Aliah rolled her eyes.

"I came out here, because while I may be a woman, I still have an opinion and I'd just as soon not have you off discussing me without being present to speak for myself."

Blane folded his arms over his chest as did her father. While her father raised his brow, Blane curled his lips into an amused smile.

"What do ye think we're discussing?" Blane asked.

"Didn't I just make myself clear?" she asked, hands on her hips.

Blane shook his head, mirth dancing in his eyes.

"You brought my father out here to ask..." She faltered. Mayhap she was wrong. Oh, how mortifying! What if Blane had simply wanted to tell her father about their journey and now she'd gone and assumed that he'd wanted to marry her. Swallowing hard, she was at a loss for words and wished for nothing more than to sink into the ground.

"I shall leave the two of you alone. I'm famished and in need of a dram ot Magnus' good whisky " Her father started to walk away.

Aliah's eyes widened further. To be so nonchalant... She'd definitely gotten things wrong. The baron stopped in his tracks in front of her, put his hand on her shoulder and squeezed. He said nothing further, but continued back toward the keep.

She was unsteady, shaky. Her stomach felt like it was doing a hundred flips per second. Motion sickness after riding Mad Maiden had been better than this. Aliah wanted to run back to her chamber, to burrow beneath the blankets and sneak out at first light. How could she ever face him?

"Aliah," Blane said. Unfolding his arms, he stepped forward and took her hands in his. They were warm, sending frissons of heat through her fingers and up her arms. "When we first met, 'twas like lightning struck me. Never had I seen a woman so beautiful—and ye held an arrow aimed at my heart."

"Apologies, I didn't know—"

"Dinna apologize. Ye have heart, ye have courage. I wouldna want ye any other way."

Confusion warred within her. Was this his way of saying goodbye? Her fingers trembled slightly as did her lip which she bit to keep steady. Blane tightened his grip on her hands and rubbed his thumbs over her knuckles. Miraculously she felt calmer.

"What I'm trying to say is... I would like to know... If ye'd have me, I'd like ye to marry me. I have to travel sometimes, but I will try to make it fast and return to ye with open arms. If ye want, I'll train another to go to market, and stay here with ye. And soon I plan to speak with Magnus about setting up our own wool market. 'Twill keep me in Sutherland more of the year. I want to make ye happy. To give ye everything ye ever wished for. We can build our own home here at Dunrobin. I canna offer ye a castle, but—"

Aliah shook her head. "Stop."

Blane's face fell. In the flickering light of a nearby torch she watched his eyes darken and his lips slacken as his smiled faded.

"I don't need a castle. All I need is you. Home is where you are. If you're open to it... I would like to journey with you. My English accent is fairly decent. Maybe even better than yours." She snickered and so did he at her jest. "I would never ask you to give up on your talents. The clan needs you."

Blane's smile returned, spreading wide. His teeth glimmered in the light, and his eyes sparkled. She liked seeing him happy.

"I'd like that. Ye've already proven ye can watch my back. Sleeping under the stars with ye would be like heaven itself."

"Aye." Recalling how she'd had to take a man's life made her realize she'd yet to confess her sins. It also made her realize, for Blane, she would do it again. Laying beneath the stars with him, however brief, had been a moment of peace and tranquility that she wished to repeat. "I...love you."

Blane sucked in a breath, his arms stealing around her waist, he pulled her flush against him. He gazed intently at her, his eyes filled with passion and emotion. "I've never had a woman say that to me afore now."

Not the exact reply she was looking for... Aliah smiled, albeit a little haltingly. "I love you," she said again, this time hoping for a different verbal response from Blane.

Blane's touch stroked up her back, over her shoulders and neck until he held the sides of her face. He brought his face close to hers, his gaze never wavering. Aliah could drown within the meadow-green depths of his eyes.

"I love ye, too," he whispered. Her heart fluttered with a sense of victory and pure sentiment. "More than I thought ever possible. I've never loved another." He brushed his lips over hers, just a whisper of a kiss. "I fought these feelings. Telling myself that ye deserved better." He kissed the tip of her nose. "And I still think ye do."

Aliah shook her head. "Nay, never."

Blane chuckled, his forehead pressed to hers. "No matter how much I tried to convince myself otherwise, I kept coming back to one thing—that I was willing to give up everything for ye."

"And I you."

"My heart was so filled with bitterness. I dinna have the strength to share myself with anyone until now—with ye. I dinna think there was room for anything else. How wrong I was. Ye've conquered my heart, lass."

"I intend to conquer more than that." With that said, Aliah rose on her tiptoes and pressed her lips to Blane's. She wasn't going to let him get away without kissing her thoroughly this time.

And he did not disappoint.

At first light, the priest was brought to Aliah's chamber where she confessed and was absolved of her sins—she did leave out the part about making love to Blane before they were wed. Some things were best left only for God's ears.

As soon as the priest retreated to the great hall, Arbella and their father entered the chamber.

"Are you ready?" Arbella asked, beaming. "Now I will see you nearly every day!"

"And I shall miss you." The baron cleared his throat to hide his emotion.

Tears burned the corners of her eyes. 'Twas true that while today she would marry Blane and fulfill her desires to spend a lifetime with him, she'd also be losing the time she'd spent with her father. Asking him to move to Scotland was impossible. The man would never do it. He'd no desire to take the position of his new son-by-marriage's enemy as an English occupier, and living with them seemed out of the question, not while he still had so much spirit left in him.

"I promise to visit each time Blane and I go to the wool market."

"That would be good." Her father pulled her and Arbella into his embrace. "I shall miss you both dearly."

Aliah nodded, tears soaking into her father's tunic. "What will you do?"

His chest rumbled as he let out a laugh. "Actually... There's a lady I've been meaning to call on."

"A lady?" both sisters said at the same time.

"Aye. A widow actually. Lady Somersby. We've exchanged a few pleasantries, and I do believe I am quite... I care about her."

"Oh, father! That is wonderful news," Aliah said.

Arbella nodded emphatically. "I'm so happy that you've found someone. It's been too long that you've been alone."

"Now that you've both gone off and found love and since Samuel is occupied, I decided to do something for myself. But enough about me. 'Tis time my youngest daughter married a truly honorable man."

They descended the stairs. Outside a hard rain fell in painful pings against their flesh as they rushed to the Sutherland clan chapel. Blane and Aliah had eyes for no one but each other. His large hand encompassed hers, and the smile on his face was both charming and enticing. Not wanting to sway from tradition, several clansmen held a canopy over them as the priest led them through the exchange of vows on the chapel steps.

A grand feast ensued within the great hall.

Her husband leaned down to whisper in her ear, his breath tickling her skin. "Temptation, I've a need to take ye upstairs and bed ye properly..."

Aliah nearly choked on the wine she sipped. Liquid heat pooled within her core and tingles spiraled up her spine. Certain heat infused her cheeks, she faced him, her eyes mischievous. "And I've a need to see just what ye mean by that."

Amid cheers and hollers, Blane lifted Aliah in his arms, swirled her in a circle and headed for the stairs.

"Put me down! You're still healing."

Blane winked and whispered in her ear, "Lass, I intend to use your special medicine—your honey."

Her head fell back as she laughed and waved goodbye. At one time she would have been embarrassed, but now, in this moment, she didn't care. Blane was her husband and he had every right to carry her up stairs, and every right to ravish her. And she wanted him too, desperately. She shivered in anticipation.

For the first time they could embrace and not worry about who would notice, or how the other felt. They'd both bared their hearts and with each passing moment, Aliah found herself falling deeper still.

Carrying her into a chamber that was not her own, Blane set her down before shutting the door and barring it. But within moments she was in his arms again. Candles were lit around the masculine room, giving it a soft, romantic glow. A vase of fresh wildflowers sat on a table between two chairs.

"At last, we are alone," he said, his eyes darkening with the same passion she felt scorching her blood.

"Make love to me," she whispered, "on the bed."

"With pleasure, lass."

Blane carried her to the large four-poster bed, easily one and half times the size of her own.

"Is this your chamber?" she asked.

"Aye. I made this bed myself a few years ago. Cutting the wood helped me to deal with my anger." He flashed her a boyish grin. "That's all changed now."

Aliah grinned. "Then mayhap I will make you angry every now and then. 'Tis a beautiful piece." The pillars were carved with Celtic swirls, knots, falcons and wildcats. The surface, a deep brownish-red color, was polished to a brilliant shine.

"I'll not have to be angry to make something fine for ye."

Aliah touched his cheek, gazed into his eyes. "I love you, Blane." The words never seemed to get old and excitement still simmered through her when he vowed his own love.

"I love ye, too, *mo chridhe*."

Aliah smiled. "Do you know I speak Gaelic?"

He winked. "I happened to see the book ye were studying."

Her eyes widened and her mouth opened into an O of surprise. "You knew all along."

Blane nodded and placed her on the bed, coming over her in one single fluid movement. She liked the weight of him on her and her body awakened, remembering his touch and what pleasure it brought. He settled his mouth on hers, kissing her tenderly, lovingly as his hands explored the expanse of her ribs, her breasts. But it wasn't what she wanted. Now that they could savor every moment, Aliah wanted to be skin to skin.

She gave Blane's chest a little shove. When he knelt upon his heels, his knees sinking into the mattress, he looked down at her with confusion. Aliah came to kneel in front of him, her knees touching his.

"I want to feel you against me," she said boldly.

Blane grinned wickedly. "There's the temptress."

He helped her undress, and in his haste ripped her gown on one shoulder. In retaliation, Aliah yanked on the ties of his shirt, but nothing happened.

"Sutherland wools are unmatched," he teased.

Aliah rolled her eyes, and set about retaliating in a different way. She kissed his throat, nipping at his tender flesh. Blane breathed deeply, moaning. Her fingernails scraped over his bare knees, beneath his plaid over his thighs until she reached his thick, hard shaft. Gripping him, she marveled once more at the silky texture. Blane groaned deep in the back of his throat, wasting no time in divesting himself of his garments. But still she didn't let him go. Instead, she delighted in tempting him with her mouth. Fever ignited when his thick velvet length slid over her tongue and only intensified by the carnal sounds issuing from his lips.

"Och, lass, ye are temptation itself."

He nudged her back, crawling over her until he settled the hot length of his entire body on hers. Aliah was instantly wrapped in warmth and a haze of sensuality. Skin to skin was definitely superior to being clothed.

They moved slowly, each exploring the other with leisure. Aliah discovered that Blane was ticklish along his ribs if she slowly scraped her nails over his flesh. He shivered with each stroke. Blane also found how sensitive her back was as he rolled her onto her belly and kissed the length of her spine, pausing at each vertebra to breathe hotly on her skin. By the time he reached her lower back, Aliah was a trembling, boneless mass.

Her husband was right. It did get better and better.

While she was lying on her belly, he used his knees to gently spread her thighs apart, settling his thick member at her slick entrance.

"Is this...possible?" she asked, turning her head in order to gaze at him behind her.

"Oh, aye, love," he said softly as he sank inside her.

They both cried out as he filled her, touching her in a way that was completely different than before. Most definitely possible. Blane used steady, excruciatingly slow strokes to torture her with pleasure for what seemed like hours. Her entire body trembled, her skin afire. He kissed her back, gently sucked at her shoulders and neck. His fingers trailed over her arms, pulling them to rest on the pillows above her head, and threading them through her own.

Aliah gasped with each stroke of his shaft, feeling like she might break apart at any moment. She writhed beneath him, lifting her buttocks to match his thrusts.

"Are ye close?" he whispered in her ear.

"Aye," she whimpered. With just one more nudge, she'd surely fall off the precipice.

Blane withdrew, leaving a breeze of cool air on her hot rear. Gripping her hips, he urged her to roll over. "I want to look into your eyes as ye find your fulfillment."

Aliah had never heard anything more stimulating. She nodded, hooking her feet to the back of his legs and spreading her thighs, she urged him to enter her once more. When he did, she arched her back, crying out in pure ecstasy. The time for slow and steady had met its end. Blane thrust hard and deep. What she thought was close to climax before was nothing compared to the fire he built in her now.

Blane held himself up on his elbows and Aliah wrapped her arms around his neck, careful to avoid his injured shoulder. Blane's gaze smoldered with her own. Moments later, she felt rapture as it encompassed her entire being, wave after wave wracking her body.

"Blane!" she cried out, working to keep her gaze steady on his.

"*Mo chridhe*," he answered as his body shuddered over hers.

As they lay there, limbs entwined, Aliah decided that life could not get any better than this. If Blane had never come to retrieve her, she'd never have known what she was missing. 'Twas a terrifying thought. One that made her hug him tighter and thank God for small miracles.

A swift breeze blew, making the furs at the windows flap against the walls. There was a noticeable draft wafting around the room.

"'Tis chillier in here than before," Aliah remarked.

Blane laughed. "Nay, I think 'tis simply we were otherwise distracted." He rose and lit a brazier—the metal clanging with each stick of wood he placed in it. Her eyes were riveted to his solid, naked form, the breadth of his shoulders and his height mesmerizing. Swarthy skin covered corded muscle. Even with the wounds on his thigh and shoulder, the man was breathtaking, exquisite. "Once the new keep is built, the chambers will each have a hearth." He glanced up at her, excitement curling his lips. "Hopefully by then, our own manor home will be built."

Already Aliah could feel warmth from the small fire. She wasn't sure though if it was in fact the flames, or the heated gaze of her husband. Desire sparked anew. She curled her fingers, beckoning him back to bed. Blane obliged, pulling her into his embrace. She rested her head on his uninjured shoulder.

"On our journey, you mentioned having a falconry at your home." Aliah stroked her fingers over Blane's chest, watching his muscles rise and fall with each breath. "You meant Dunrobin didn't you?"

"Aye. Would ye like to hunt with me tomorrow?" he asked.

"As long as it isn't raining."

Blane rolled onto his side, propping his head up on his elbow as he gazed down at her. "Now what kind of an adventure would that be? I say we go no matter the weather."

She grinned up at him, running her hand down his belly. "I suppose if I have to be stranded in a storm, there's no one I'd rather be with."

Blane winked, his smile turning carnal as his hand smoothed over her nude hip. "We'll have to keep each other warm."

"A task I will most enthusiastically take to heart." And with that she kissed him soundly, wondering if he'd be amenable to a steamy bath for two.

"The End"

If you enjoyed **THE HIGHLANDER'S CONQUEST**, *please spread the word by leaving a review on the site where you purchased your copy, or a reader site such as Goodreads or Shelfari! I love to hear from readers too, so drop me a line at* authorelizaknight@gmail.com *OR visit me on Facebook:* https://www.facebook.com/elizaknightauthor. I'm also on Twitter: @ElizaKnight *Many thanks!*

Eliza Knight

AUTHOR'S NOTE

In fiction, an author often takes creative license to bend fact around their story. I did so in this case with the Earldom of Sutherland. The original earldom was given to the Sutherland Clan in 1235, about 62 years before my story takes place. For the purposes of this family saga, it was important to shift this date slightly. Of additional note is that the family seat of the Sutherlands wasn't officially Dunrobin until the 1400's, however history shows that a castle stood on the site from the time of the earldom.

Hope you're enjoying the Stolen Bride series so far! I've certainly been enjoying weaving a tale around these fascinating characters.

Eliza Knight

The saga continues! Look for more books in <u>The Stolen Bride Series</u> coming soon!

Book Three– *The Highlander's Lady*– December 15, 2012

A Highlander tamed…

Laird Daniel Murray seeks adventure, battle and freedom for his countrymen. Putting off his duties as laird – with a promise to his that clan he'll return come spring – Daniel sets off with his men to fight alongside William Wallace and the Bruce. But soon he stumbles across an enchanting lady in need. She tantalizes him with an offer he simply can't refuse and a desire he attempts to dismiss.

A lady's passion ignited…

Escaping near death at the treacherous hands of a nearby clan, Lady Myra must find the Bruce and relay the news of an enemy within his own camp. Alone in a world full of danger and the future of her clan at stake, she must trust the handsome, charismatic Highland laird who promises to keep her safe on her journey – and sets her heart to pounding.

Together, Daniel and Myra will risk not only their lives, but their hearts while discovering the true meaning of hope and love in a world fraught with unrest.

There are six books total in The Stolen Bride Series! If you haven't read Book One, look for THE HIGHLANDER'S REWARD at most e-tailers. Check out my website, for information on future releases <u>www.elizaknight.com</u>.

ABOUT THE AUTHOR

Eliza Knight is the multi-published, award-winning, Amazon best-selling author of sizzling historical romance and erotic romance. While not reading, writing or researching for her latest book, she chases after her three children. In her spare time (if there is such a thing...) she likes daydreaming, wine-tasting, traveling, hiking, staring at the stars, watching movies, shopping and visiting with family and friends. She lives atop a small mountain, and enjoys cold winter nights when she can curl up in front of a roaring fire with her own knight in shining armor. Visit Eliza at www.elizaknight.com or her historical blog History Undressed: www.historyundressed.com

CPSIA information can be obtained
at www.ICGtesting.com
Printed in the USA
FSHW010618311219
65615FS